JUSTICE LEAGUE UNLIMITED
UNITED THEY STAND

Written by:
Adam Beechen

Colored by:
Heroic Age

Illustrated by:
Carlo Barberi
Ethen Beavers
Walden Wong

Lettered by:
Phil Balsman
Pat Brosseau
Nick J. Napolitano

Superman created by **Jerry Siegel** and **Joe Shuster**

Batman created by **Bob Kane**

Wonder Woman created by **William Moulton Marston**

Dan DiDio
VP-Executive Editor

Tom Palmer, Jr.
Editor-original series

Jeanine Schaefer
Assistant Editor-original series

Scott Nybakken
Editor-collected edition

Robbin Brosterman
Senior Art Director

Paul Levitz
President & Publisher

Georg Brewer
VP-Design & Retail Product
Development

Richard Bruning
Senior VP-Creative Director

Patrick Caldon
Senior VP-Finance & Operations

Chris Caramalis
VP-Finance

Terri Cunningham
VP-Managing Editor

Stephanie Fierman
Senior VP-Sales & Marketing

Alison Gill
VP-Manufacturing

Rich Johnson
VP-Book Trade Sales

Hank Kanalz
VP-General Manager, WildStorm

Lillian Laserson
Senior VP & General Counsel

Jim Lee
Editorial Director-WildStorm

Paula Lowitt
Senior VP-Business & Legal Affairs

David McKillips
VP-Advertising & Custom Publishing

John Nee
VP-Business Development

Gregory Noveck
Senior VP-Creative Affairs

Cheryl Rubin
Senior VP-Brand Management

Bob Wayne
VP-Sales

JUSTICE LEAGUE UNLIMITED VOL. 1: UNITED THEY STAND

DC Comics, 1700 Broadway, New York, NY 10019
A Warner Bros. Entertainment Company.
Printed in Canada. First Printing.
ISBN: 1-4012-0512-7
Publication design by John J. Hill.

WB SHIELD ™ & © Warner Bros. Entertainment Inc.
(s05)

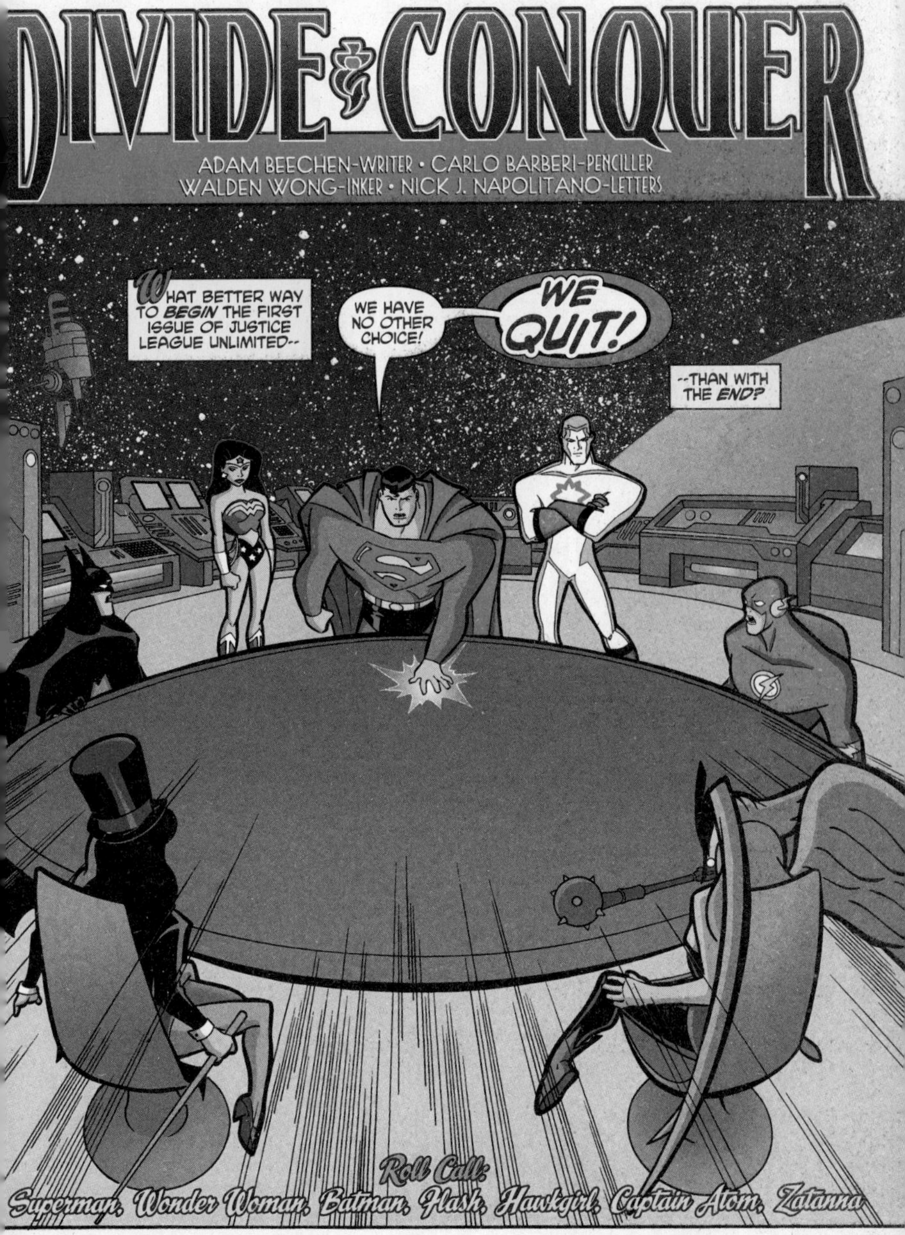
DIVIDE & CONQUER
ADAM BEECHEN-WRITER • CARLO BARBERI-PENCILLER
WALDEN WONG-INKER • NICK J. NAPOLITANO-LETTERS
WHAT BETTER WAY TO *BEGIN* THE FIRST ISSUE OF JUSTICE LEAGUE UNLIMITED--
WE HAVE NO OTHER CHOICE!
WE QUIT!
--THAN WITH THE *END*?
Roll Call:
Superman, Wonder Woman, Batman, Flash, Hawkgirl, Captain Atom, Zatanna

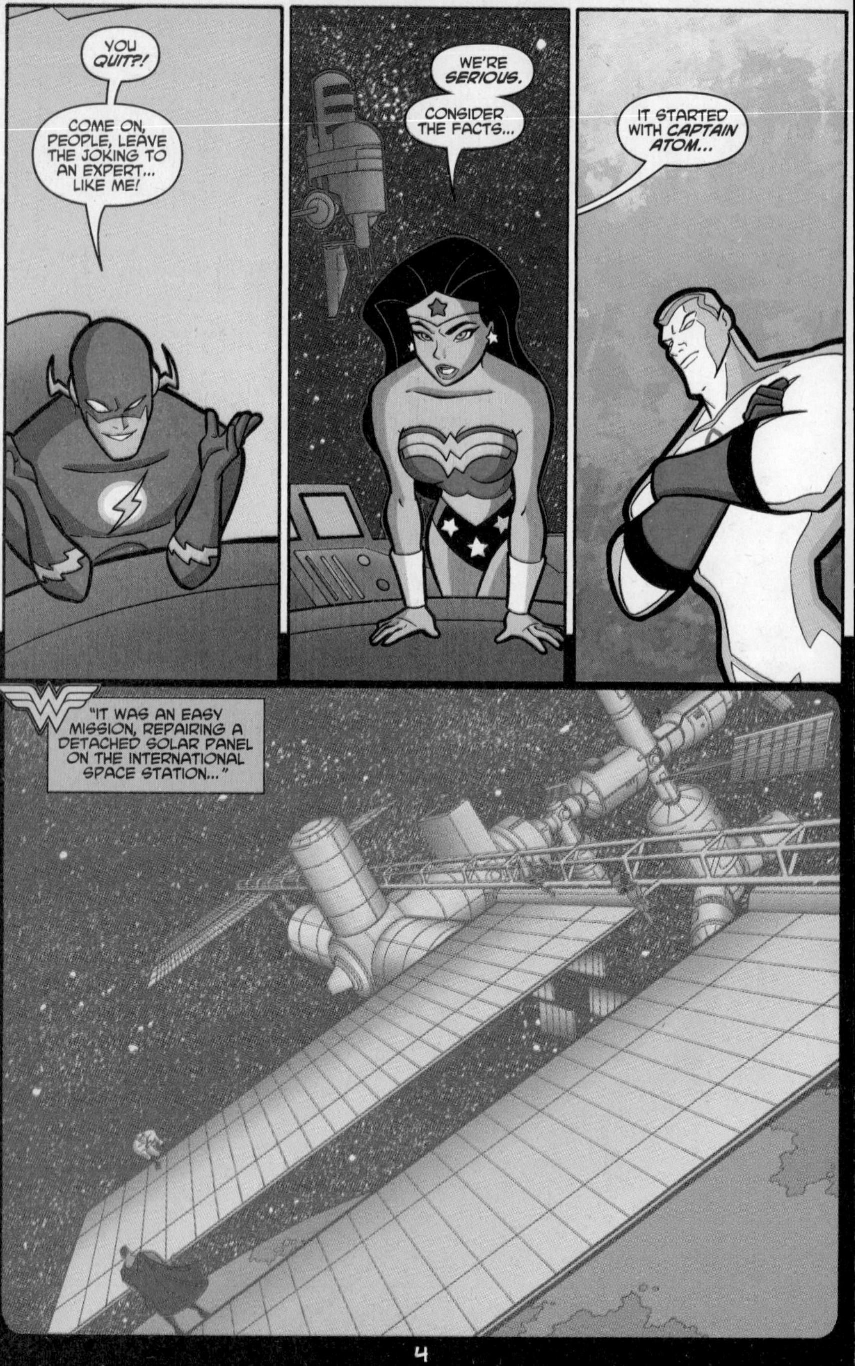
YOU QUIT?!
COME ON, PEOPLE, LEAVE THE JOKING TO AN EXPERT... LIKE ME!
WE'RE SERIOUS.
CONSIDER THE FACTS...
IT STARTED WITH CAPTAIN ATOM...
"IT WAS AN EASY MISSION, REPAIRING A DETACHED SOLAR PANEL ON THE INTERNATIONAL SPACE STATION..."

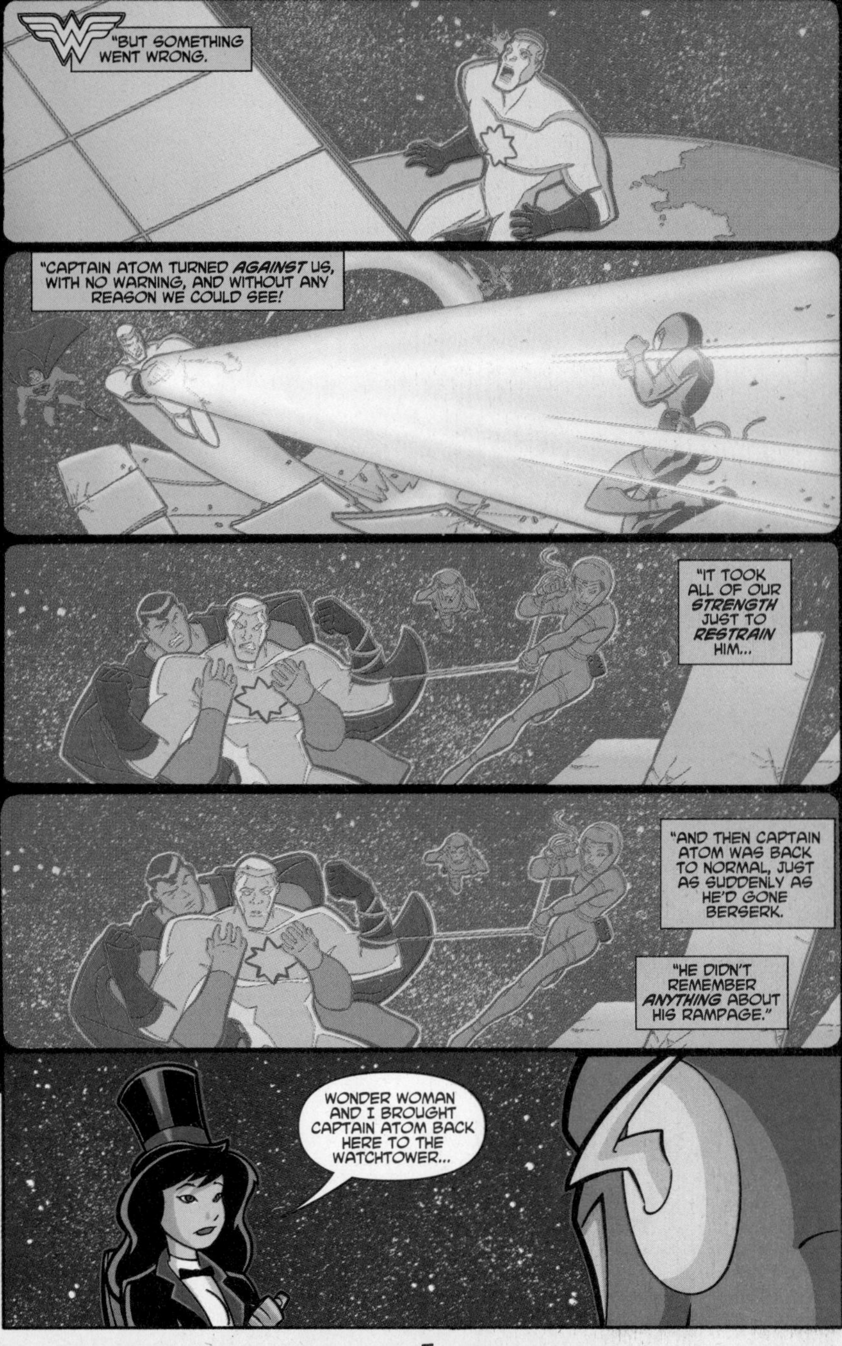
"BUT SOMETHING WENT WRONG.
"CAPTAIN ATOM TURNED AGAINST US, WITH NO WARNING, AND WITHOUT ANY REASON WE COULD SEE!
"IT TOOK ALL OF OUR STRENGTH JUST TO RESTRAIN HIM...
"AND THEN CAPTAIN ATOM WAS BACK TO NORMAL, JUST AS SUDDENLY AS HE'D GONE BERSERK.
"HE DIDN'T REMEMBER ANYTHING ABOUT HIS RAMPAGE."
WONDER WOMAN AND I BROUGHT CAPTAIN ATOM BACK HERE TO THE WATCHTOWER...

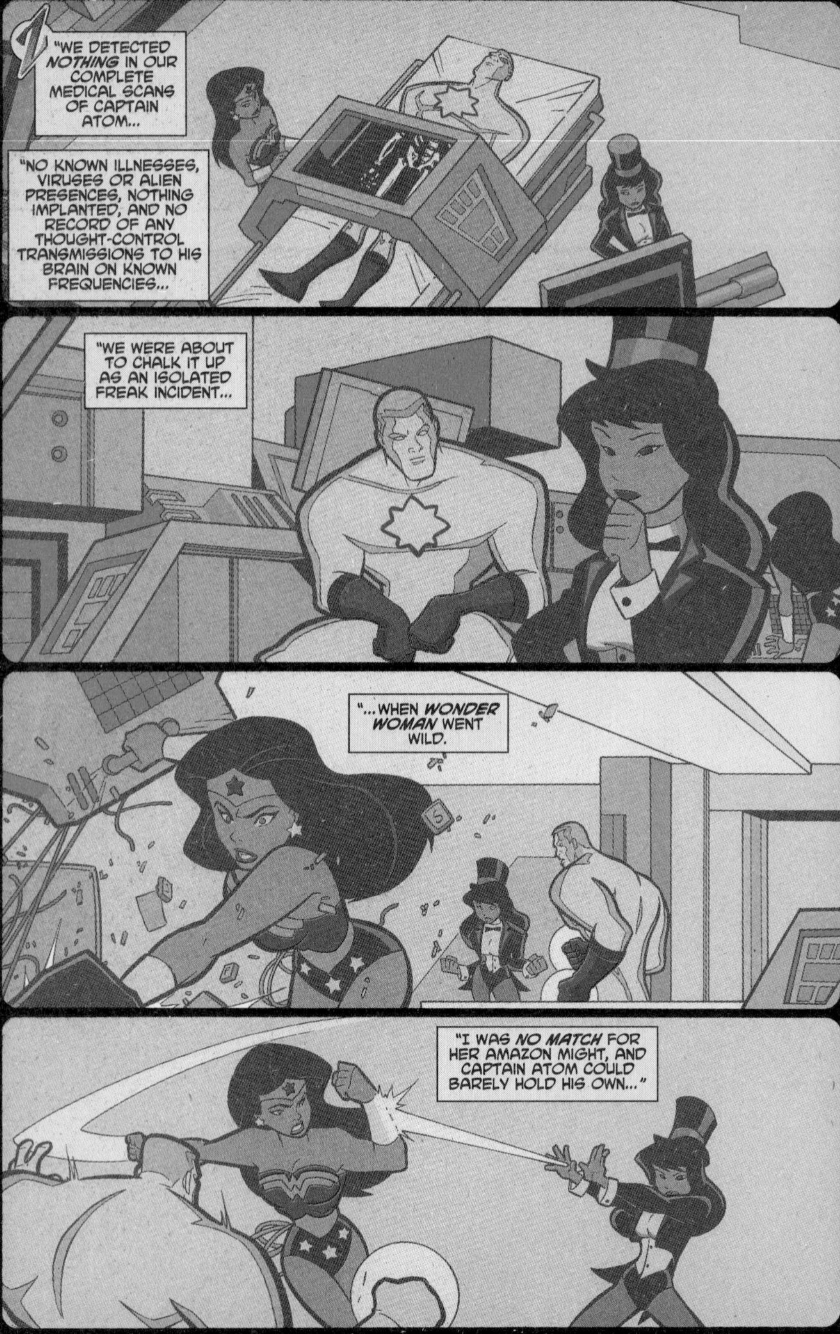
"WE DETECTED NOTHING IN OUR COMPLETE MEDICAL SCANS OF CAPTAIN ATOM...
"NO KNOWN ILLNESSES, VIRUSES OR ALIEN PRESENCES, NOTHING IMPLANTED, AND NO RECORD OF ANY THOUGHT-CONTROL TRANSMISSIONS TO HIS BRAIN ON KNOWN FREQUENCIES...
"WE WERE ABOUT TO CHALK IT UP AS AN ISOLATED FREAK INCIDENT...
"...WHEN WONDER WOMAN WENT WILD.
"I WAS NO MATCH FOR HER AMAZON MIGHT, AND CAPTAIN ATOM COULD BARELY HOLD HIS OWN..."

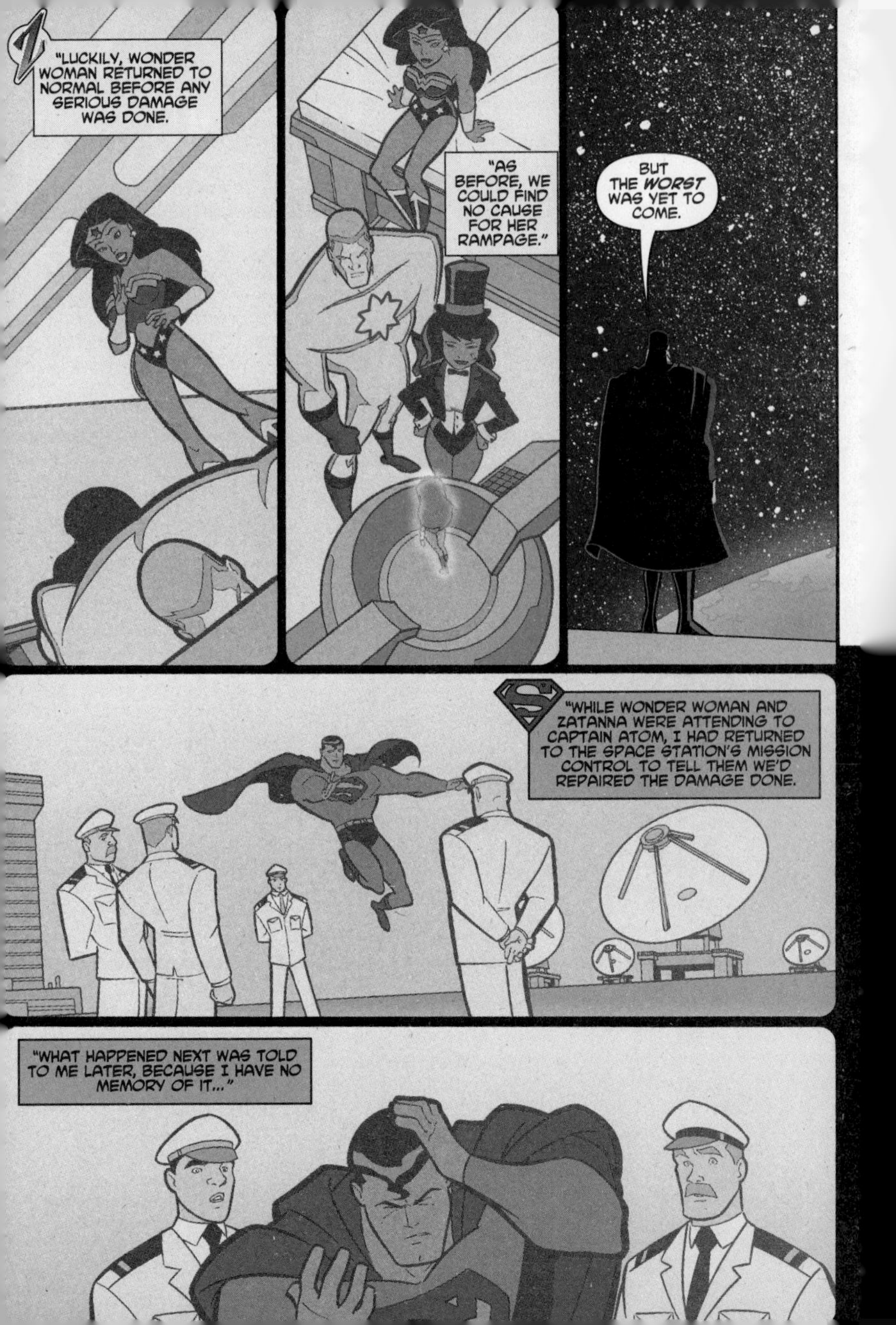
"LUCKILY, WONDER WOMAN RETURNED TO NORMAL BEFORE ANY SERIOUS DAMAGE WAS DONE.
"AS BEFORE, WE COULD FIND NO CAUSE FOR HER RAMPAGE."
BUT THE *WORST* WAS YET TO COME.
"WHILE WONDER WOMAN AND ZATANNA WERE ATTENDING TO CAPTAIN ATOM, I HAD RETURNED TO THE SPACE STATION'S MISSION CONTROL TO TELL THEM WE'D REPAIRED THE DAMAGE DONE.
"WHAT HAPPENED NEXT WAS TOLD TO ME LATER, BECAUSE I HAVE NO MEMORY OF IT..."

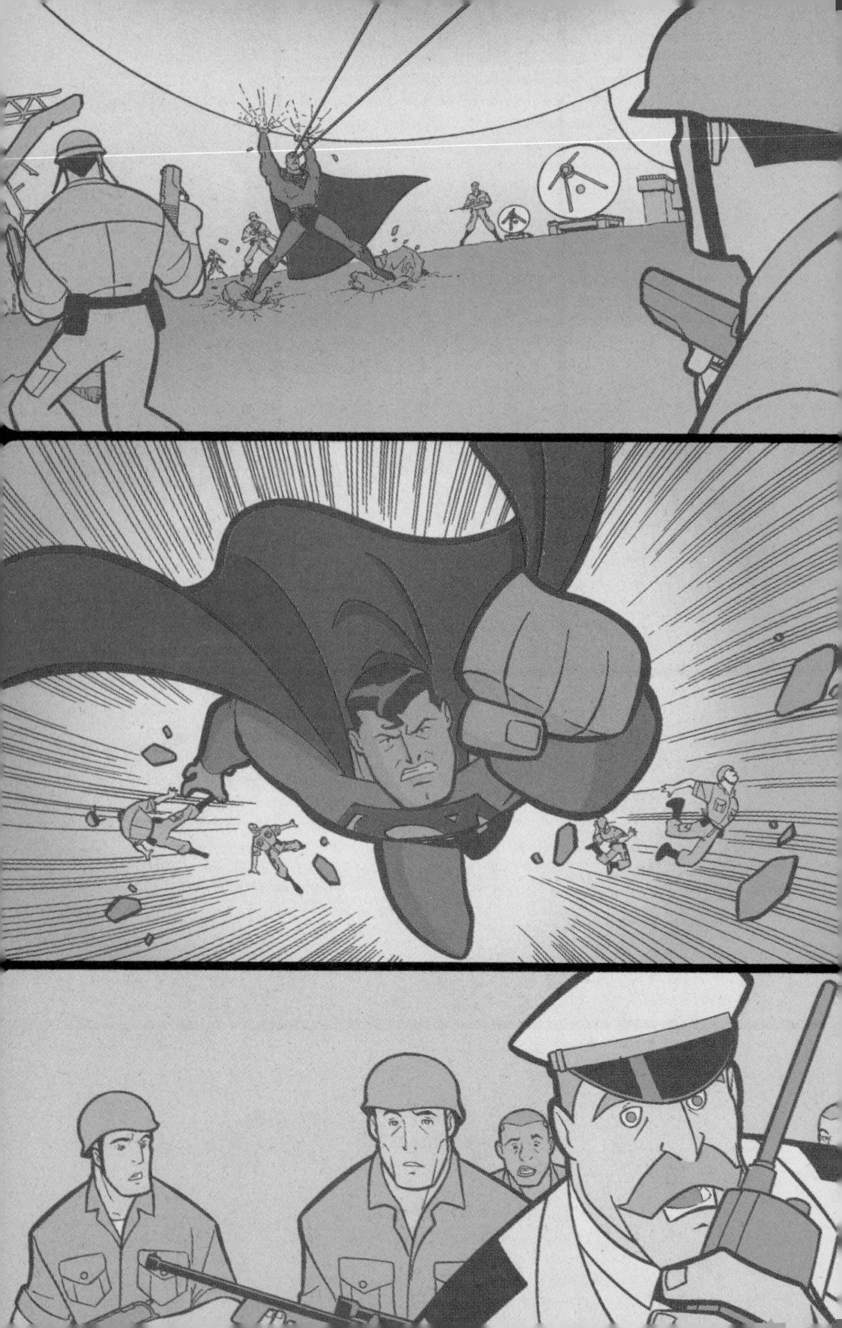

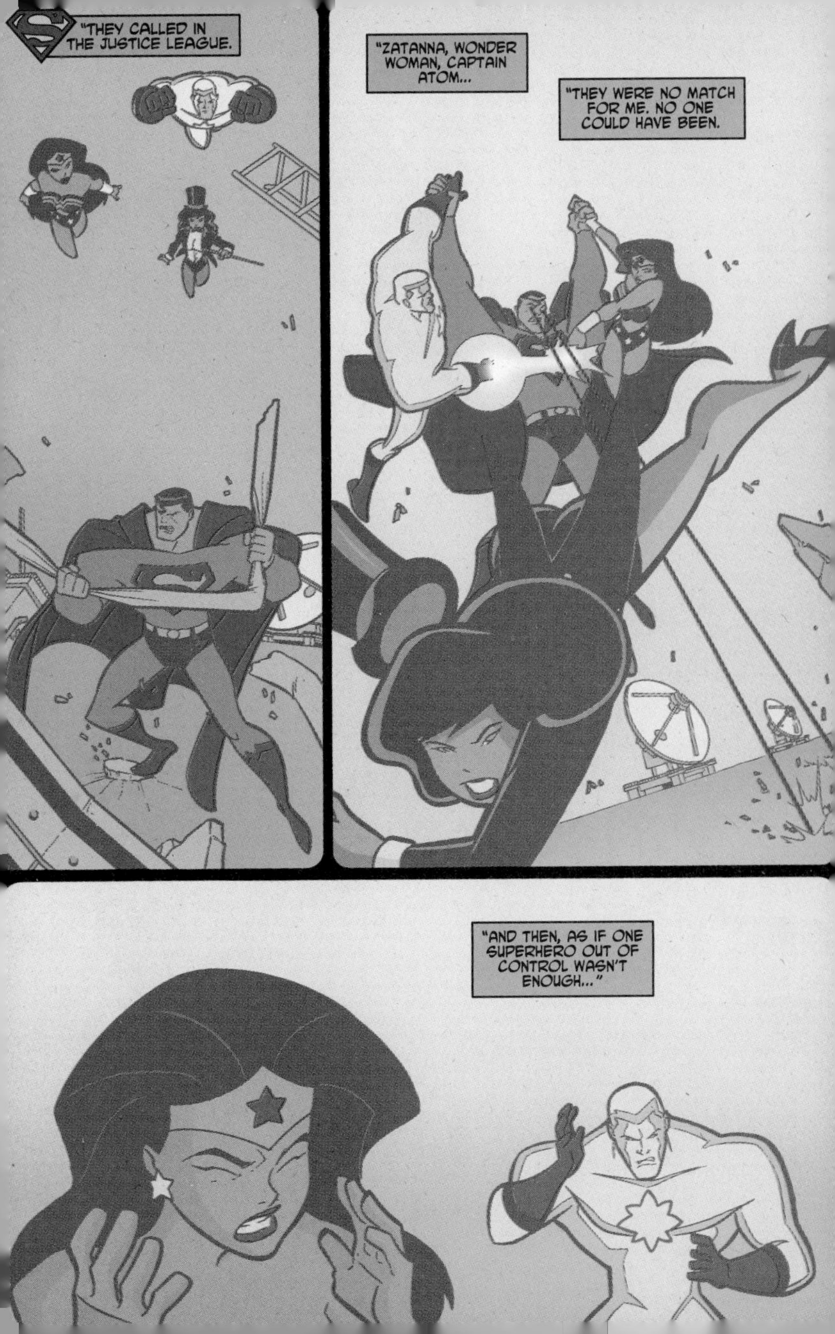
"THEY CALLED IN THE JUSTICE LEAGUE.
"ZATANNA, WONDER WOMAN, CAPTAIN ATOM...
"THEY WERE NO MATCH FOR ME. NO ONE COULD HAVE BEEN.
"AND THEN, AS IF ONE SUPERHERO OUT OF CONTROL WASN'T ENOUGH..."

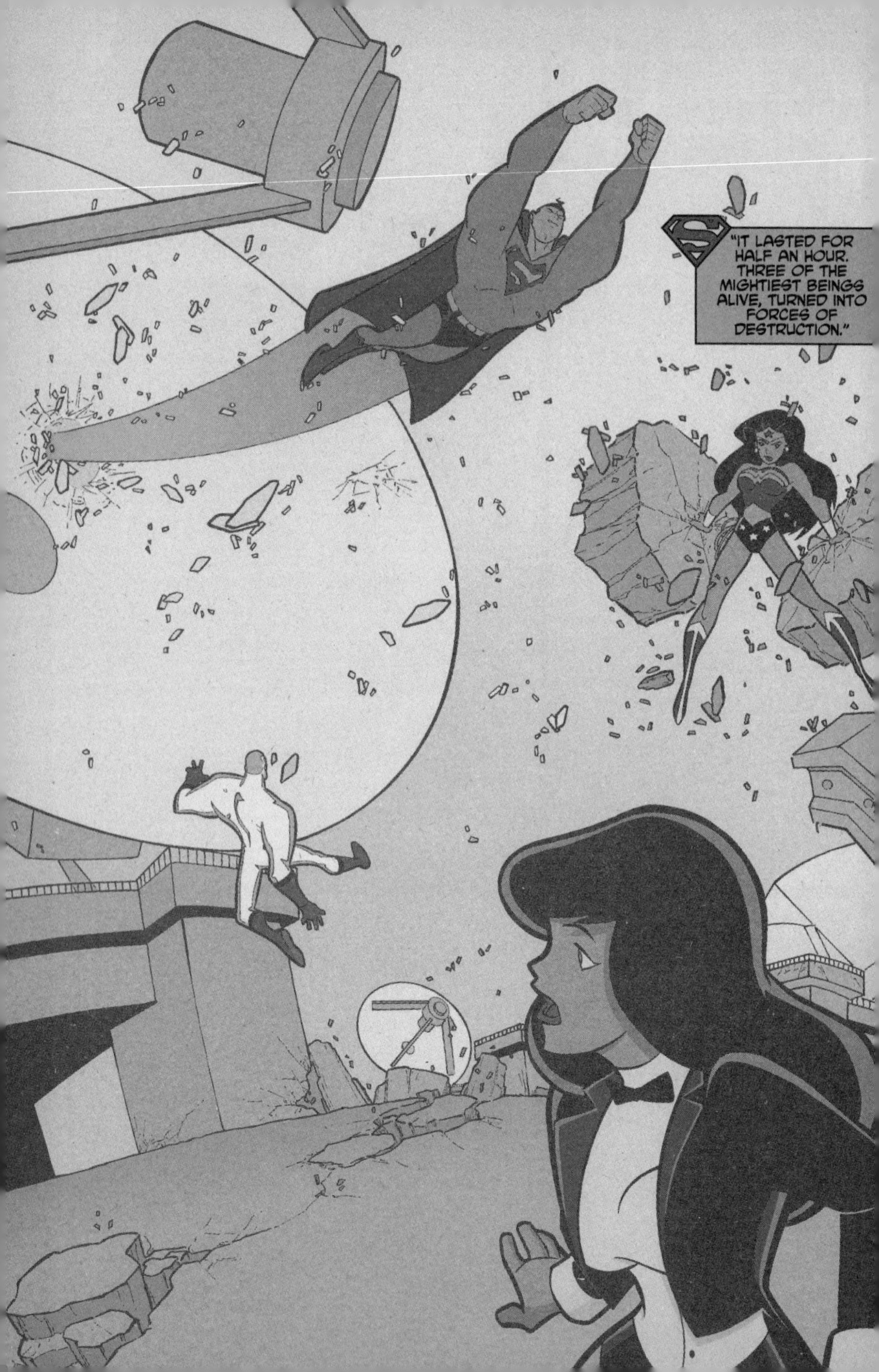
"IT LASTED FOR HALF AN HOUR. THREE OF THE MIGHTIEST BEINGS ALIVE, TURNED INTO FORCES OF DESTRUCTION."

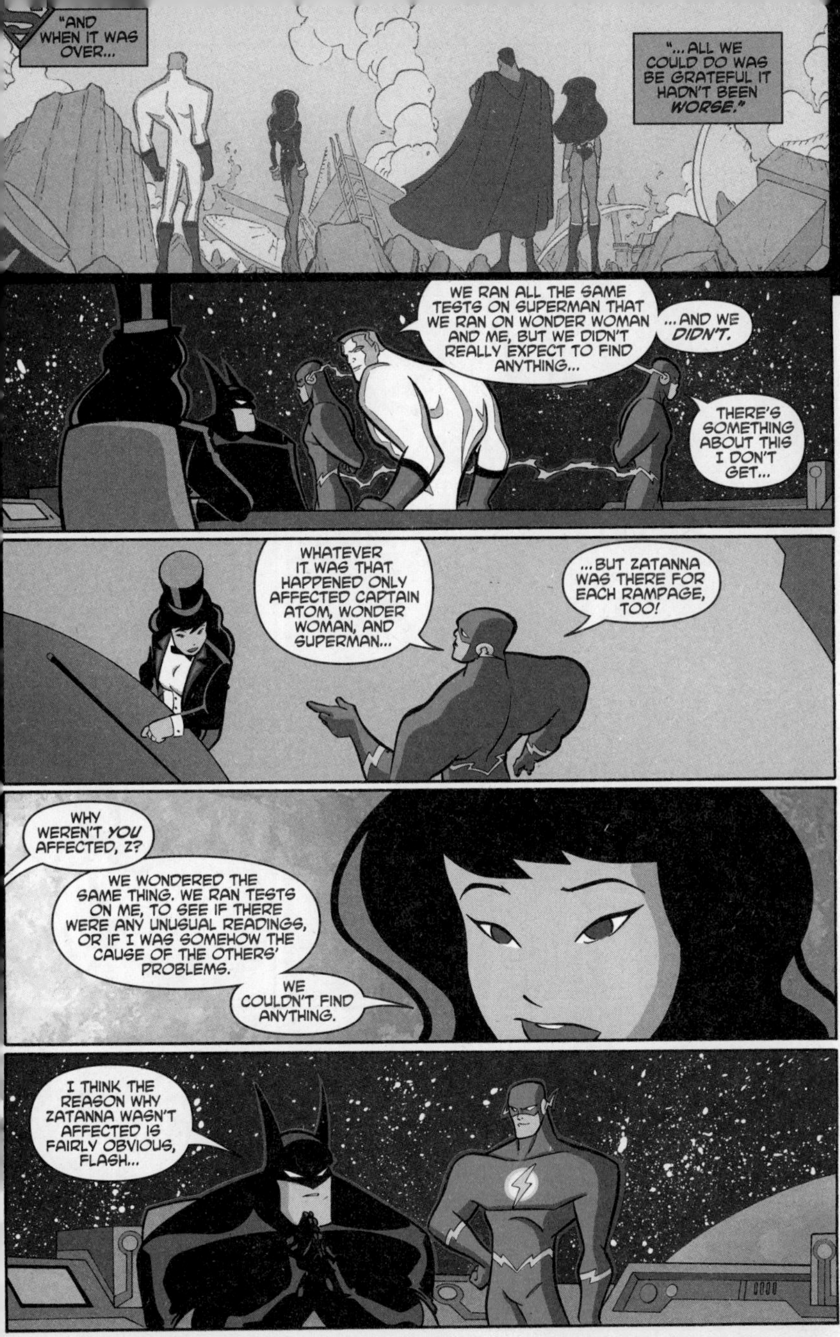
"AND WHEN IT WAS OVER...
"...ALL WE COULD DO WAS BE GRATEFUL IT HADN'T BEEN WORSE."
WE RAN ALL THE SAME TESTS ON SUPERMAN THAT WE RAN ON WONDER WOMAN AND ME, BUT WE DIDN'T REALLY EXPECT TO FIND ANYTHING...
...AND WE DIDN'T.
THERE'S SOMETHING ABOUT THIS I DON'T GET...
WHATEVER IT WAS THAT HAPPENED ONLY AFFECTED CAPTAIN ATOM, WONDER WOMAN, AND SUPERMAN...
...BUT ZATANNA WAS THERE FOR EACH RAMPAGE, TOO!
WHY WEREN'T YOU AFFECTED, Z?
WE WONDERED THE SAME THING. WE RAN TESTS ON ME, TO SEE IF THERE WERE ANY UNUSUAL READINGS, OR IF I WAS SOMEHOW THE CAUSE OF THE OTHERS' PROBLEMS.
WE COULDN'T FIND ANYTHING.
I THINK THE REASON WHY ZATANNA WASN'T AFFECTED IS FAIRLY OBVIOUS, FLASH...

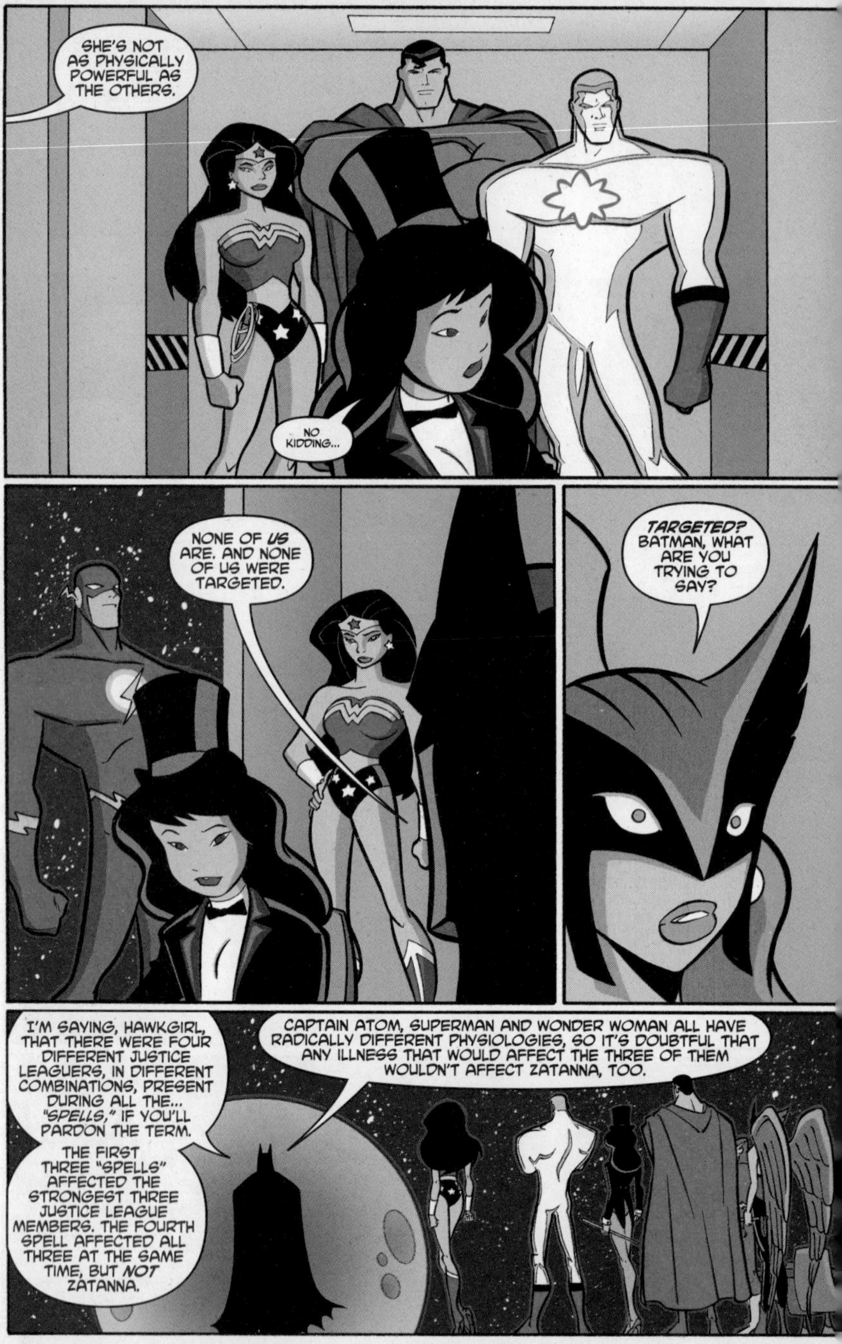
SHE'S NOT AS PHYSICALLY POWERFUL AS THE OTHERS.
NO KIDDING...
NONE OF *US* ARE. AND NONE OF US WERE TARGETED.
TARGETED? BATMAN, WHAT ARE YOU TRYING TO SAY?
I'M SAYING, HAWKGIRL, THAT THERE WERE FOUR DIFFERENT JUSTICE LEAGUERS, IN DIFFERENT COMBINATIONS, PRESENT DURING ALL THE... *"SPELLS,"* IF YOU'LL PARDON THE TERM.
THE FIRST THREE "SPELLS" AFFECTED THE STRONGEST THREE JUSTICE LEAGUE MEMBERS. THE FOURTH SPELL AFFECTED ALL THREE AT THE SAME TIME, BUT *NOT* ZATANNA.
CAPTAIN ATOM, SUPERMAN AND WONDER WOMAN ALL HAVE RADICALLY DIFFERENT PHYSIOLOGIES, SO IT'S DOUBTFUL THAT ANY ILLNESS THAT WOULD AFFECT THE THREE OF THEM WOULDN'T AFFECT ZATANNA, TOO.

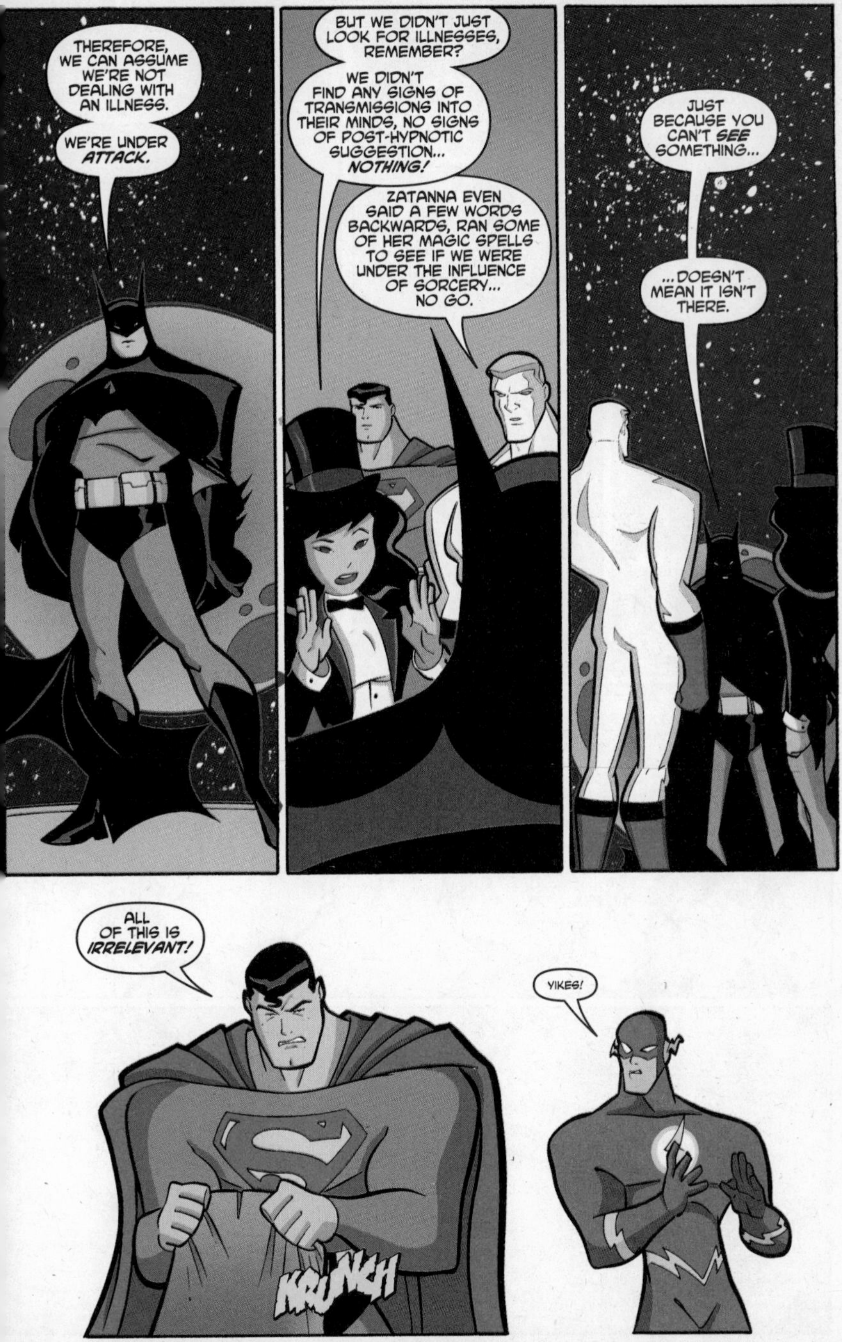
THEREFORE, WE CAN ASSUME WE'RE NOT DEALING WITH AN ILLNESS.
WE'RE UNDER *ATTACK.*
BUT WE DIDN'T JUST LOOK FOR ILLNESSES, REMEMBER?
WE DIDN'T FIND ANY SIGNS OF TRANSMISSIONS INTO THEIR MINDS, NO SIGNS OF POST-HYPNOTIC SUGGESTION... *NOTHING!*
ZATANNA EVEN SAID A FEW WORDS BACKWARDS, RAN SOME OF HER MAGIC SPELLS TO SEE IF WE WERE UNDER THE INFLUENCE OF SORCERY... NO GO.
JUST BECAUSE YOU CAN'T *SEE* SOMETHING...
...DOESN'T MEAN IT ISN'T THERE.
ALL OF THIS IS *IRRELEVANT!*
YIKES!
KRUNCH

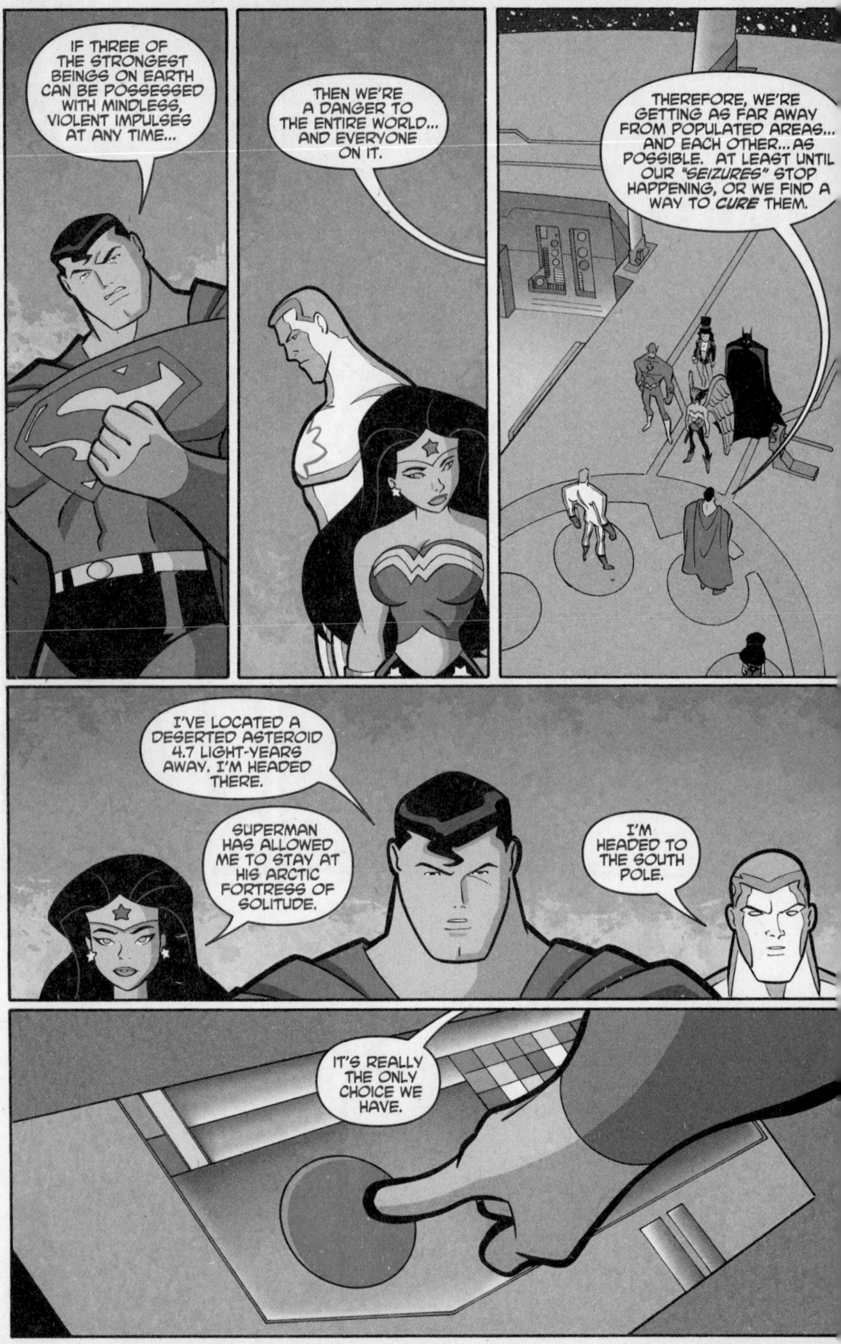
IF THREE OF THE STRONGEST BEINGS ON EARTH CAN BE POSSESSED WITH MINDLESS, VIOLENT IMPULSES AT ANY TIME...
THEN WE'RE A DANGER TO THE ENTIRE WORLD... AND EVERYONE ON IT.
THEREFORE, WE'RE GETTING AS FAR AWAY FROM POPULATED AREAS... AND EACH OTHER... AS POSSIBLE. AT LEAST UNTIL OUR "SEIZURES" STOP HAPPENING, OR WE FIND A WAY TO CURE THEM.
I'VE LOCATED A DESERTED ASTEROID 4.7 LIGHT-YEARS AWAY. I'M HEADED THERE.
SUPERMAN HAS ALLOWED ME TO STAY AT HIS ARCTIC FORTRESS OF SOLITUDE.
I'M HEADED TO THE SOUTH POLE.
IT'S REALLY THE ONLY CHOICE WE HAVE.

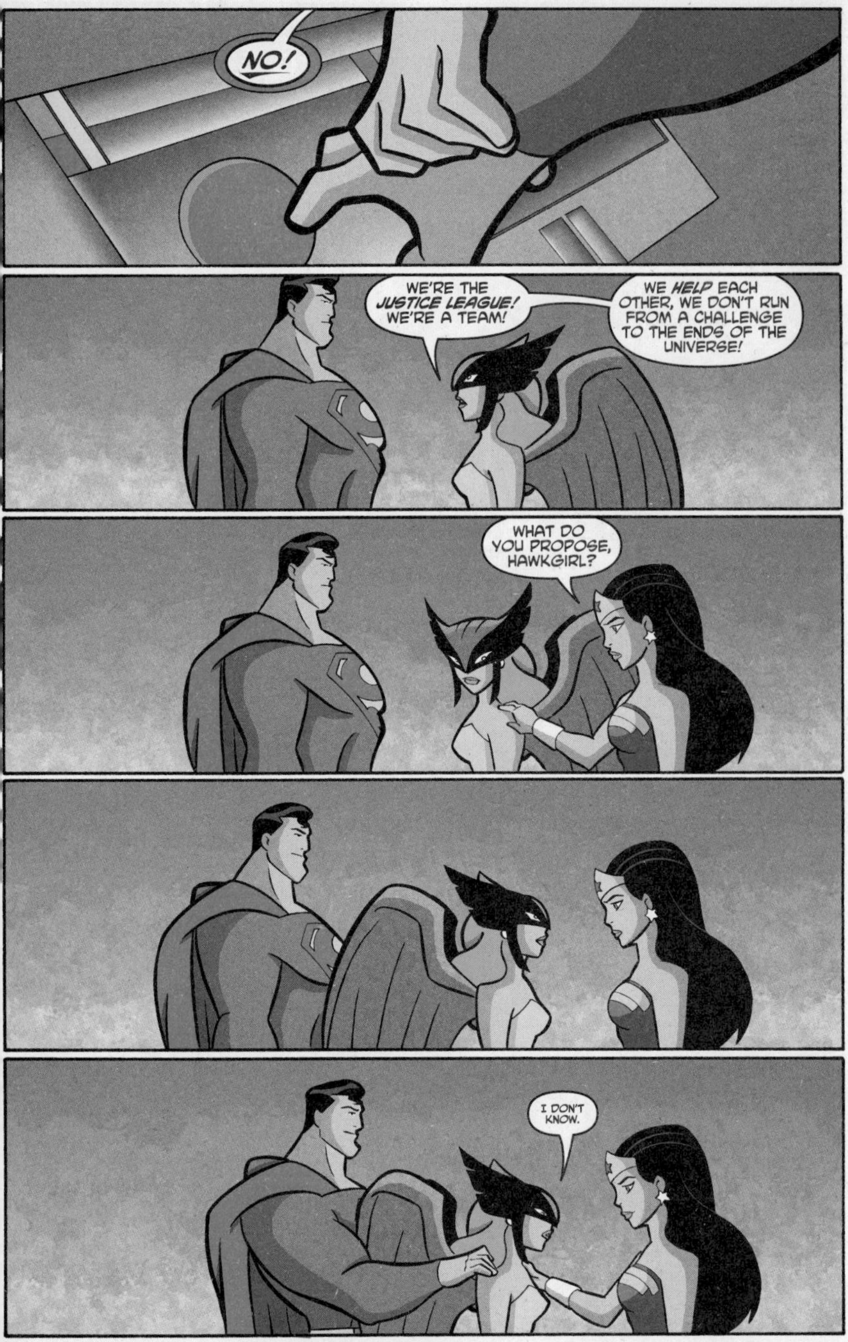
NO!
WE'RE THE JUSTICE LEAGUE! WE'RE A TEAM!
WE HELP EACH OTHER, WE DON'T RUN FROM A CHALLENGE TO THE ENDS OF THE UNIVERSE!
WHAT DO YOU PROPOSE, HAWKGIRL?
I DON'T KNOW.

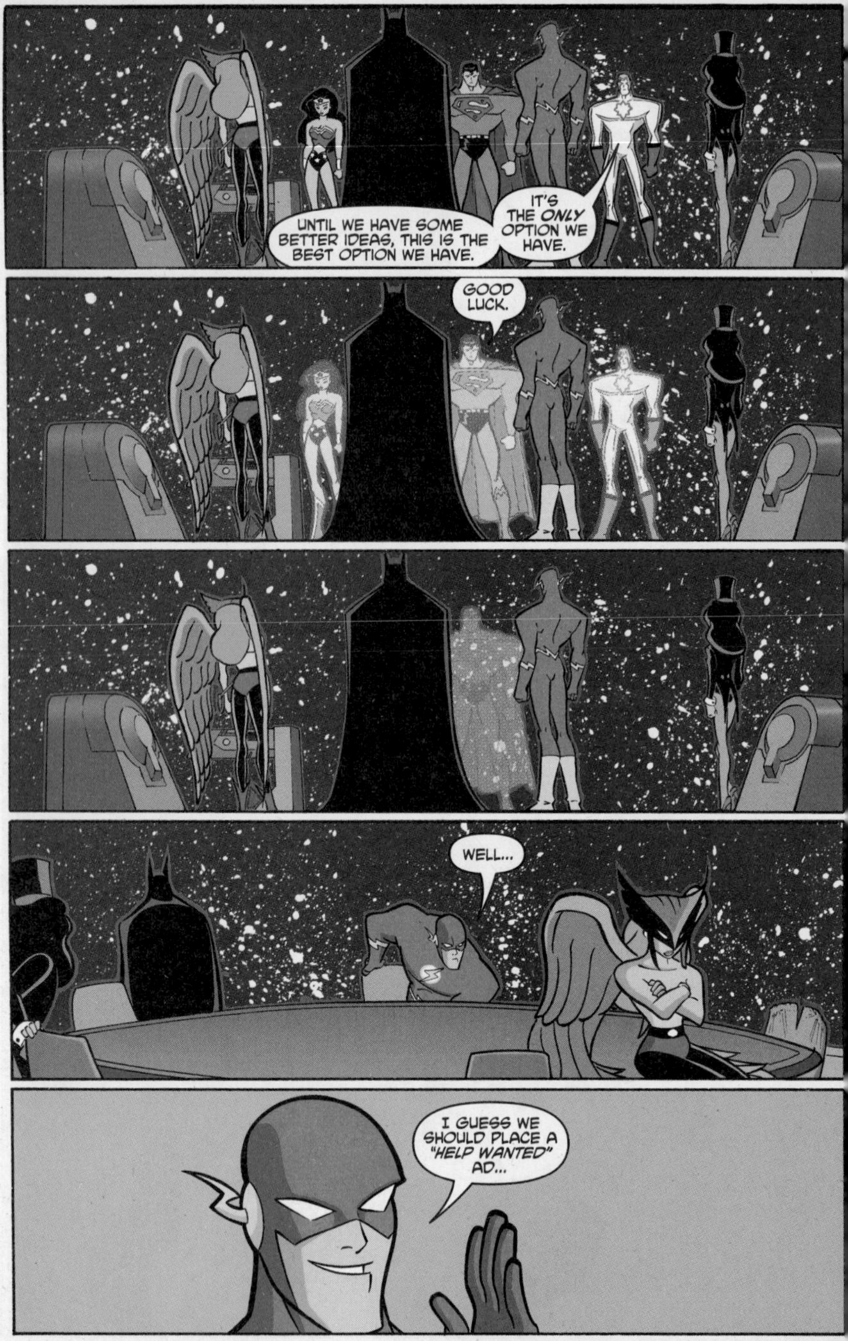
UNTIL WE HAVE SOME BETTER IDEAS, THIS IS THE BEST OPTION WE HAVE.
IT'S THE *ONLY* OPTION WE HAVE.
GOOD LUCK.
WELL...
I GUESS WE SHOULD PLACE A *"HELP WANTED"* AD...

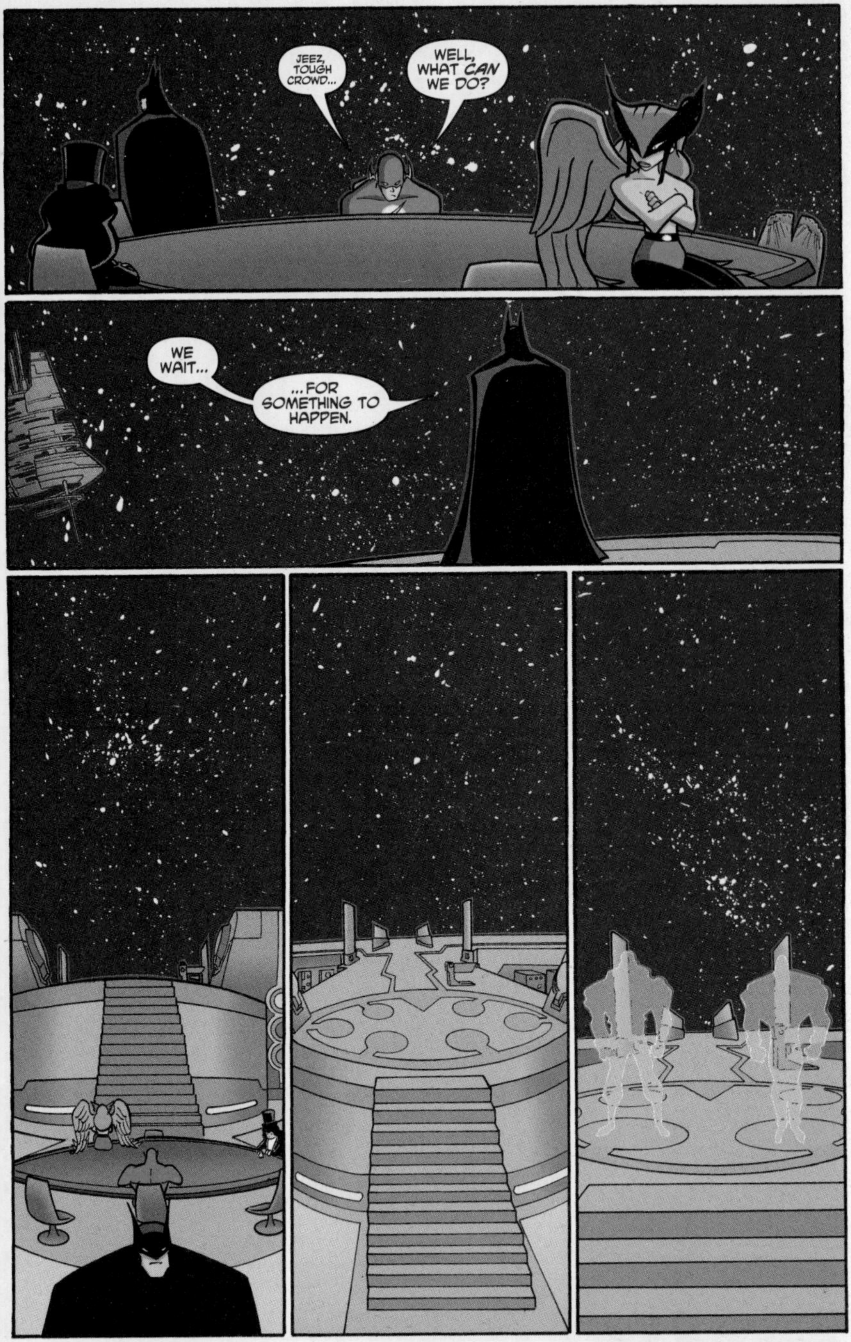
JEEZ, TOUGH CROWD...
WELL, WHAT CAN WE DO?
WE WAIT...
...FOR SOMETHING TO HAPPEN.

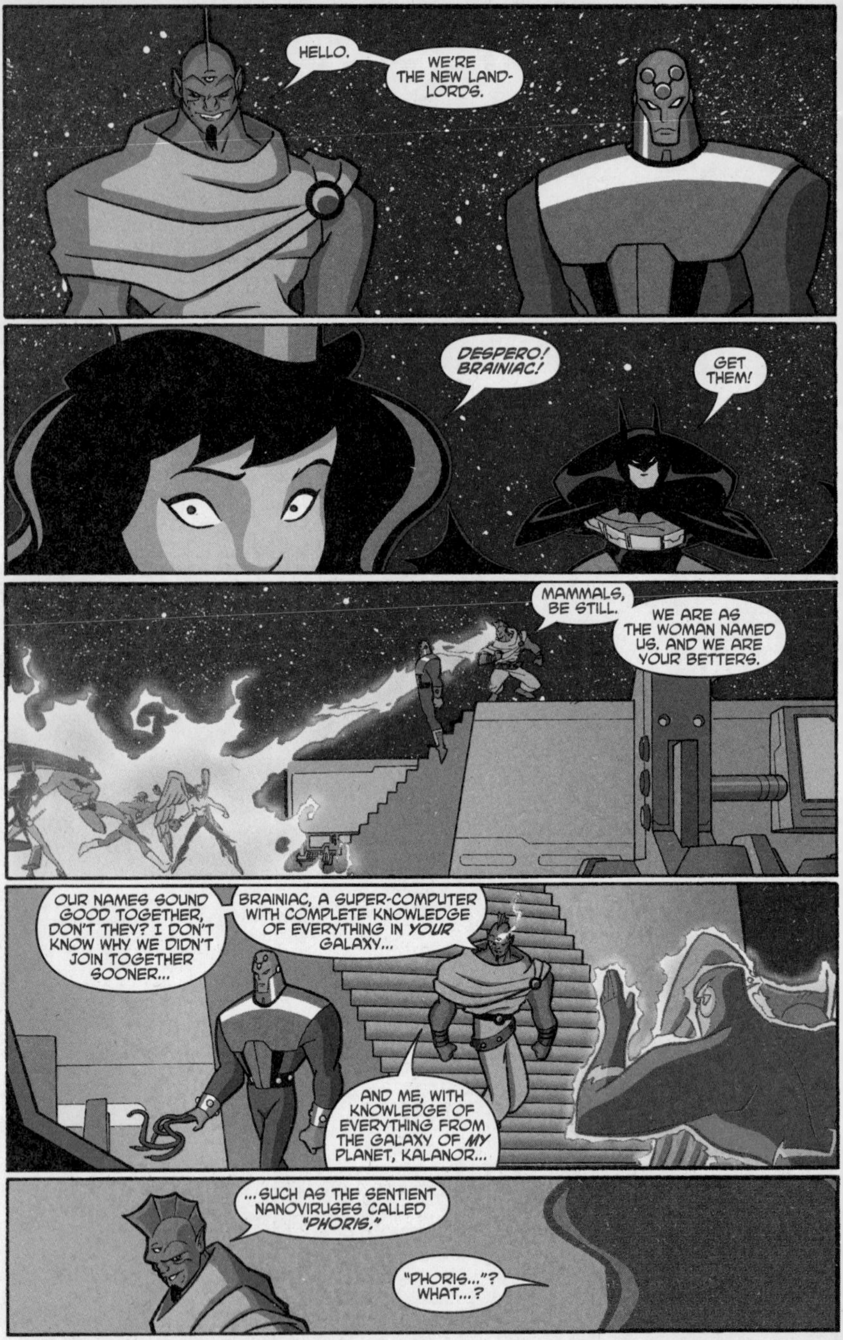
HELLO.
WE'RE THE NEW LAND-LORDS.
DESPERO! BRAINIAC!
GET THEM!
MAMMALS, BE STILL.
WE ARE AS THE WOMAN NAMED US. AND WE ARE YOUR BETTERS.
OUR NAMES SOUND GOOD TOGETHER, DON'T THEY? I DON'T KNOW WHY WE DIDN'T JOIN TOGETHER SOONER...
BRAINIAC, A SUPER-COMPUTER WITH COMPLETE KNOWLEDGE OF EVERYTHING IN YOUR GALAXY...
AND ME, WITH KNOWLEDGE OF EVERYTHING FROM THE GALAXY OF MY PLANET, KALANOR...
...SUCH AS THE SENTIENT NANOVIRUSES CALLED "PHORIS."
"PHORIS..."? WHAT...?

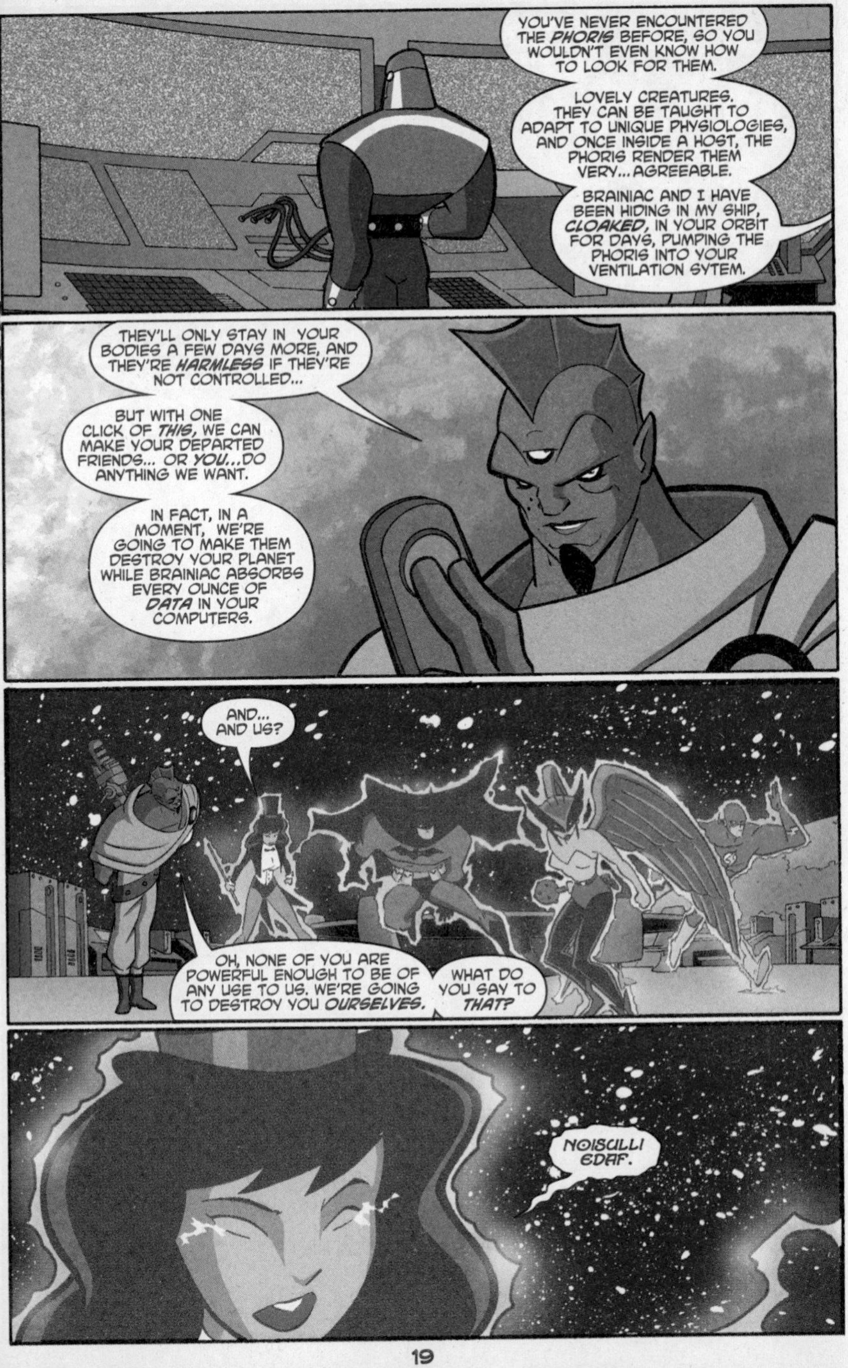
YOU'VE NEVER ENCOUNTERED THE *PHORIS* BEFORE, SO YOU WOULDN'T EVEN KNOW HOW TO LOOK FOR THEM.
LOVELY CREATURES. THEY CAN BE TAUGHT TO ADAPT TO UNIQUE PHYSIOLOGIES, AND ONCE INSIDE A HOST, THE PHORIS RENDER THEM VERY... AGREEABLE.
BRAINIAC AND I HAVE BEEN HIDING IN MY SHIP, *CLOAKED,* IN YOUR ORBIT FOR DAYS, PUMPING THE PHORIS INTO YOUR VENTILATION SYTEM.
THEY'LL ONLY STAY IN YOUR BODIES A FEW DAYS MORE, AND THEY'RE *HARMLESS* IF THEY'RE NOT CONTROLLED...
BUT WITH ONE CLICK OF *THIS,* WE CAN MAKE YOUR DEPARTED FRIENDS... OR *YOU*...DO ANYTHING WE WANT.
IN FACT, IN A MOMENT, WE'RE GOING TO MAKE THEM DESTROY YOUR PLANET WHILE BRAINIAC ABSORBS EVERY OUNCE OF *DATA* IN YOUR COMPUTERS.
AND... AND US?
OH, NONE OF YOU ARE POWERFUL ENOUGH TO BE OF ANY USE TO US. WE'RE GOING TO DESTROY YOU *OURSELVES.*
WHAT DO YOU SAY TO *THAT?*
NOISULLI EDAF.

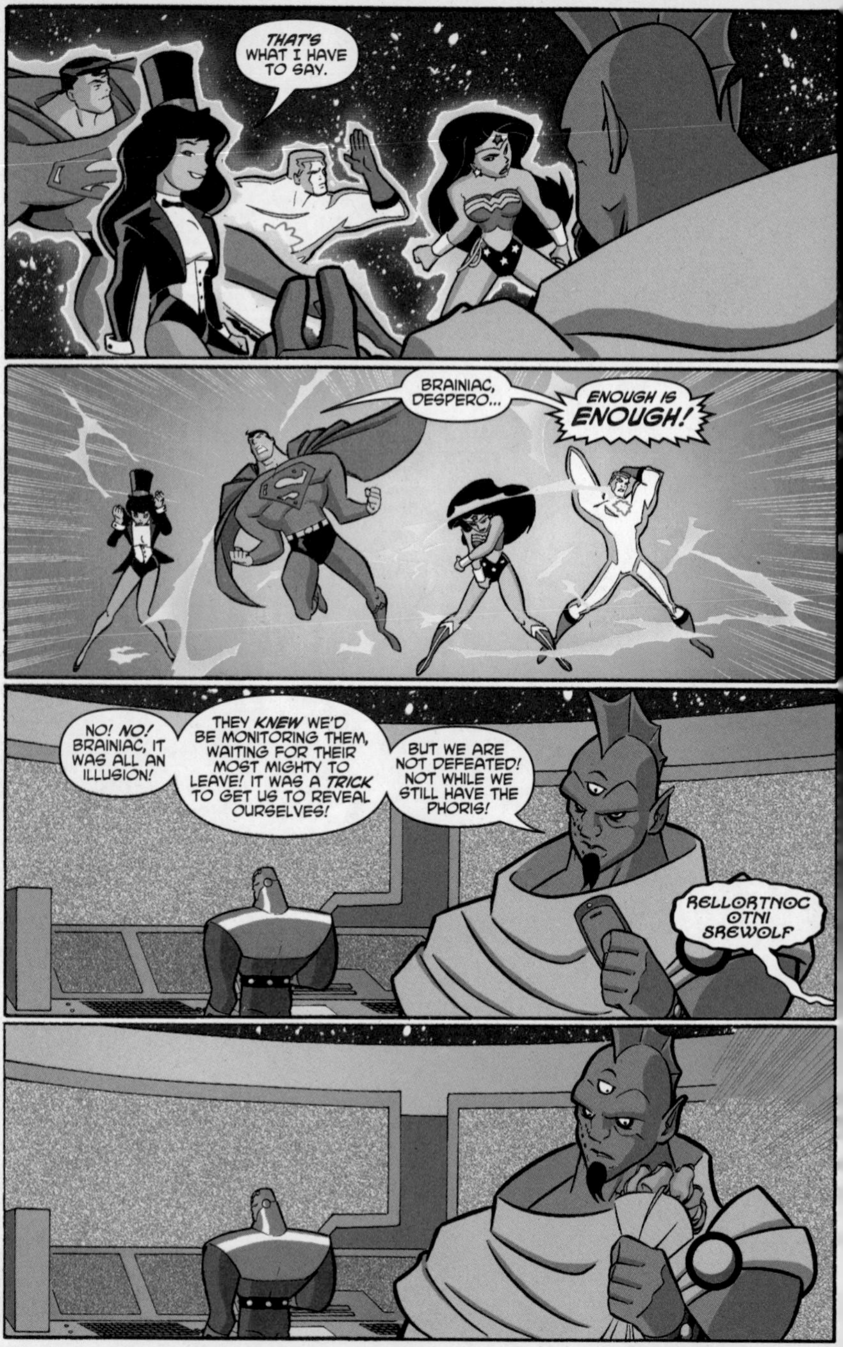
THAT'S WHAT I HAVE TO SAY.
BRAINIAC, DESPERO...
ENOUGH IS ENOUGH!
NO! NO! BRAINIAC, IT WAS ALL AN ILLUSION!
THEY KNEW WE'D BE MONITORING THEM, WAITING FOR THEIR MOST MIGHTY TO LEAVE! IT WAS A TRICK TO GET US TO REVEAL OURSELVES!
BUT WE ARE NOT DEFEATED! NOT WHILE WE STILL HAVE THE PHORIS!
RELLORTNOC OTNI SREWOLF

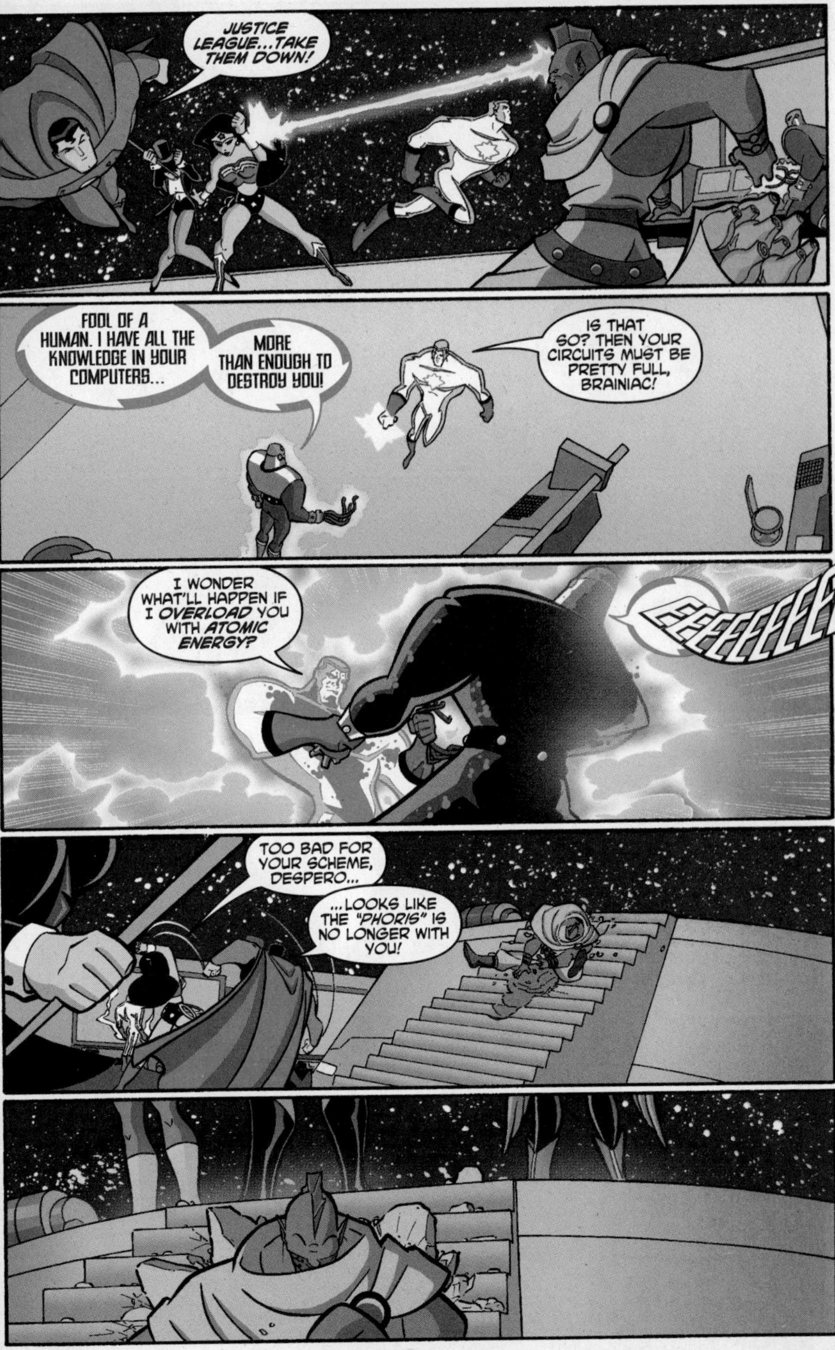

JUSTICE LEAGUE...TAKE THEM DOWN!
FOOL OF A HUMAN. I HAVE ALL THE KNOWLEDGE IN YOUR COMPUTERS...
MORE THAN ENOUGH TO DESTROY YOU!
IS THAT SO? THEN YOUR CIRCUITS MUST BE PRETTY FULL, BRAINIAC!
I WONDER WHAT'LL HAPPEN IF I OVERLOAD YOU WITH ATOMIC ENERGY?
EEEEEEEEEEE
TOO BAD FOR YOUR SCHEME, DESPERO...
...LOOKS LIKE THE "PHORIS" IS NO LONGER WITH YOU!

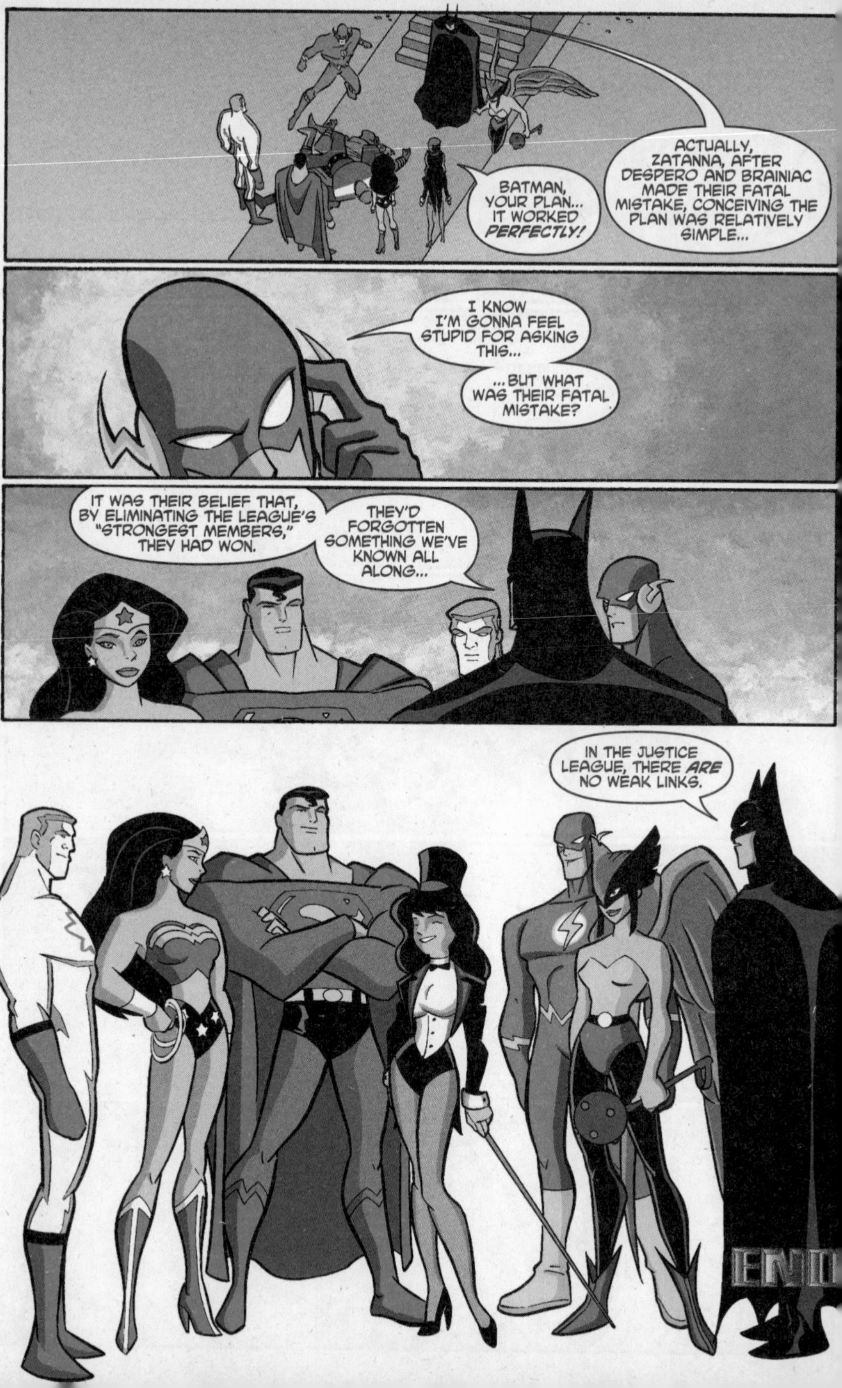
BATMAN, YOUR PLAN... IT WORKED PERFECTLY!
ACTUALLY, ZATANNA, AFTER DESPERO AND BRAINIAC MADE THEIR FATAL MISTAKE, CONCEIVING THE PLAN WAS RELATIVELY SIMPLE...
I KNOW I'M GONNA FEEL STUPID FOR ASKING THIS...
...BUT WHAT WAS THEIR FATAL MISTAKE?
IT WAS THEIR BELIEF THAT, BY ELIMINATING THE LEAGUE'S "STRONGEST MEMBERS," THEY HAD WON.
THEY'D FORGOTTEN SOMETHING WE'VE KNOWN ALL ALONG...
IN THE JUSTICE LEAGUE, THERE ARE NO WEAK LINKS.
END

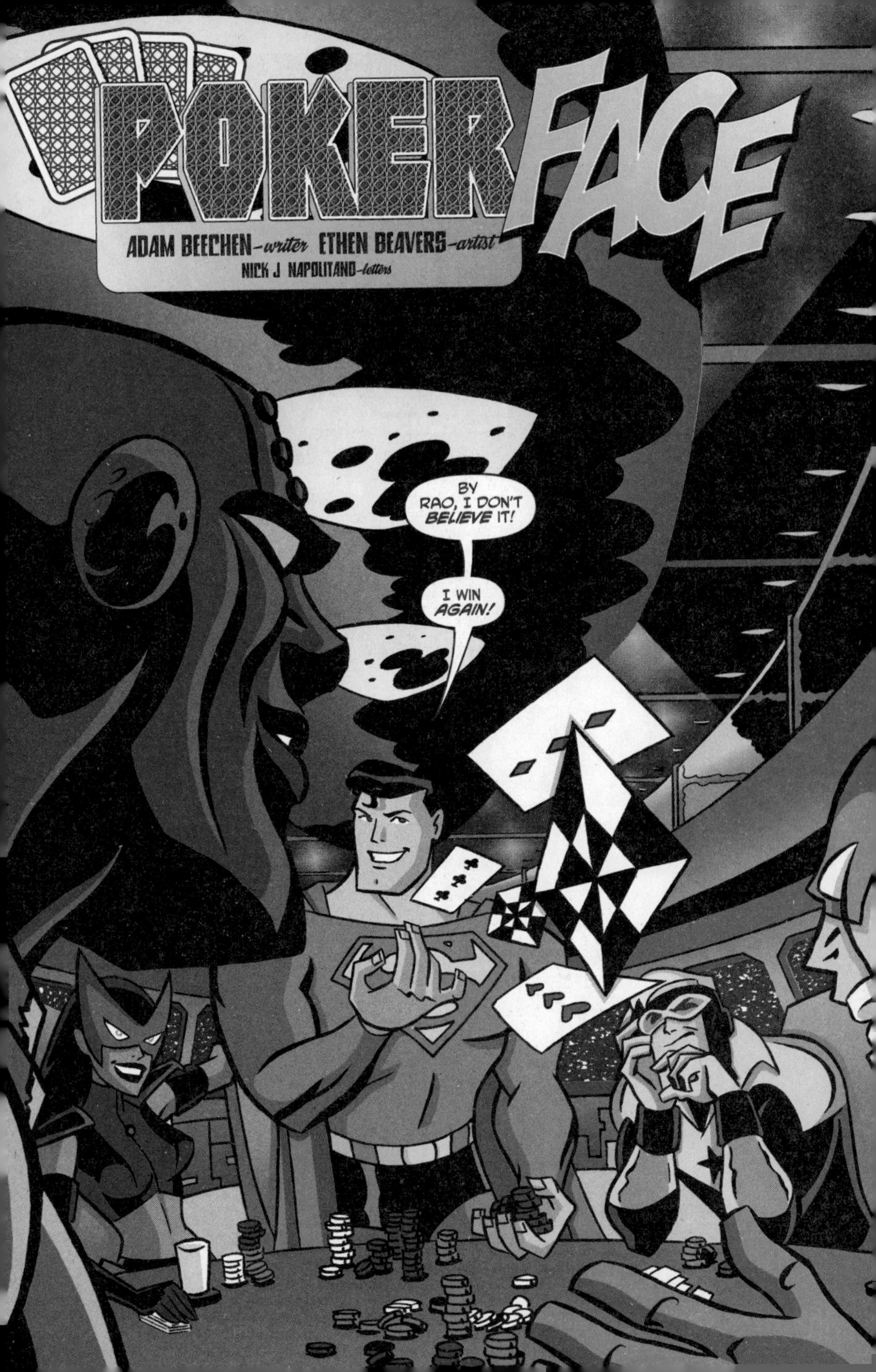
POKER FACE
ADAM BEECHEN–writer ETHEN BEAVERS–artist
NICK J NAPOLITANO–letters
BY RAO, I DON'T BELIEVE IT!
I WIN AGAIN!

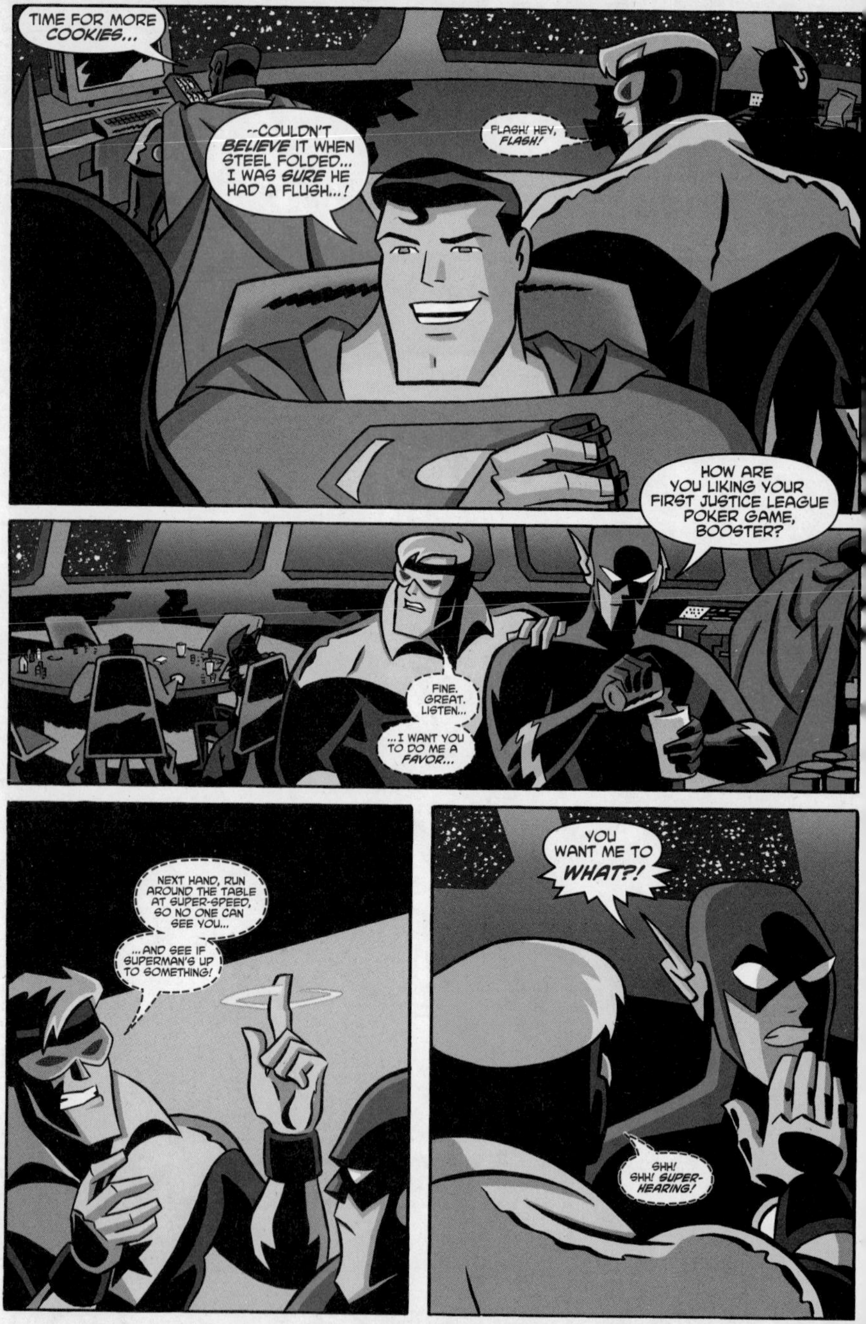

TIME FOR MORE COOKIES...
--COULDN'T BELIEVE IT WHEN STEEL FOLDED... I WAS SURE HE HAD A FLUSH...!
FLASH! HEY, FLASH!
HOW ARE YOU LIKING YOUR FIRST JUSTICE LEAGUE POKER GAME, BOOSTER?
FINE. GREAT. LISTEN...
...I WANT YOU TO DO ME A FAVOR...
NEXT HAND, RUN AROUND THE TABLE AT SUPER-SPEED, SO NO ONE CAN SEE YOU...
...AND SEE IF SUPERMAN'S UP TO SOMETHING!
YOU WANT ME TO WHAT?!
SHH! SHH! SUPER-HEARING!

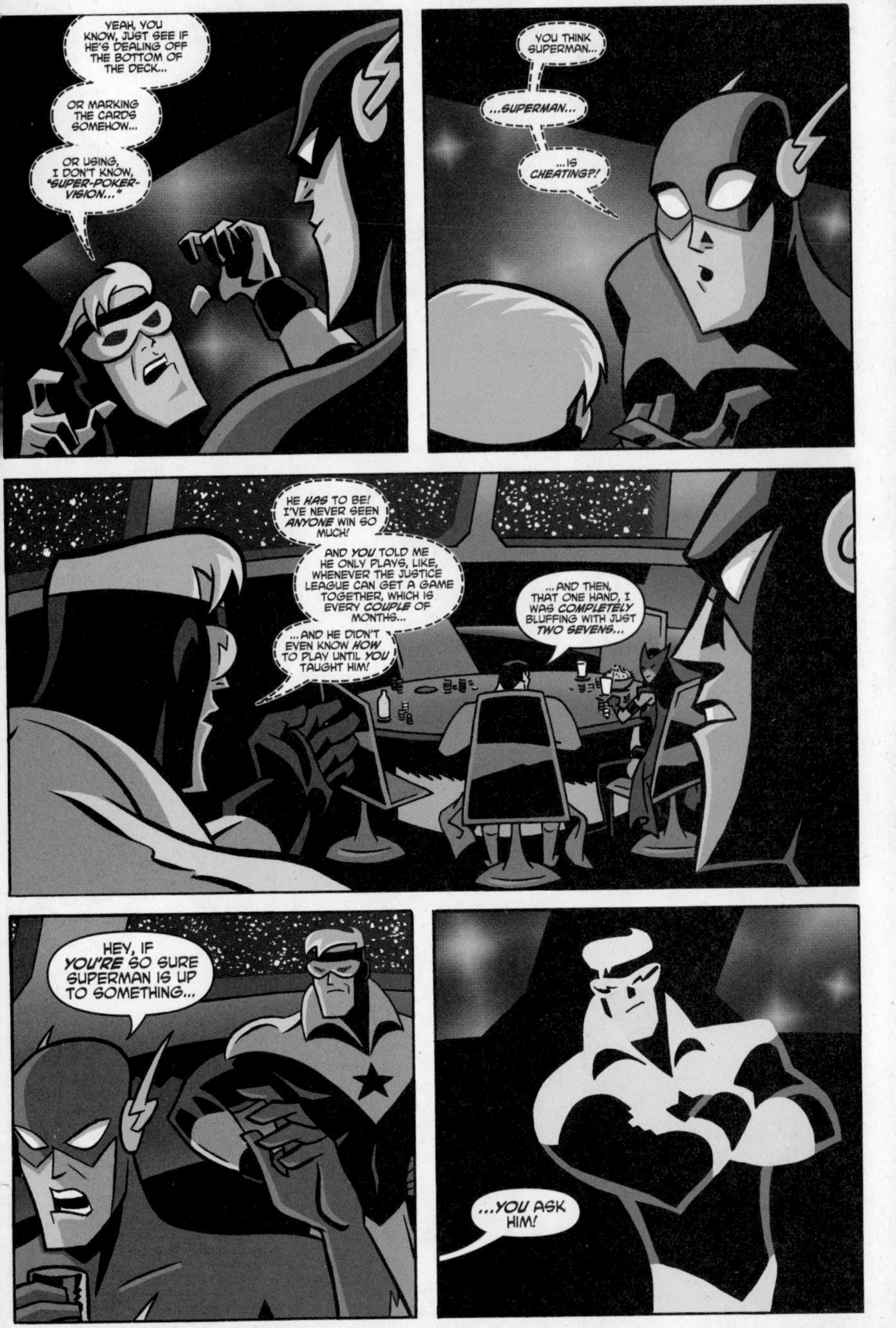
YEAH, YOU KNOW, JUST SEE IF HE'S DEALING OFF THE BOTTOM OF THE DECK...
OR MARKING THE CARDS SOMEHOW...
OR USING, I DON'T KNOW, "SUPER-POKER-VISION..."
YOU THINK SUPERMAN...
...SUPERMAN...
...IS CHEATING?!
HE HAS TO BE! I'VE NEVER SEEN ANYONE WIN SO MUCH!
AND YOU TOLD ME HE ONLY PLAYS, LIKE, WHENEVER THE JUSTICE LEAGUE CAN GET A GAME TOGETHER, WHICH IS EVERY COUPLE OF MONTHS...
...AND HE DIDN'T EVEN KNOW HOW TO PLAY UNTIL YOU TAUGHT HIM!
...AND THEN, THAT ONE HAND, I WAS COMPLETELY BLUFFING WITH JUST TWO SEVENS...
HEY, IF YOU'RE SO SURE SUPERMAN IS UP TO SOMETHING...
...YOU ASK HIM!

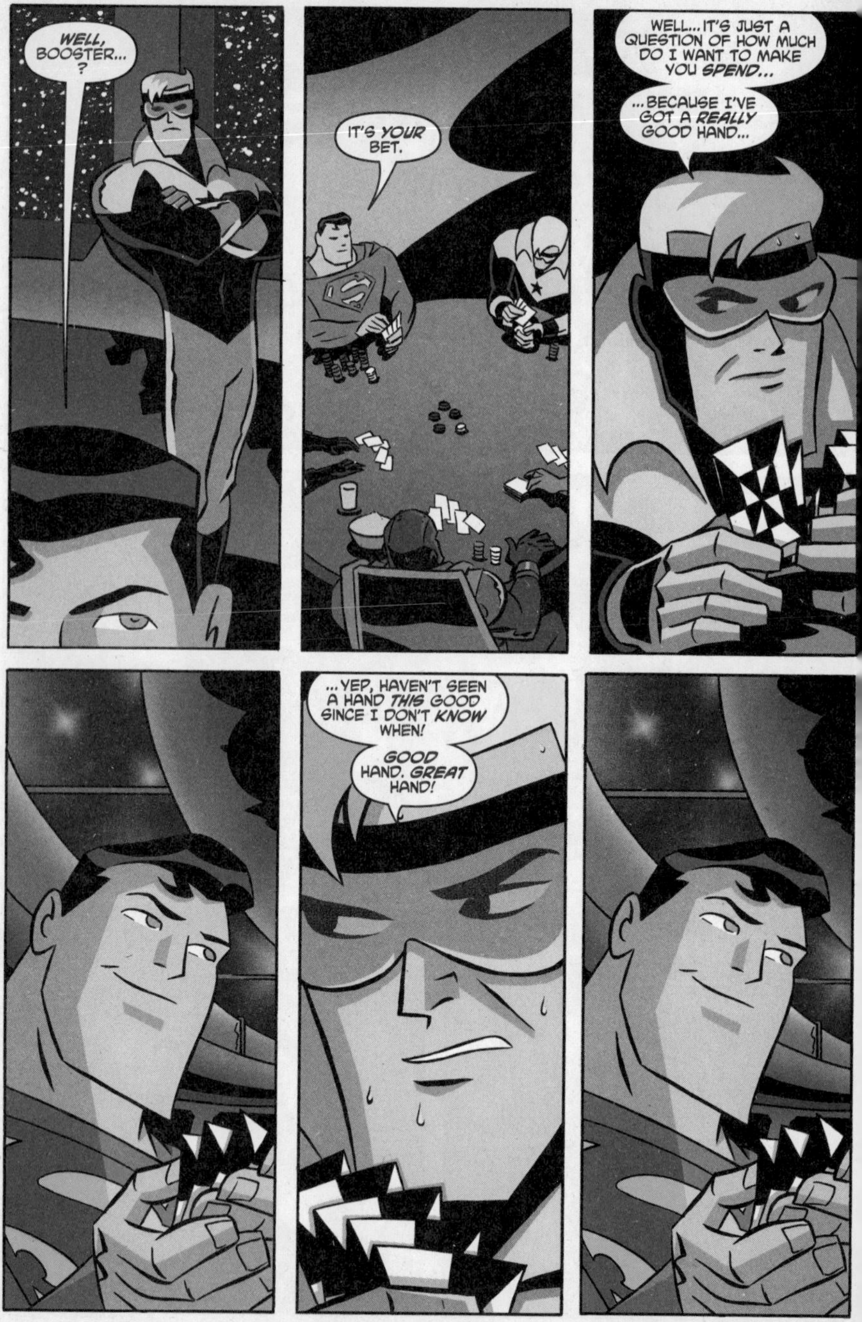
WELL, BOOSTER... ?
IT'S YOUR BET.
WELL... IT'S JUST A QUESTION OF HOW MUCH DO I WANT TO MAKE YOU SPEND...
...BECAUSE I'VE GOT A REALLY GOOD HAND...
...YEP, HAVEN'T SEEN A HAND THIS GOOD SINCE I DON'T KNOW WHEN!
GOOD HAND. GREAT HAND!

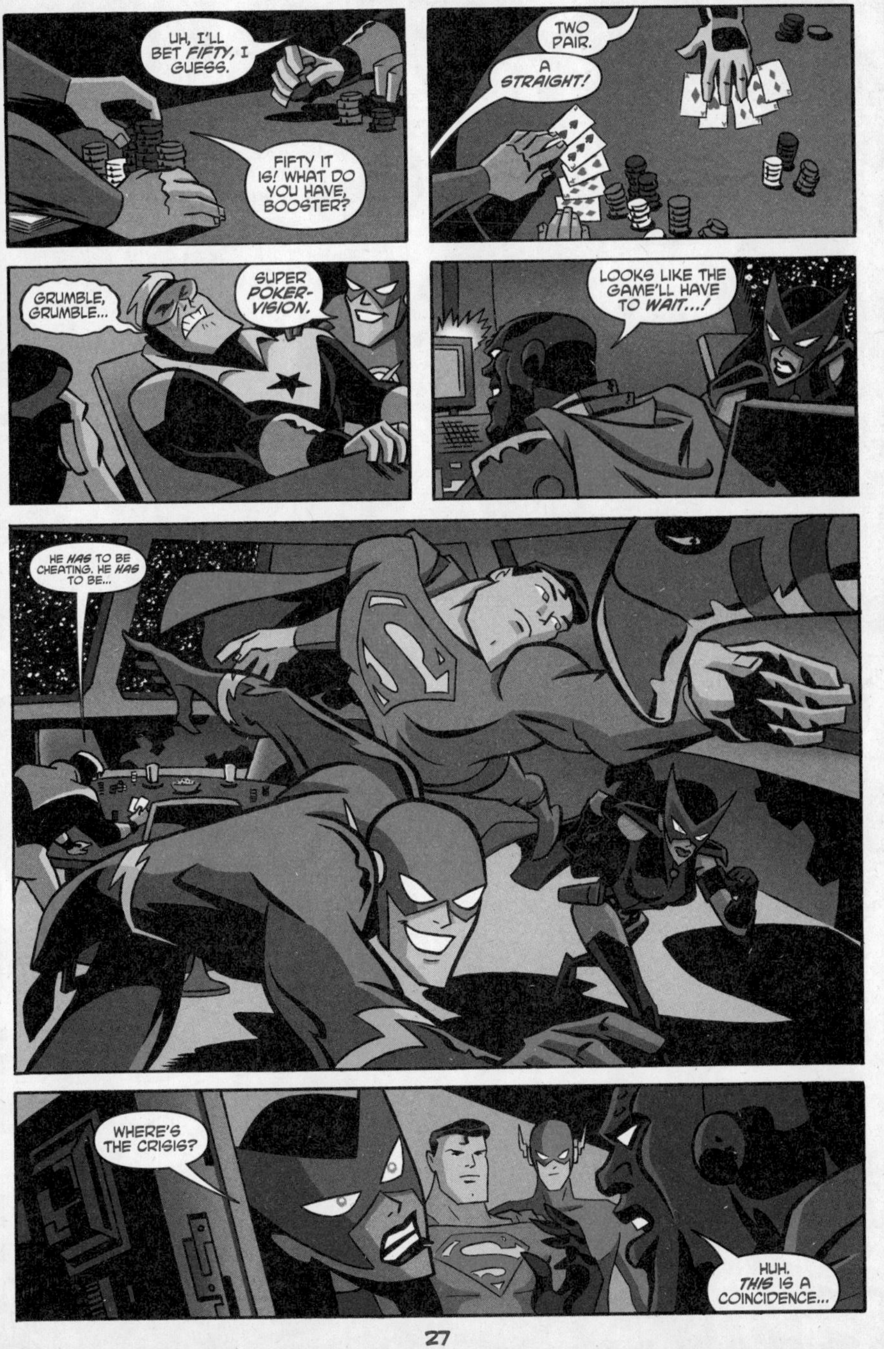
UH, I'LL BET FIFTY, I GUESS.
FIFTY IT IS! WHAT DO YOU HAVE, BOOSTER?
TWO PAIR.
A STRAIGHT!
GRUMBLE, GRUMBLE...
SUPER POKER-VISION.
LOOKS LIKE THE GAME'LL HAVE TO WAIT...!
HE HAS TO BE CHEATING. HE HAS TO BE...
WHERE'S THE CRISIS?
HUH. THIS IS A COINCIDENCE...

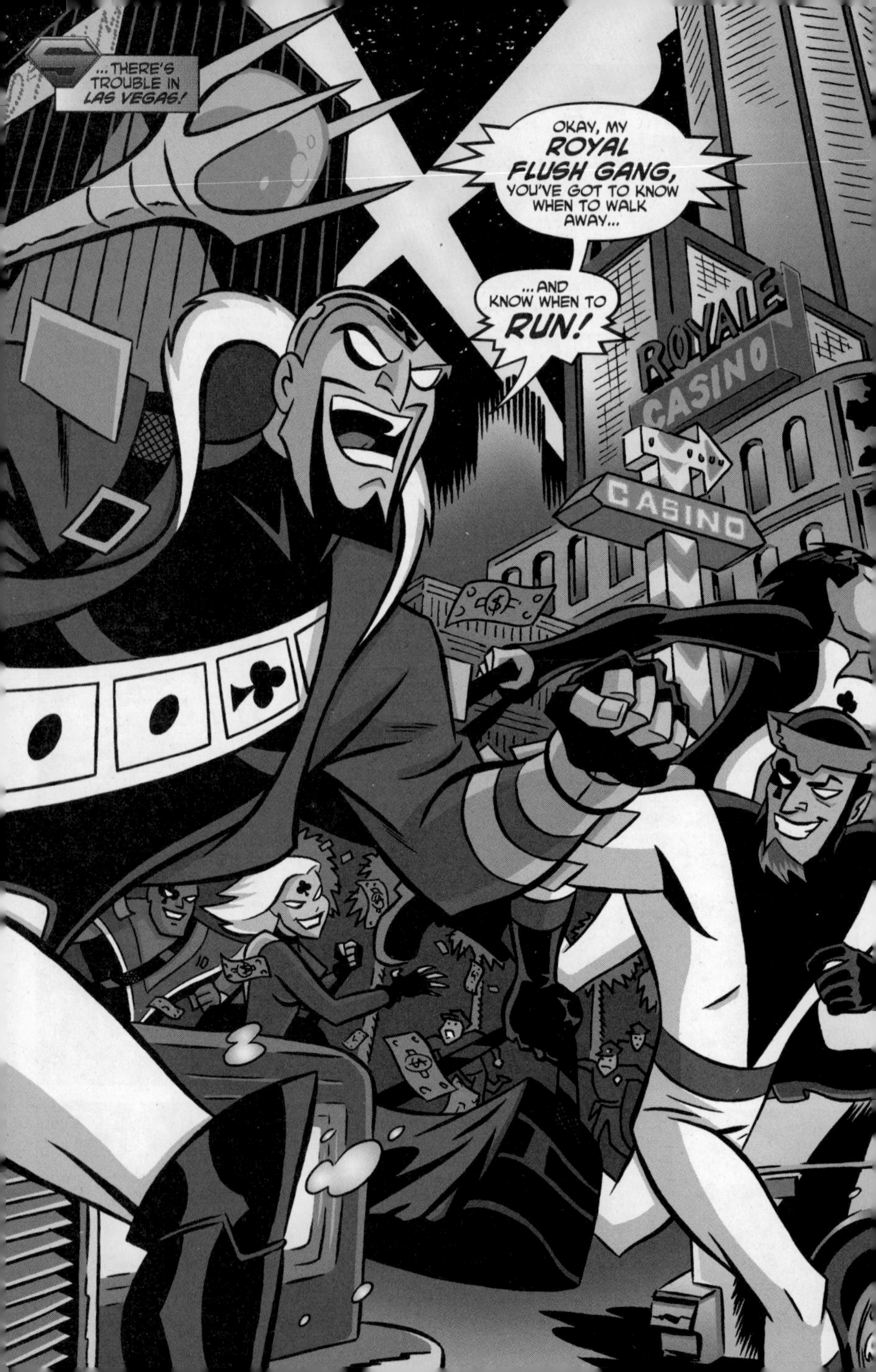
...THERE'S TROUBLE IN LAS VEGAS!
OKAY, MY ROYAL FLUSH GANG, YOU'VE GOT TO KNOW WHEN TO WALK AWAY...
...AND KNOW WHEN TO RUN!
ROYALE CASINO
CASINO

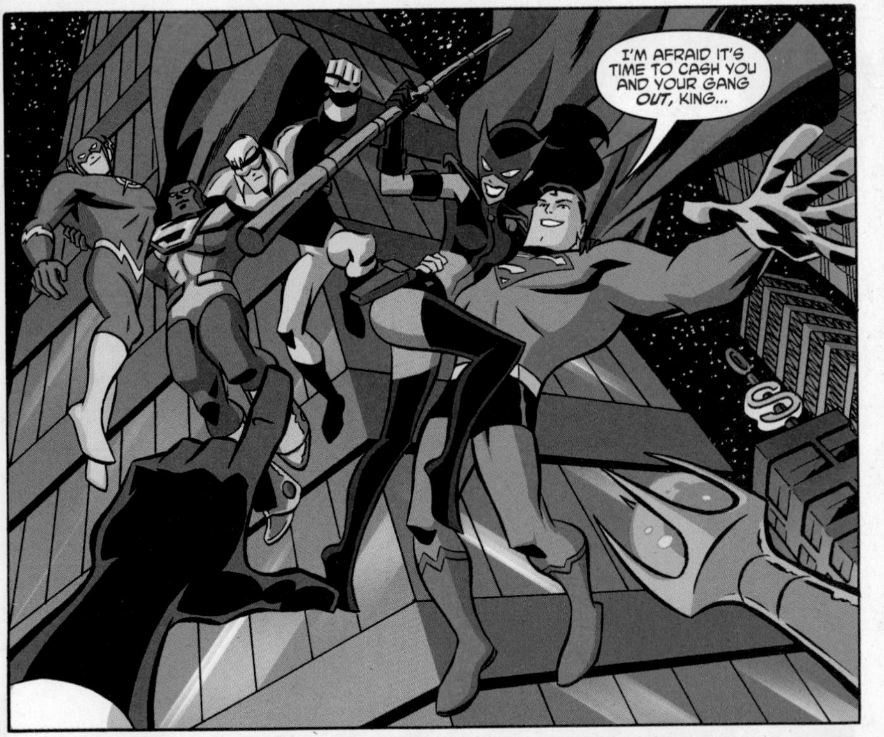
I'M AFRAID IT'S TIME TO CASH YOU AND YOUR GANG *OUT*, KING...

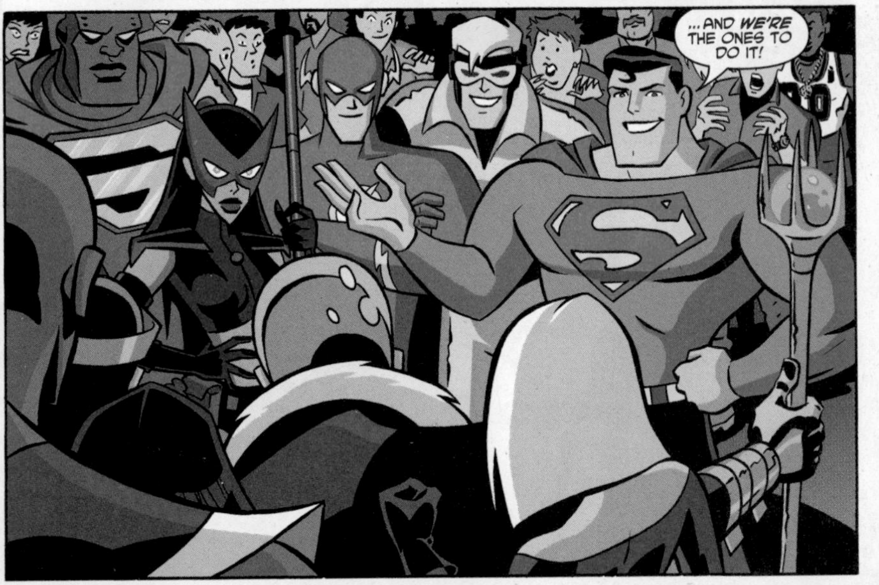
...AND *WE'RE* THE ONES TO DO IT!

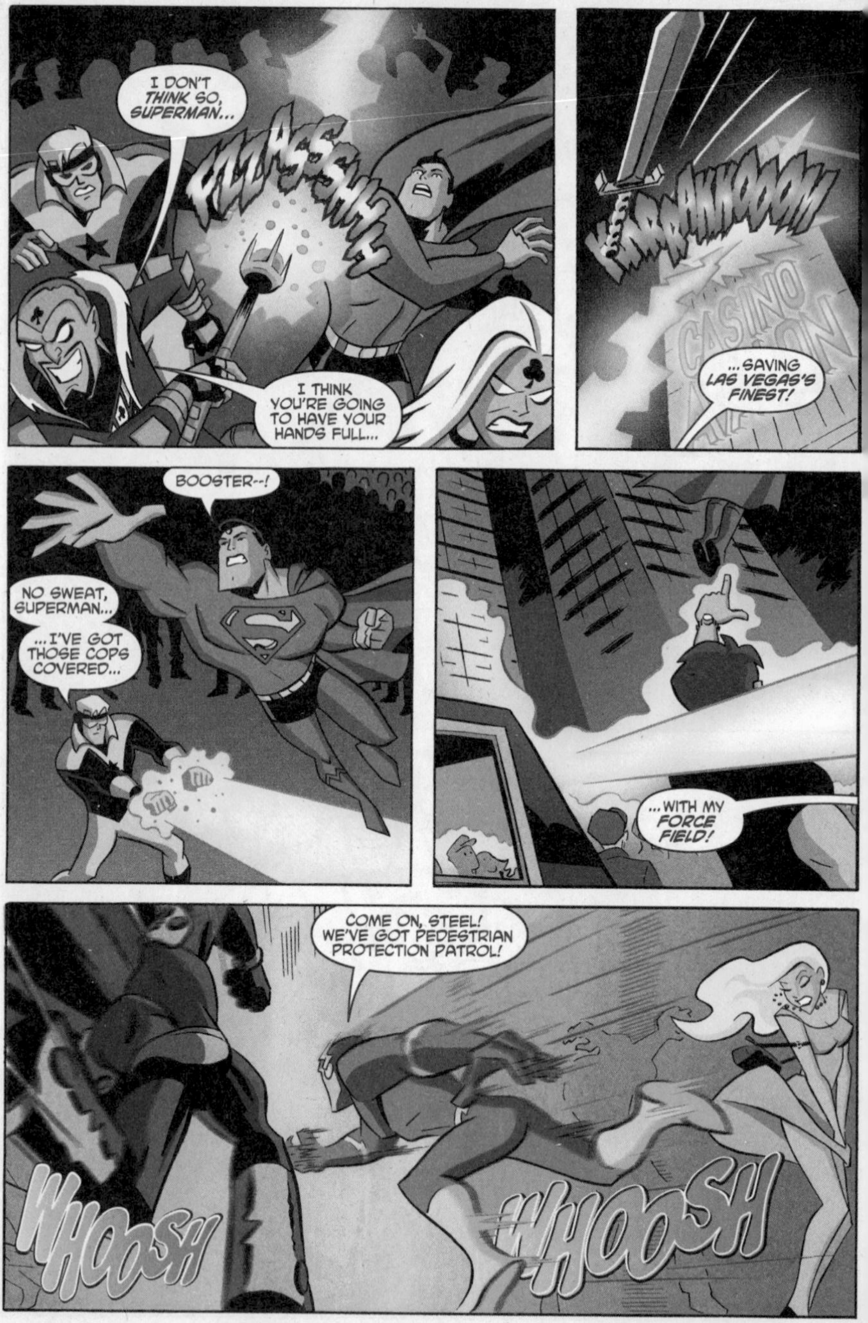
I DON'T THINK SO, SUPERMAN...
FZZASSSHH
I THINK YOU'RE GOING TO HAVE YOUR HANDS FULL...
KRRAKKOOOM
CASINO
...SAVING LAS VEGAS'S FINEST!
BOOSTER--!
NO SWEAT, SUPERMAN...
...I'VE GOT THOSE COPS COVERED...
...WITH MY FORCE FIELD!
COME ON, STEEL! WE'VE GOT PEDESTRIAN PROTECTION PATROL!
WHOOSH
WHOOSH

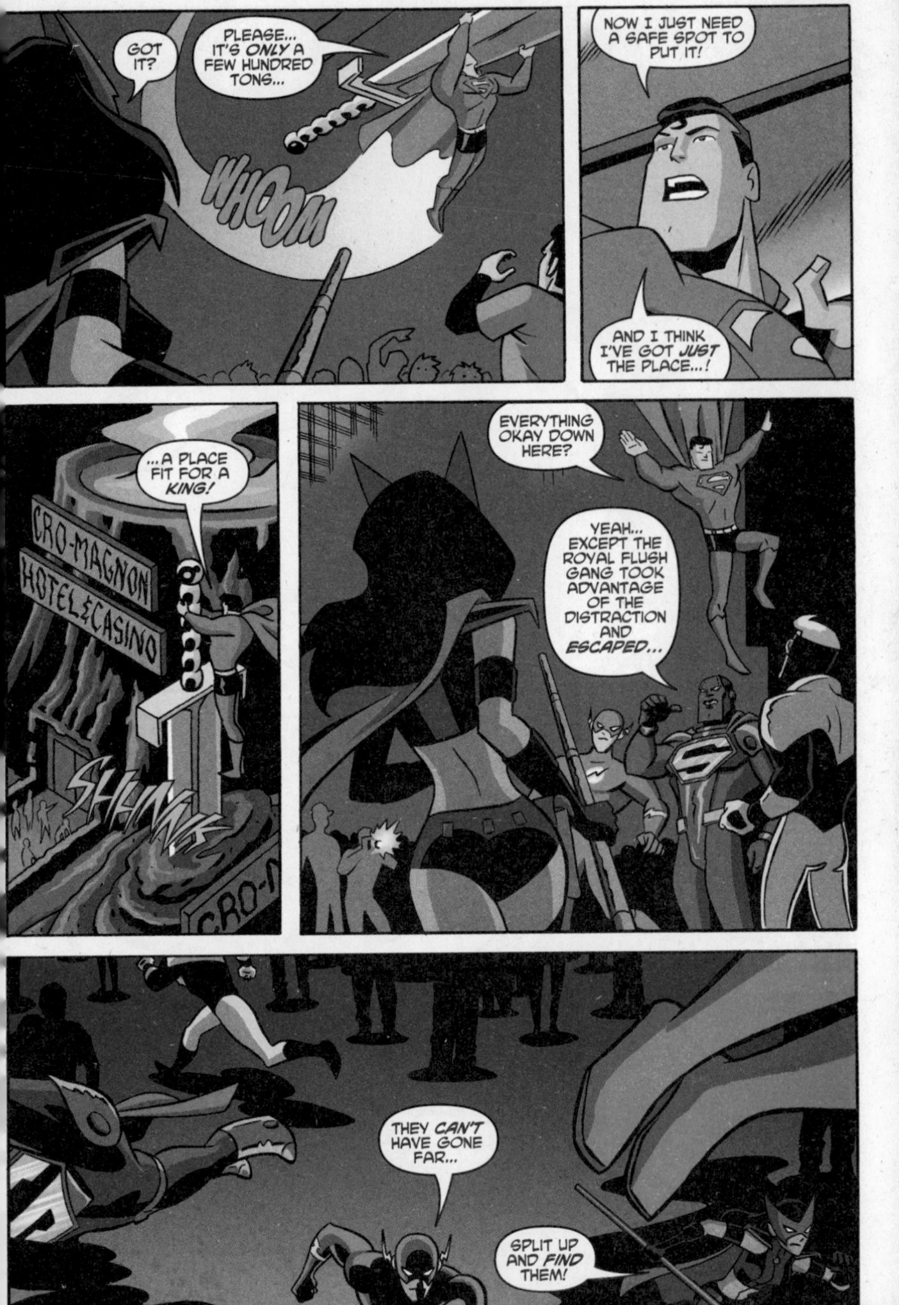
GOT IT?
PLEASE... IT'S ONLY A FEW HUNDRED TONS...
WHOOM
NOW I JUST NEED A SAFE SPOT TO PUT IT!
AND I THINK I'VE GOT JUST THE PLACE...!
...A PLACE FIT FOR A KING!
CRO-MAGNON
HOTEL&CASINO
SHUNK
EVERYTHING OKAY DOWN HERE?
YEAH... EXCEPT THE ROYAL FLUSH GANG TOOK ADVANTAGE OF THE DISTRACTION AND ESCAPED...
THEY CAN'T HAVE GONE FAR...
SPLIT UP AND FIND THEM!

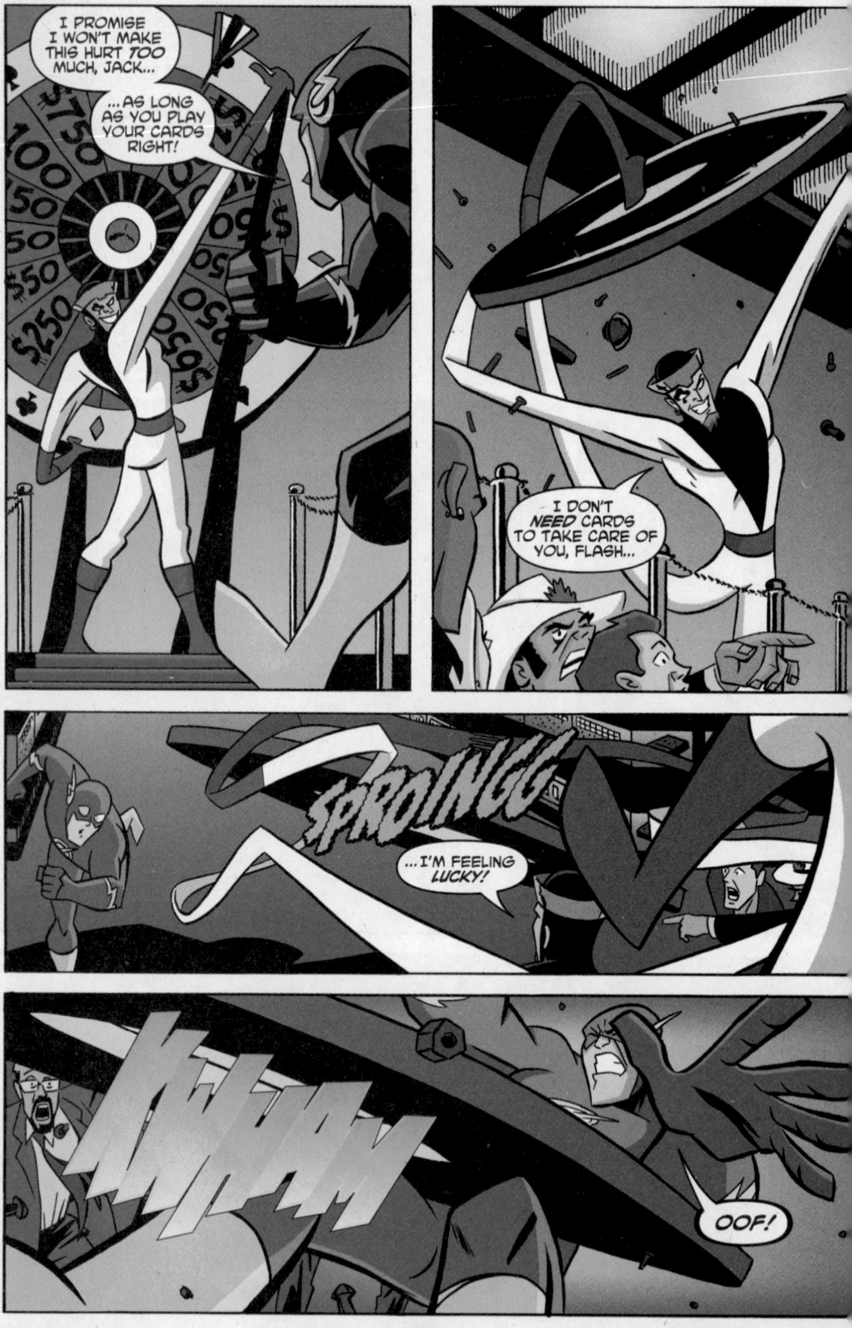
I PROMISE I WON'T MAKE THIS HURT *TOO* MUCH, JACK...
...AS LONG AS YOU PLAY YOUR CARDS RIGHT!
I DON'T *NEED* CARDS TO TAKE CARE OF YOU, FLASH...
SPROINGG
...I'M FEELING *LUCKY!*
WHAM
OOF!

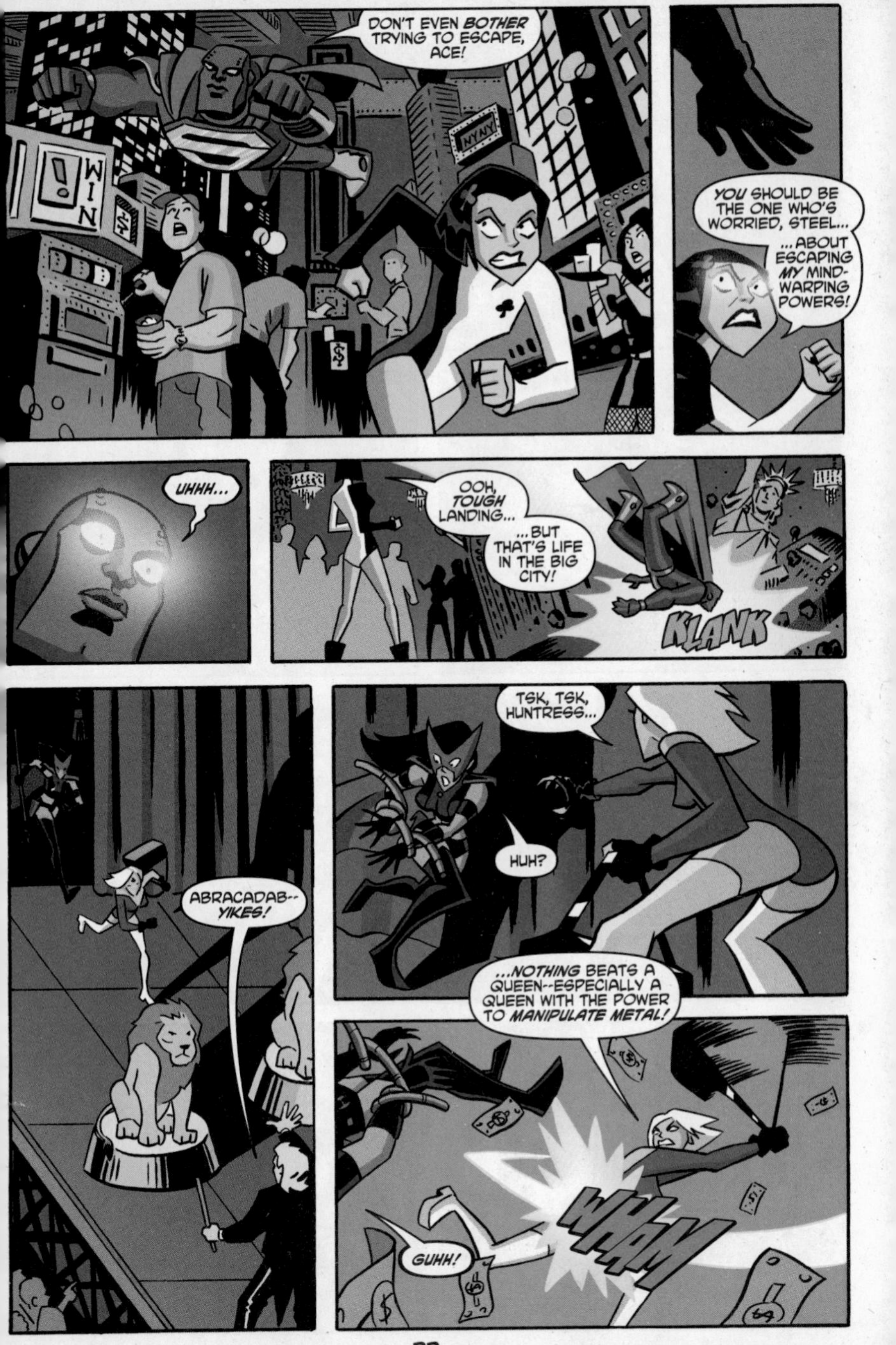
DON'T EVEN BOTHER TRYING TO ESCAPE, ACE!
WIN
NY NY
YOU SHOULD BE THE ONE WHO'S WORRIED, STEEL...
...ABOUT ESCAPING MY MIND-WARPING POWERS!
UHHH...
OOH, TOUGH LANDING...
...BUT THAT'S LIFE IN THE BIG CITY!
KLANK
ABRACADAB-- YIKES!
TSK, TSK, HUNTRESS...
HUH?
...NOTHING BEATS A QUEEN--ESPECIALLY A QUEEN WITH THE POWER TO MANIPULATE METAL!
WHAM
GUHH!

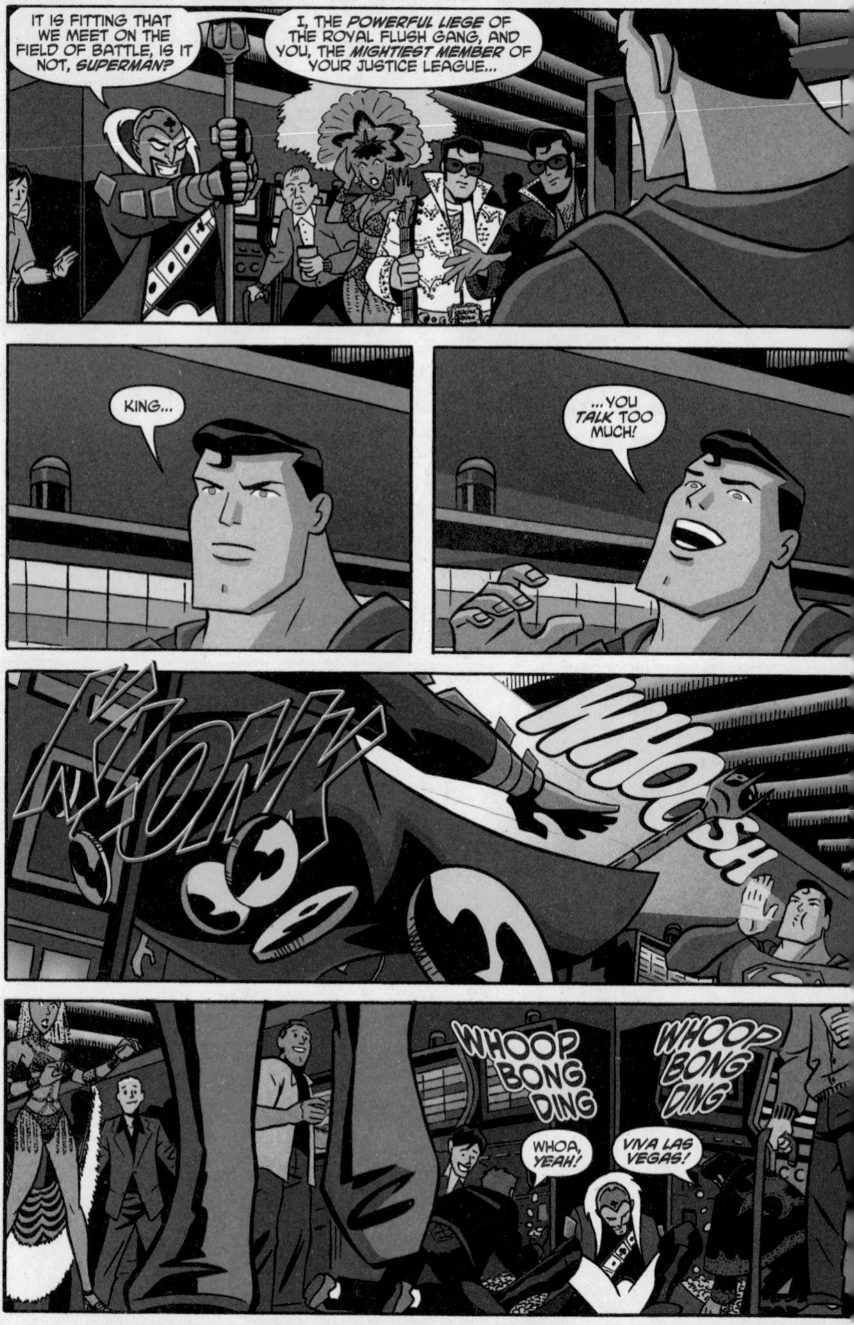
IT IS FITTING THAT WE MEET ON THE FIELD OF BATTLE, IS IT NOT, *SUPERMAN?*
I, THE *POWERFUL LIEGE* OF THE ROYAL FLUSH GANG, AND YOU, THE *MIGHTIEST MEMBER* OF YOUR JUSTICE LEAGUE...
KING...
...YOU *TALK* TOO MUCH!
KLONK
WHOOSH
WHOOP BONG DING
WHOOP BONG DING
WHOA, YEAH!
VIVA LAS VEGAS!

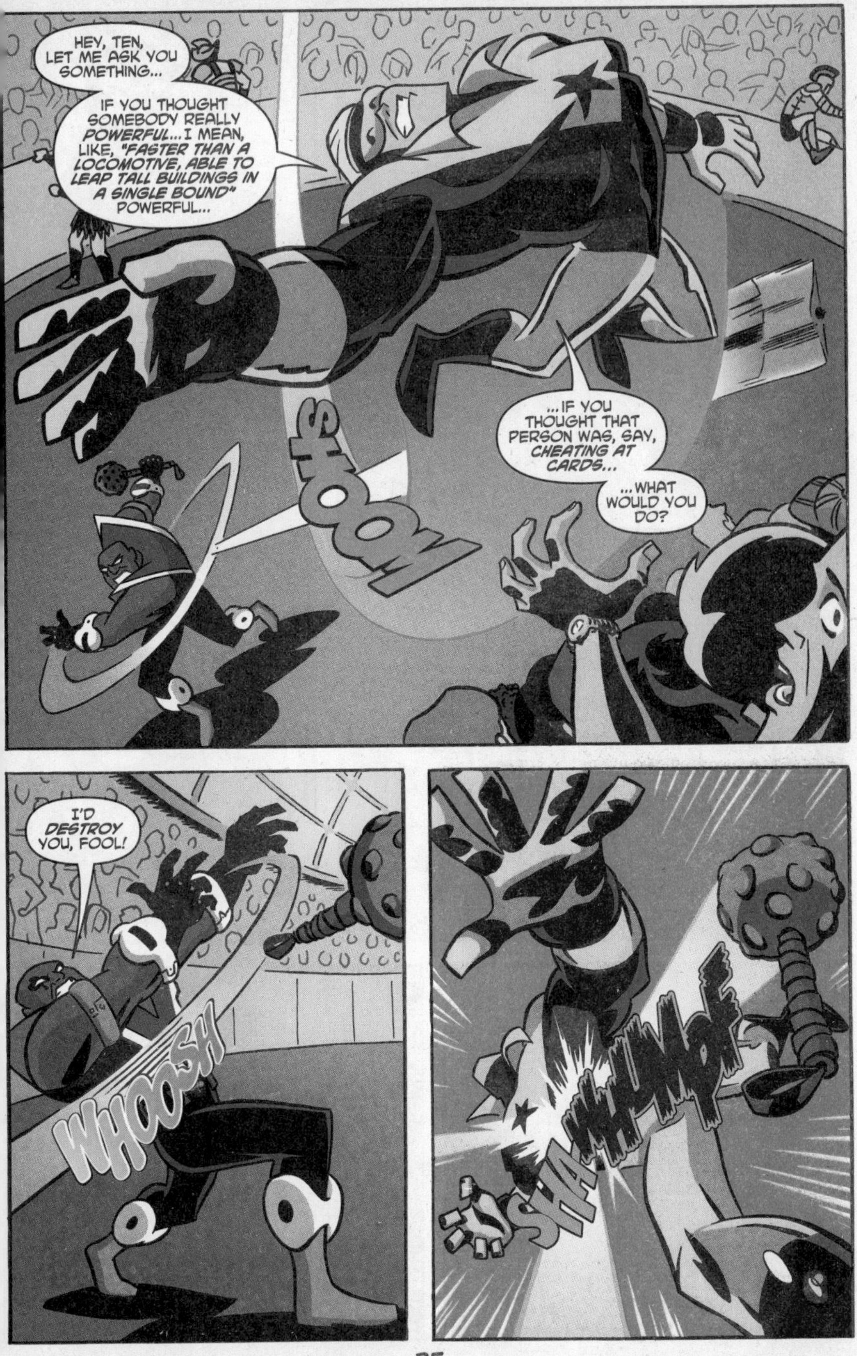
HEY, TEN, LET ME ASK YOU SOMETHING...
IF YOU THOUGHT SOMEBODY REALLY *POWERFUL*...I MEAN, LIKE, *"FASTER THAN A LOCOMOTIVE, ABLE TO LEAP TALL BUILDINGS IN A SINGLE BOUND"* POWERFUL...
SHOOOM
...IF YOU THOUGHT THAT PERSON WAS, SAY, *CHEATING AT CARDS*...
...WHAT WOULD YOU DO?
I'D *DESTROY* YOU, FOOL!
WHOOSH
SHA-WHUMP

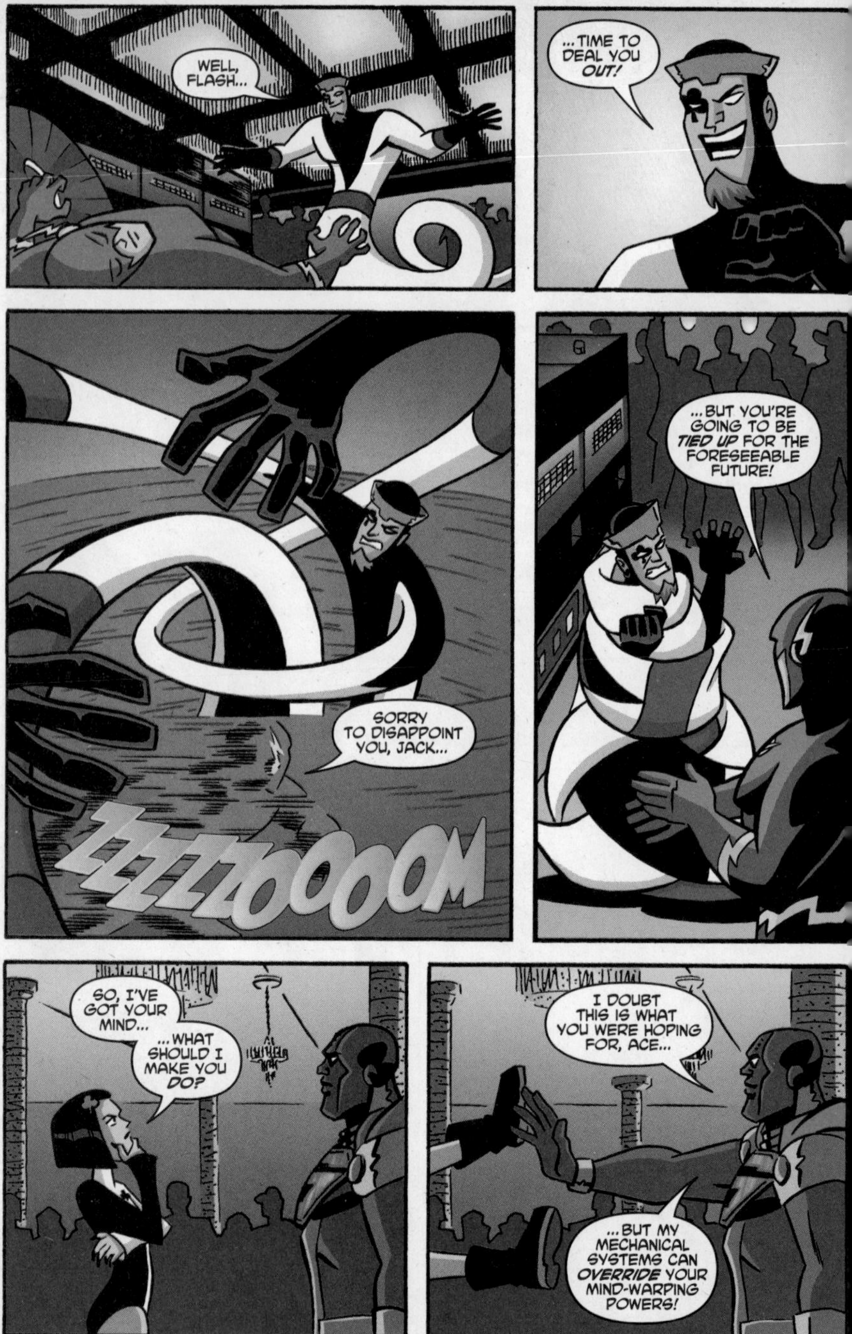
WELL, FLASH...
...TIME TO DEAL YOU OUT!
SORRY TO DISAPPOINT YOU, JACK...
ZZZZZOOOOOM
...BUT YOU'RE GOING TO BE TIED UP FOR THE FORESEEABLE FUTURE!
SO, I'VE GOT YOUR MIND...
...WHAT SHOULD I MAKE YOU DO?
I DOUBT THIS IS WHAT YOU WERE HOPING FOR, ACE...
...BUT MY MECHANICAL SYSTEMS CAN OVERRIDE YOUR MIND-WARPING POWERS!

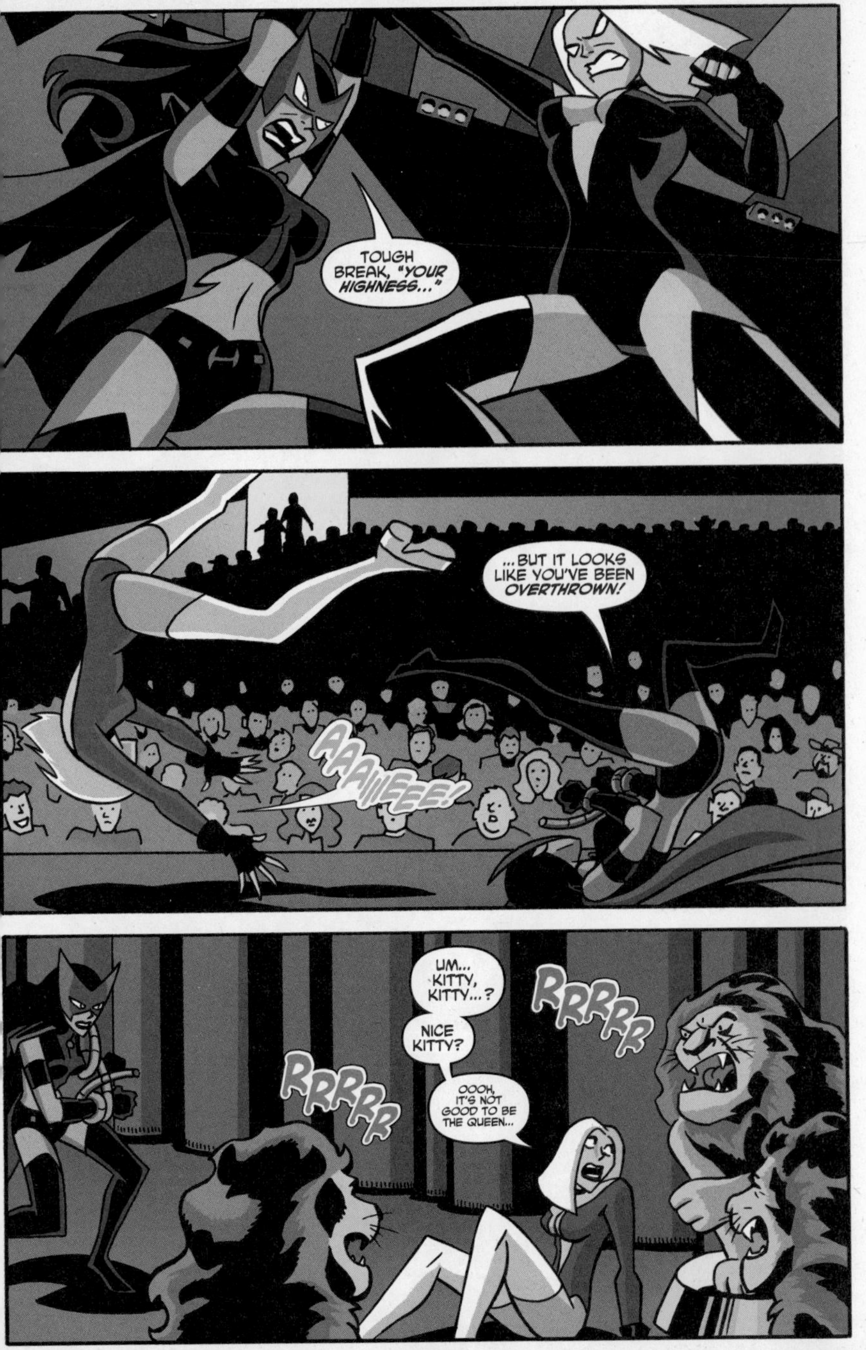

TOUGH BREAK, "YOUR HIGHNESS..."
...BUT IT LOOKS LIKE YOU'VE BEEN OVERTHROWN!
AAAIIIEEEE!
UM... KITTY, KITTY...?
NICE KITTY?
RRRRR
RRRRR
OOOH, IT'S NOT GOOD TO BE THE QUEEN...

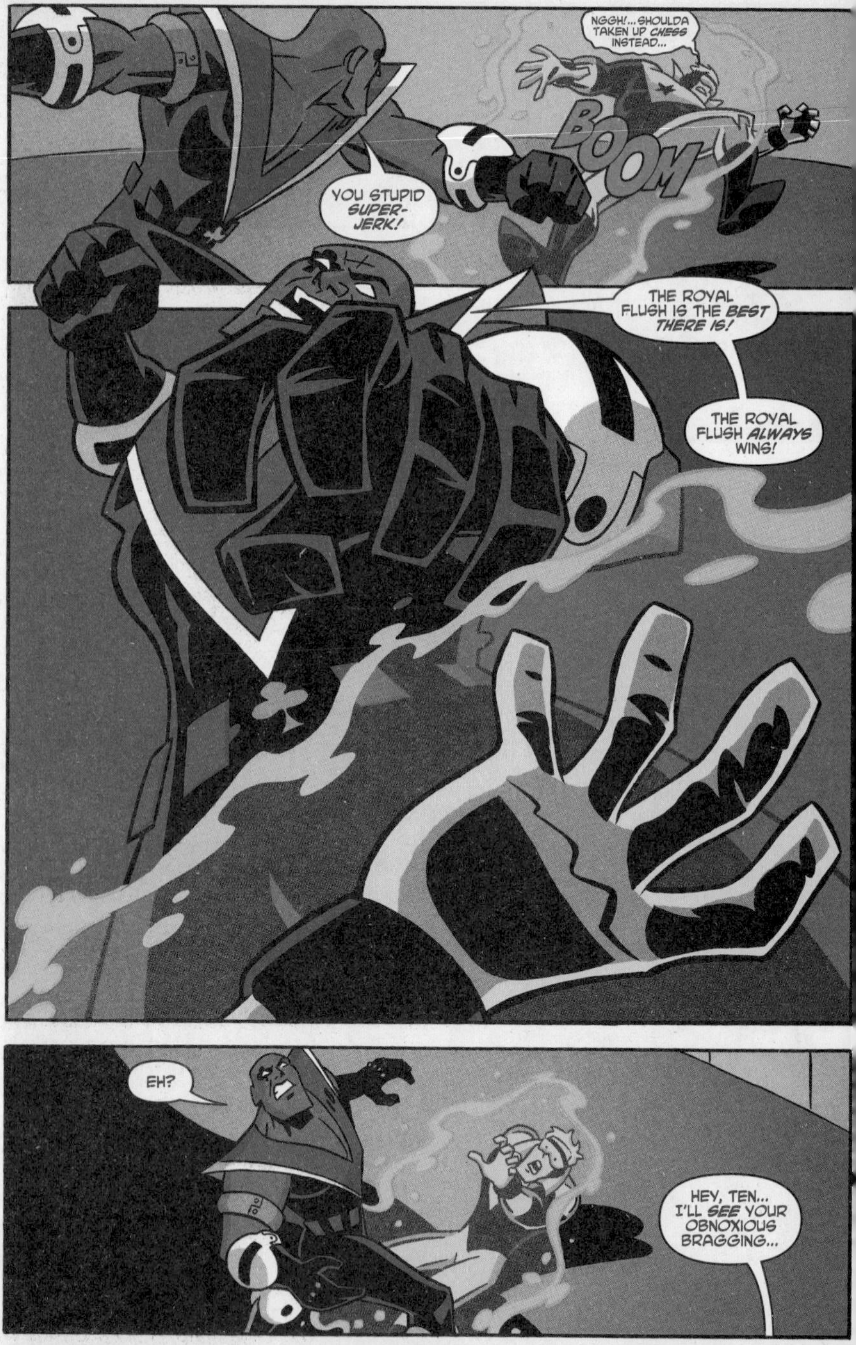
NGGH!...SHOULDA TAKEN UP CHESS INSTEAD...
BOOM
YOU STUPID SUPER-JERK!
THE ROYAL FLUSH IS THE BEST THERE IS!
THE ROYAL FLUSH ALWAYS WINS!
EH?
HEY, TEN... I'LL SEE YOUR OBNOXIOUS BRAGGING...

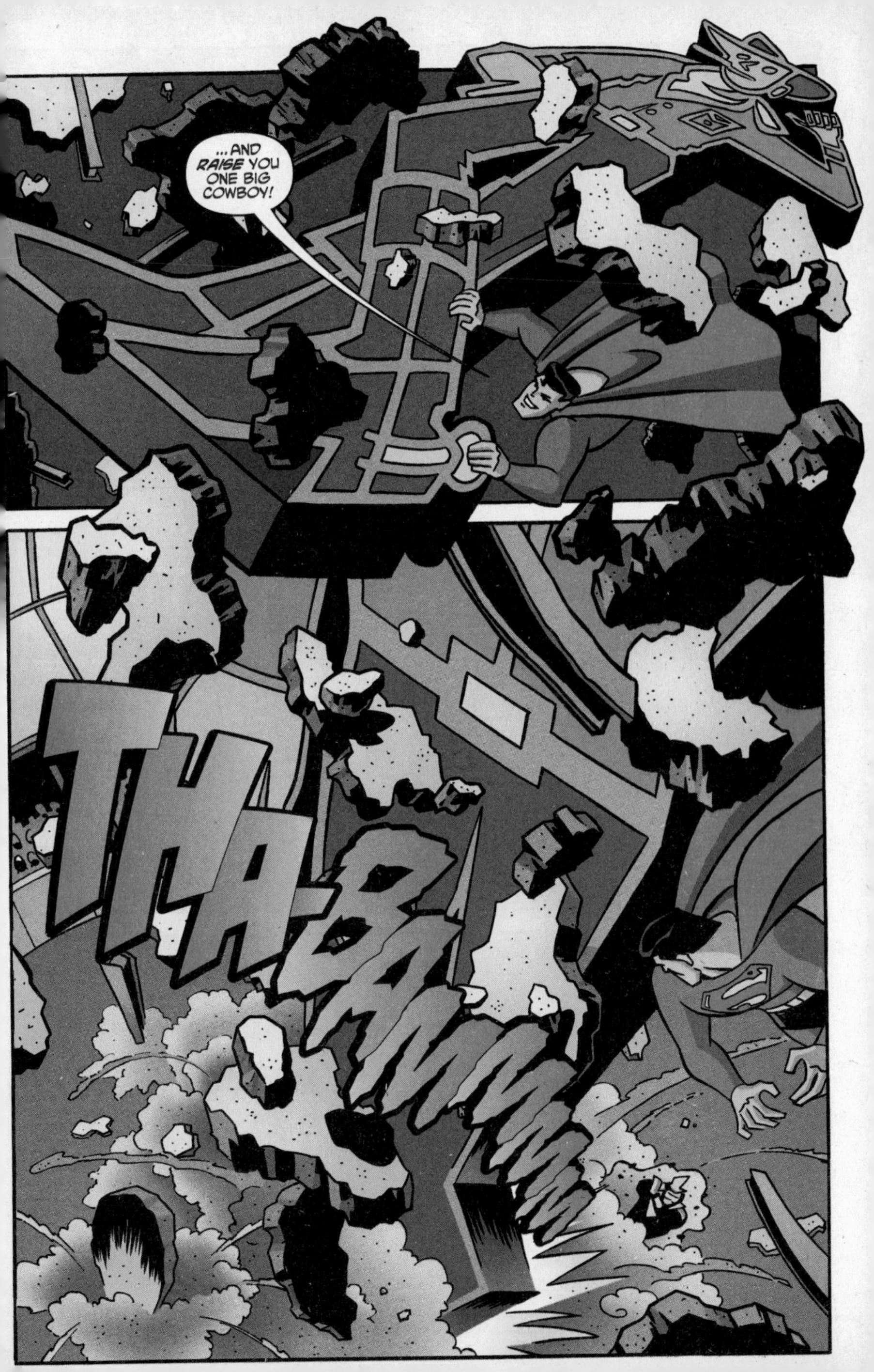
...AND RAISE YOU ONE BIG COWBOY!
THA-BAMM

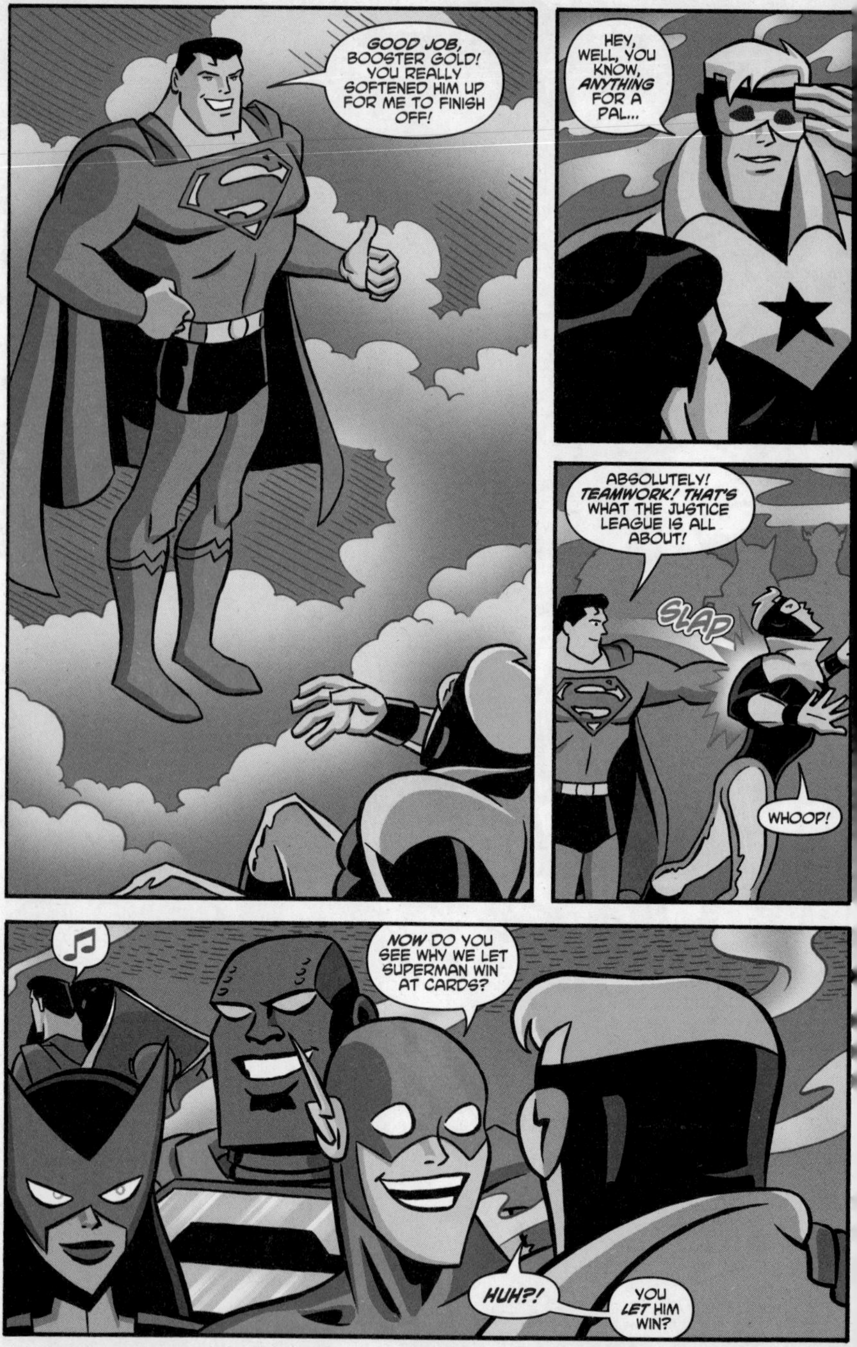
GOOD JOB, BOOSTER GOLD! YOU REALLY SOFTENED HIM UP FOR ME TO FINISH OFF!
HEY, WELL, YOU KNOW, ANYTHING FOR A PAL...
ABSOLUTELY! TEAMWORK! THAT'S WHAT THE JUSTICE LEAGUE IS ALL ABOUT!
SLAP
WHOOP!
NOW DO YOU SEE WHY WE LET SUPERMAN WIN AT CARDS?
HUH?!
YOU LET HIM WIN?

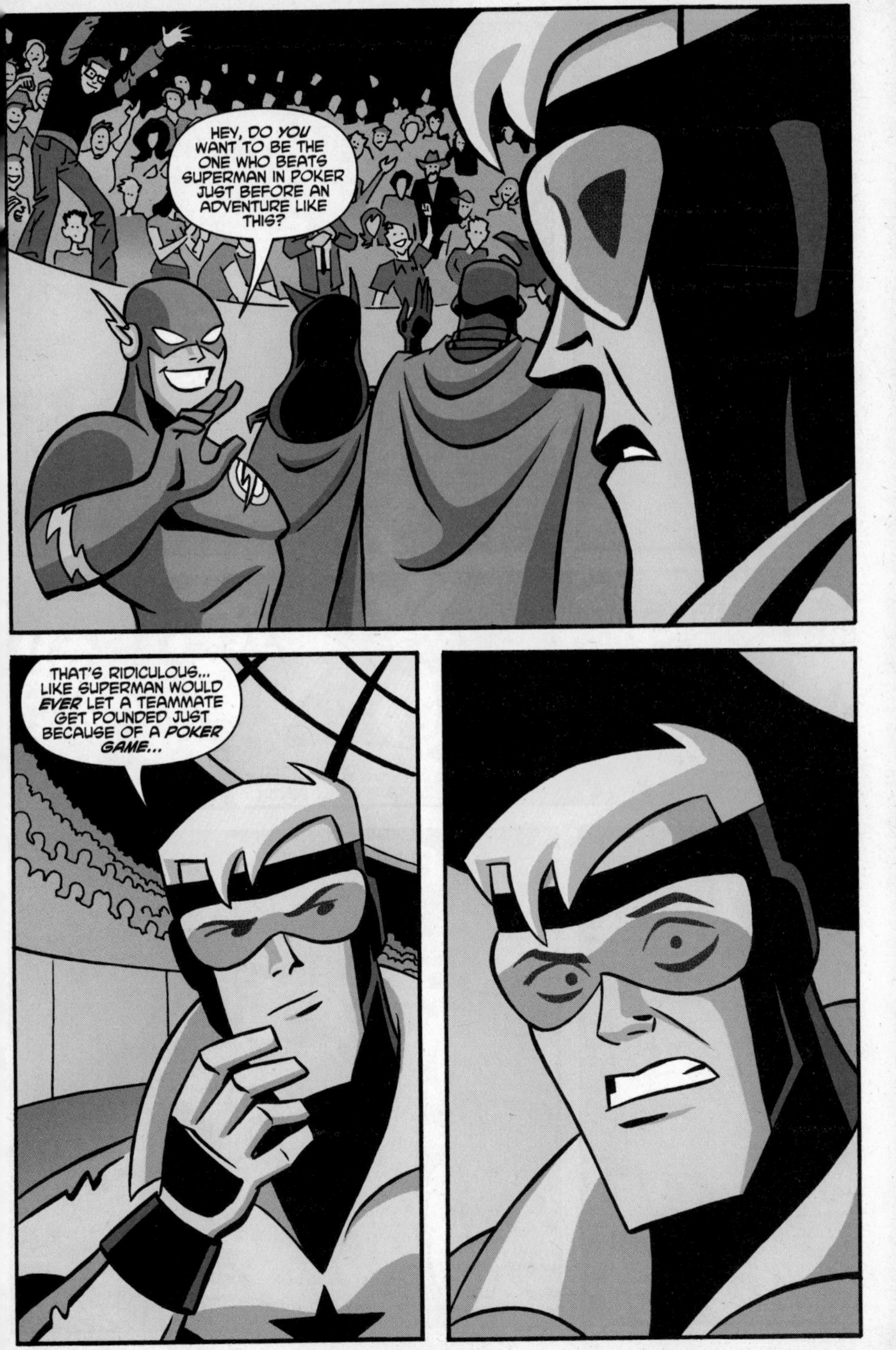
HEY, DO YOU WANT TO BE THE ONE WHO BEATS SUPERMAN IN POKER JUST BEFORE AN ADVENTURE LIKE THIS?
THAT'S RIDICULOUS... LIKE SUPERMAN WOULD EVER LET A TEAMMATE GET POUNDED JUST BECAUSE OF A POKER GAME...

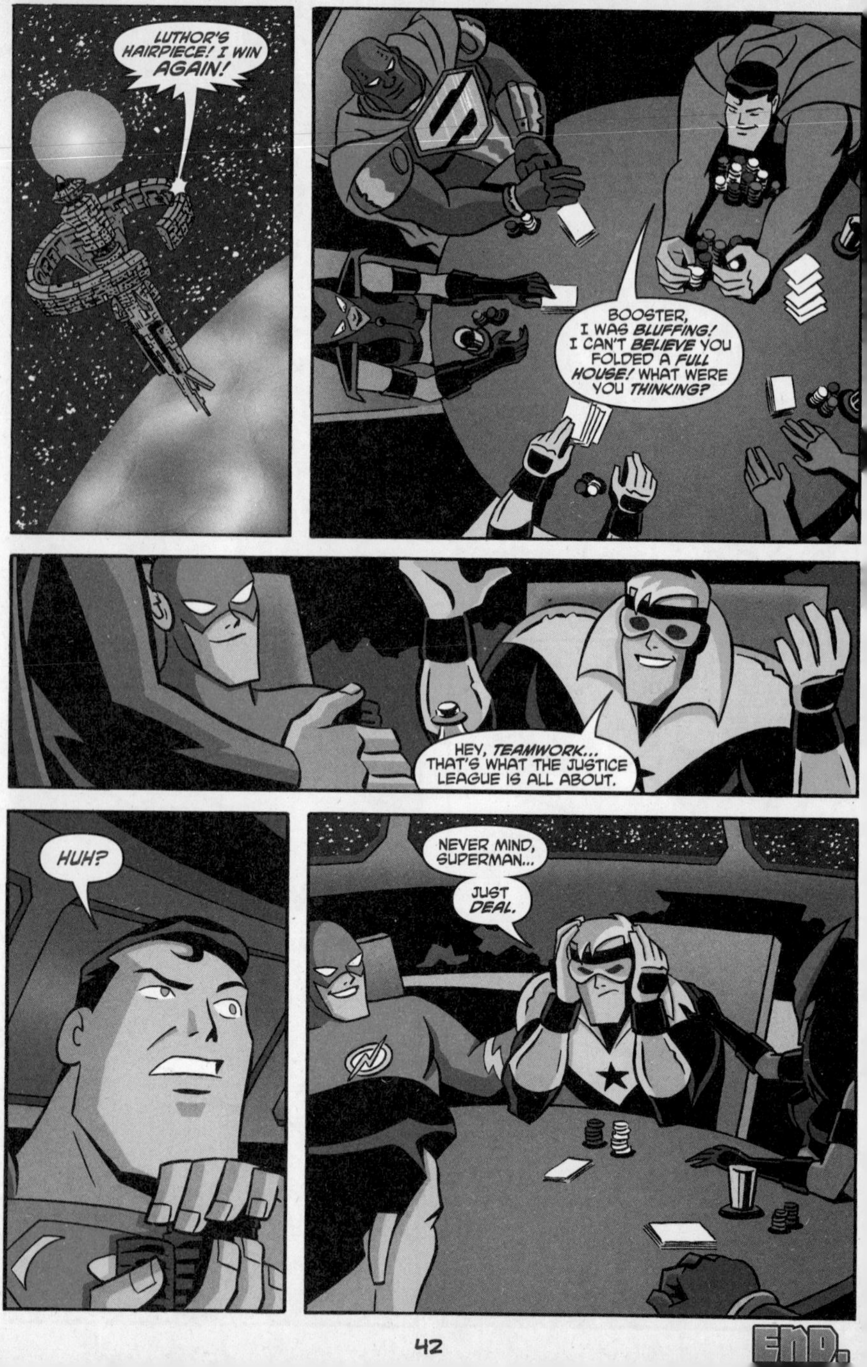
LUTHOR'S HAIRPIECE! I WIN AGAIN!
BOOSTER, I WAS BLUFFING! I CAN'T BELIEVE YOU FOLDED A FULL HOUSE! WHAT WERE YOU THINKING?
HEY, TEAMWORK... THAT'S WHAT THE JUSTICE LEAGUE IS ALL ABOUT.
HUH?
NEVER MIND, SUPERMAN...
JUST DEAL.
END.

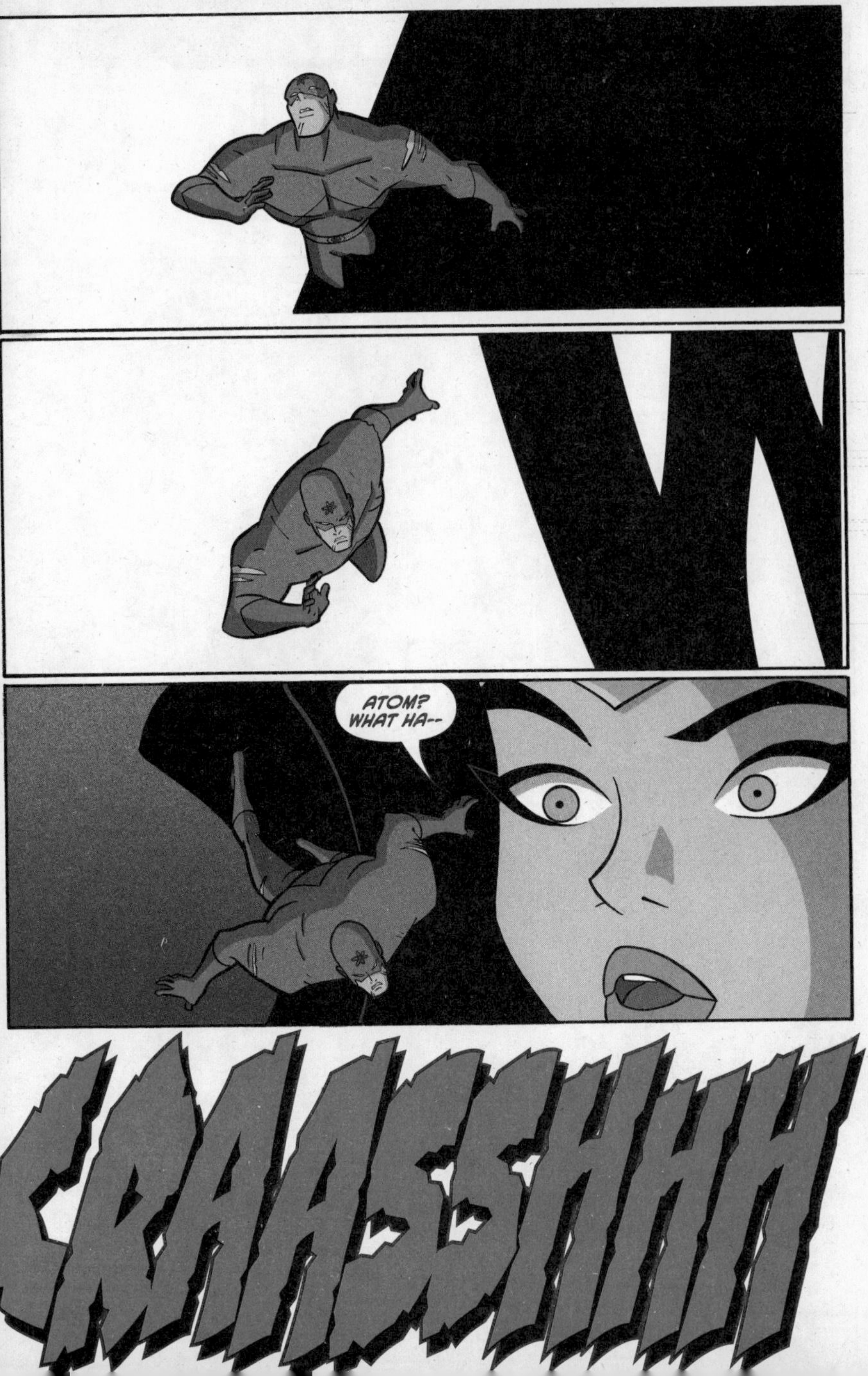
ATOM?
WHAT HA--
CRAASHHH

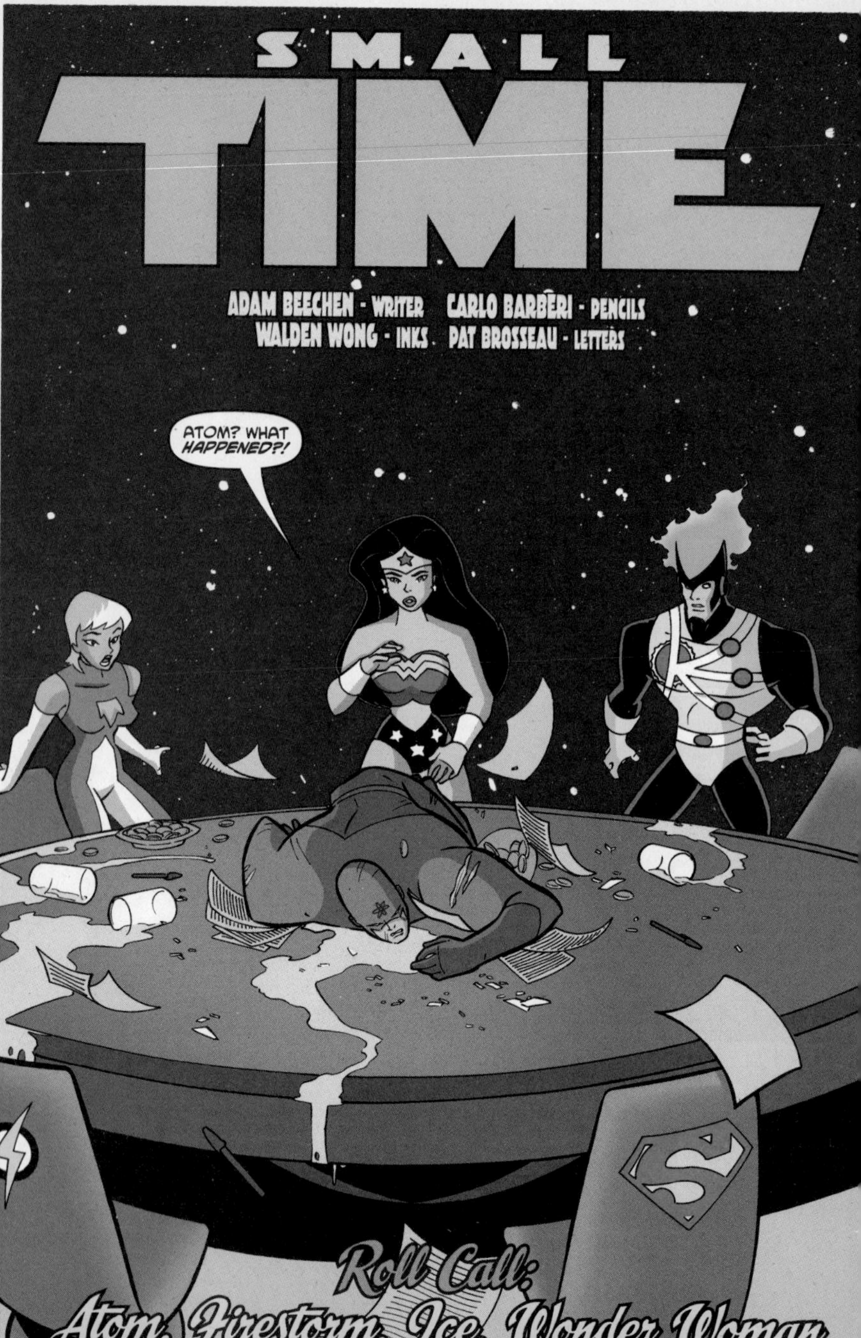
SMALL TIME
ADAM BEECHEN - WRITER CARLO BARBERI - PENCILS
WALDEN WONG - INKS PAT BROSSEAU - LETTERS
ATOM? WHAT HAPPENED?!
Roll Call:
Atom, Firestorm, Ice, Wonder Woman

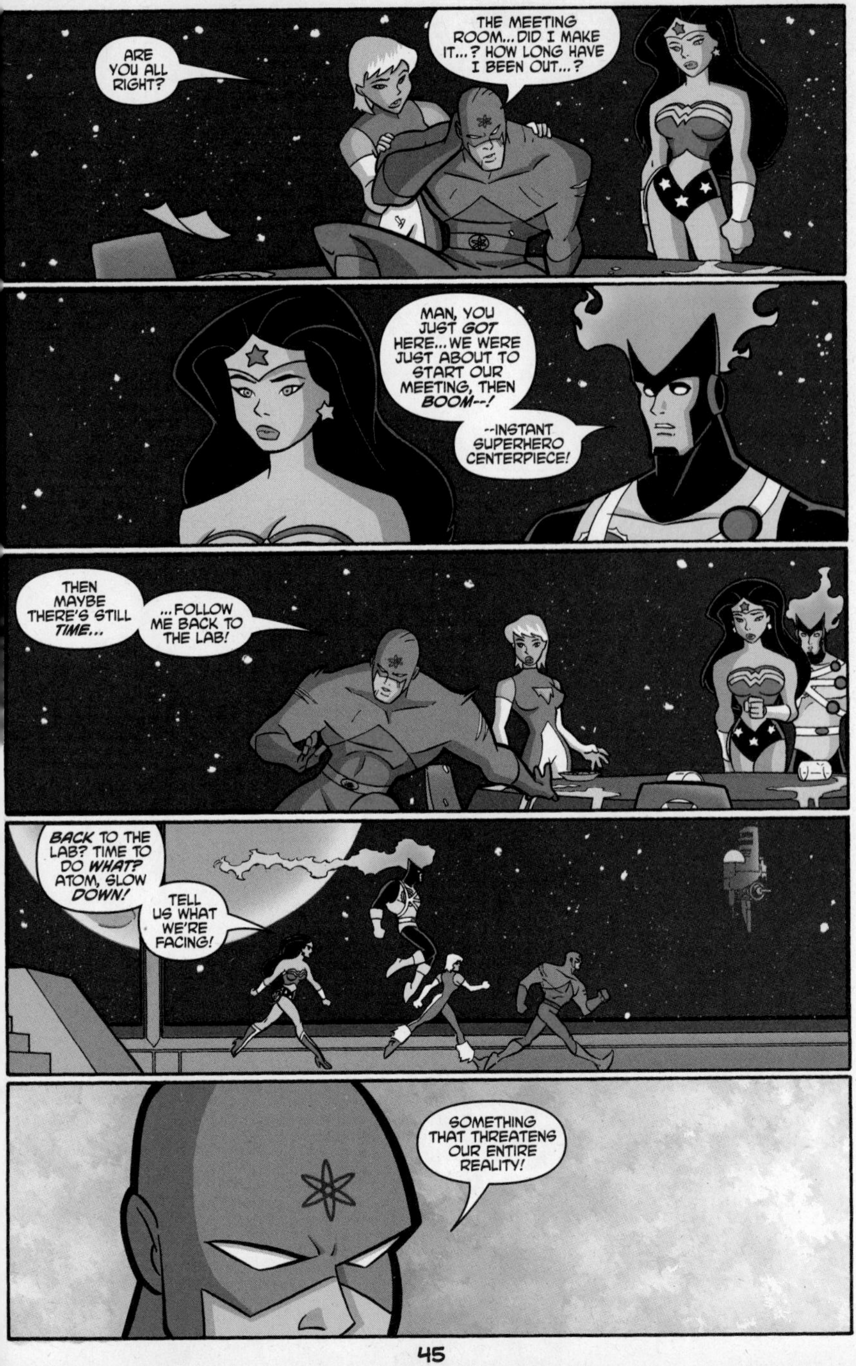

ARE YOU ALL RIGHT?
THE MEETING ROOM... DID I MAKE IT...? HOW LONG HAVE I BEEN OUT...?
MAN, YOU JUST GOT HERE... WE WERE JUST ABOUT TO START OUR MEETING, THEN BOOM--!
--INSTANT SUPERHERO CENTERPIECE!
THEN MAYBE THERE'S STILL TIME...
...FOLLOW ME BACK TO THE LAB!
BACK TO THE LAB? TIME TO DO WHAT? ATOM, SLOW DOWN!
TELL US WHAT WE'RE FACING!
SOMETHING THAT THREATENS OUR ENTIRE REALITY!

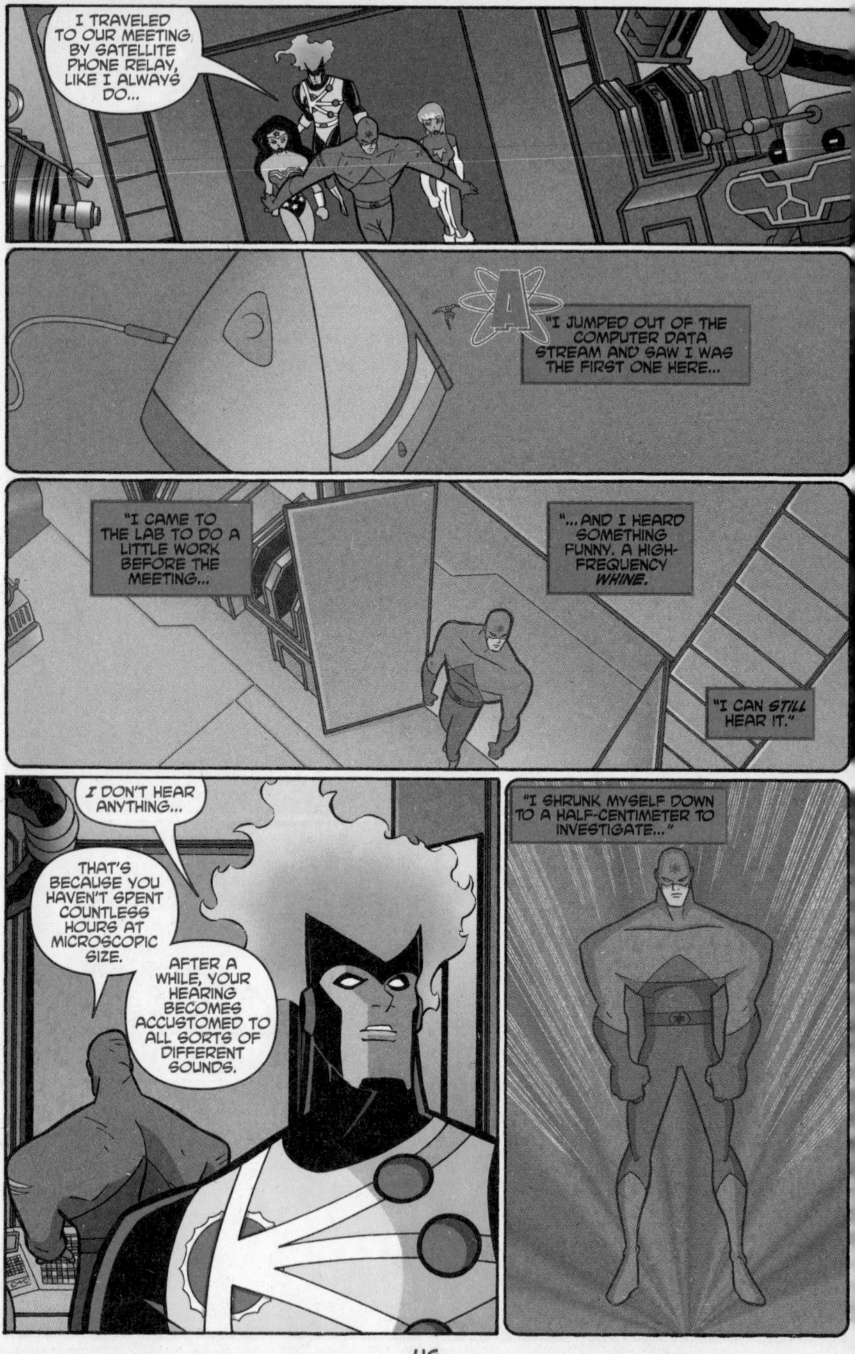

I TRAVELED TO OUR MEETING BY SATELLITE PHONE RELAY, LIKE I ALWAYS DO...
"I JUMPED OUT OF THE COMPUTER DATA STREAM AND SAW I WAS THE FIRST ONE HERE...
"I CAME TO THE LAB TO DO A LITTLE WORK BEFORE THE MEETING...
"...AND I HEARD SOMETHING FUNNY. A HIGH-FREQUENCY *WHINE.*
"I CAN *STILL* HEAR IT."
I DON'T HEAR ANYTHING...
THAT'S BECAUSE YOU HAVEN'T SPENT COUNTLESS HOURS AT MICROSCOPIC SIZE.
AFTER A WHILE, YOUR HEARING BECOMES ACCUSTOMED TO ALL SORTS OF DIFFERENT SOUNDS.
"I SHRUNK MYSELF DOWN TO A HALF-CENTIMETER TO INVESTIGATE..."

"...AND I FOUND THE *SOURCE* OF THE WHINE BEHIND THE PHANTOM ZONE PROJECTOR..."

"THE *WHAT?*"

"IT'S A MACHINE USED BY *KRYPTONIANS* TO SEND CRIMINALS TO A *LIMBO DIMENSION.*"

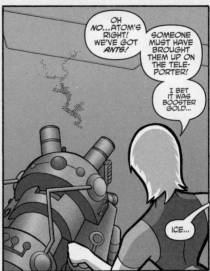

OH NO...ATOM'S RIGHT! WE'VE GOT *ANTS!*

SOMEONE MUST HAVE BROUGHT THEM UP ON THE TELE-PORTER!

I BET IT WAS BOOSTER GOLD...

ICE...

THEY'RE TOO *SMALL* TO BE ANTS.

AND ANTS DON'T WHINE. THOSE *AREN'T* ANTS.

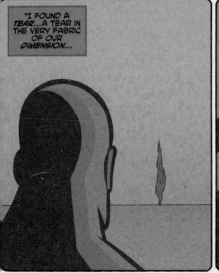

"I FOUND A *TEAR*...A TEAR IN THE VERY FABRIC OF OUR *DIMENSION*..."

"...JUST LARGE ENOUGH FOR *THEM* TO FIT THROUGH!"

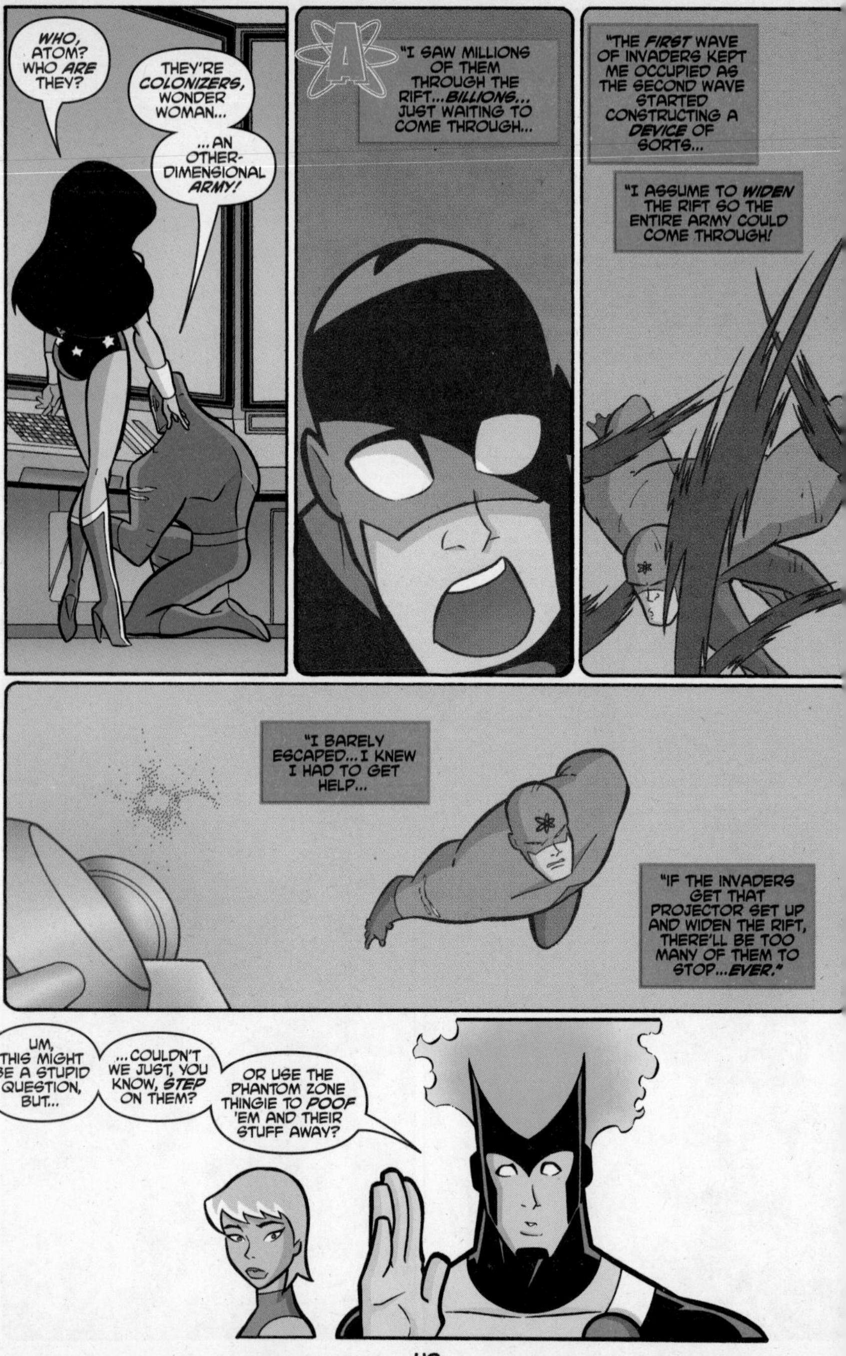
WHO, ATOM? WHO ARE THEY?
THEY'RE COLONIZERS, WONDER WOMAN...
...AN OTHER-DIMENSIONAL ARMY!
"I SAW MILLIONS OF THEM THROUGH THE RIFT...BILLIONS... JUST WAITING TO COME THROUGH...
"THE FIRST WAVE OF INVADERS KEPT ME OCCUPIED AS THE SECOND WAVE STARTED CONSTRUCTING A DEVICE OF SORTS...
"I ASSUME TO WIDEN THE RIFT SO THE ENTIRE ARMY COULD COME THROUGH!
"I BARELY ESCAPED...I KNEW I HAD TO GET HELP...
"IF THE INVADERS GET THAT PROJECTOR SET UP AND WIDEN THE RIFT, THERE'LL BE TOO MANY OF THEM TO STOP...EVER."
UM, THIS MIGHT BE A STUPID QUESTION, BUT...
...COULDN'T WE JUST, YOU KNOW, STEP ON THEM?
OR USE THE PHANTOM ZONE THINGIE TO POOF 'EM AND THEIR STUFF AWAY?

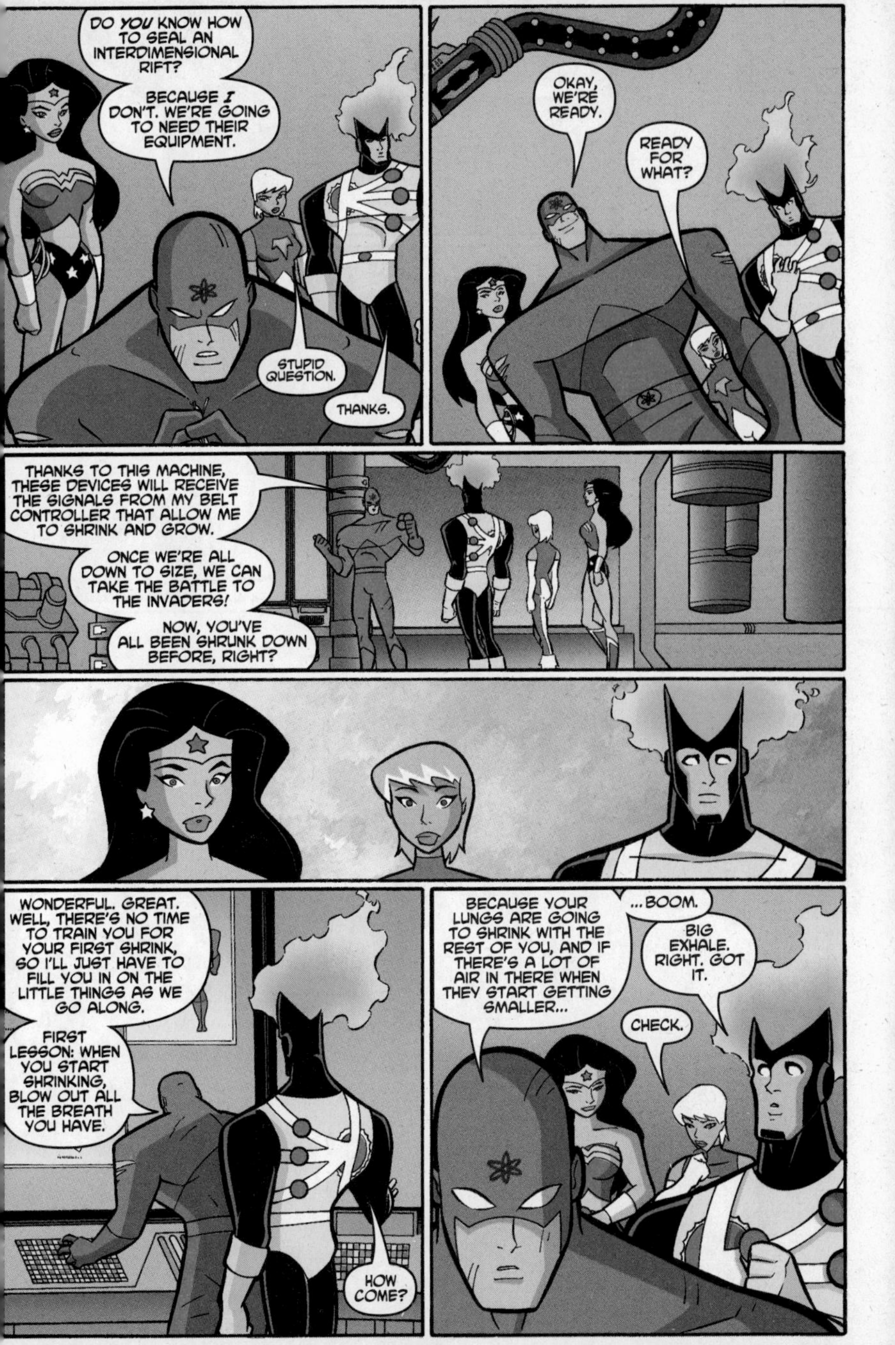
DO YOU KNOW HOW TO SEAL AN INTERDIMENSIONAL RIFT?
BECAUSE I DON'T. WE'RE GOING TO NEED THEIR EQUIPMENT.
STUPID QUESTION.
THANKS.
OKAY, WE'RE READY.
READY FOR WHAT?
THANKS TO THIS MACHINE, THESE DEVICES WILL RECEIVE THE SIGNALS FROM MY BELT CONTROLLER THAT ALLOW ME TO SHRINK AND GROW.
ONCE WE'RE ALL DOWN TO SIZE, WE CAN TAKE THE BATTLE TO THE INVADERS!
NOW, YOU'VE ALL BEEN SHRUNK DOWN BEFORE, RIGHT?
WONDERFUL. GREAT. WELL, THERE'S NO TIME TO TRAIN YOU FOR YOUR FIRST SHRINK, SO I'LL JUST HAVE TO FILL YOU IN ON THE LITTLE THINGS AS WE GO ALONG.
FIRST LESSON: WHEN YOU START SHRINKING, BLOW OUT ALL THE BREATH YOU HAVE.
HOW COME?
BECAUSE YOUR LUNGS ARE GOING TO SHRINK WITH THE REST OF YOU, AND IF THERE'S A LOT OF AIR IN THERE WHEN THEY START GETTING SMALLER...
...BOOM.
BIG EXHALE. RIGHT. GOT IT.
CHECK.

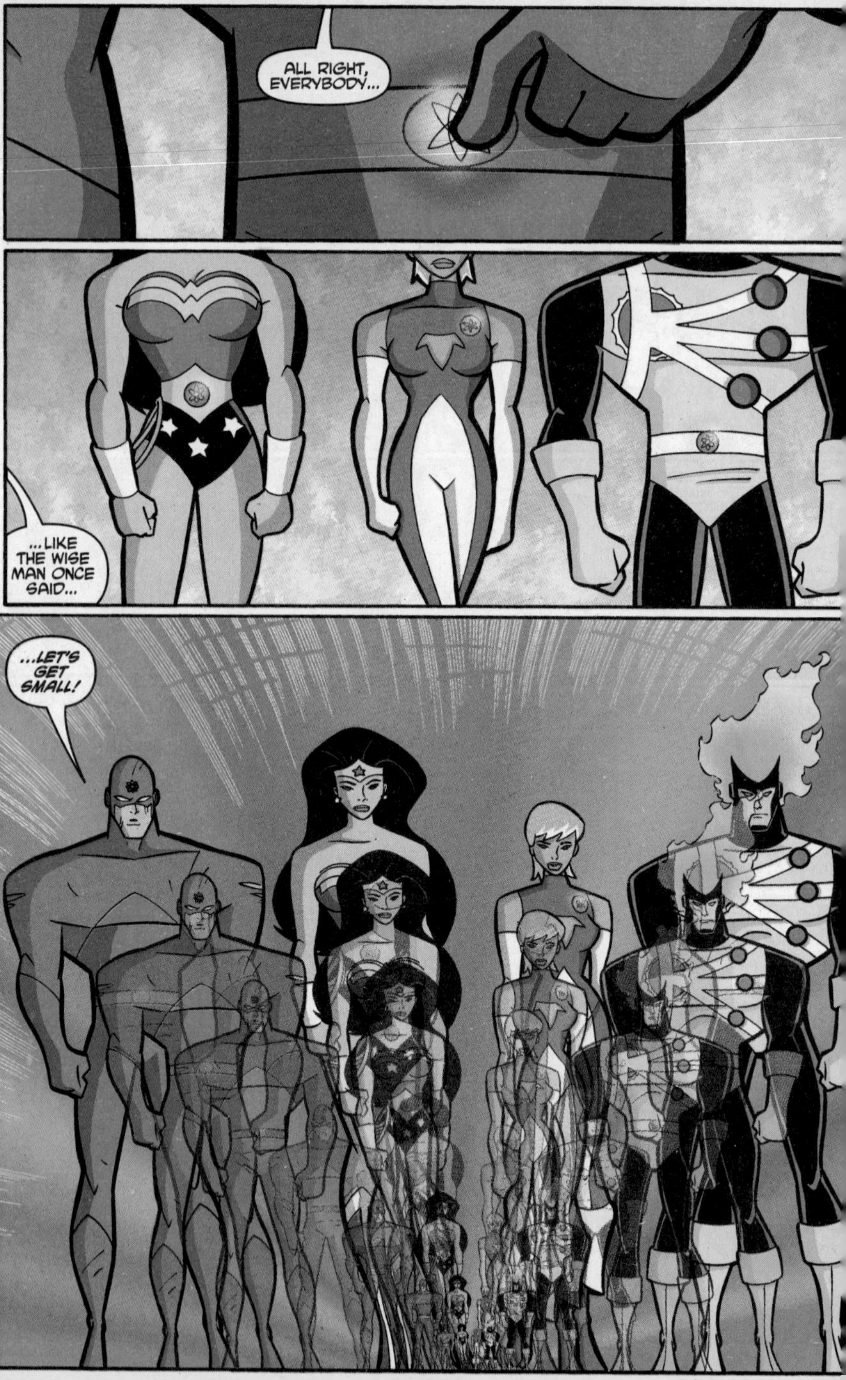
ALL RIGHT, EVERYBODY...
...LIKE THE WISE MAN ONCE SAID...
...LET'S GET SMALL!

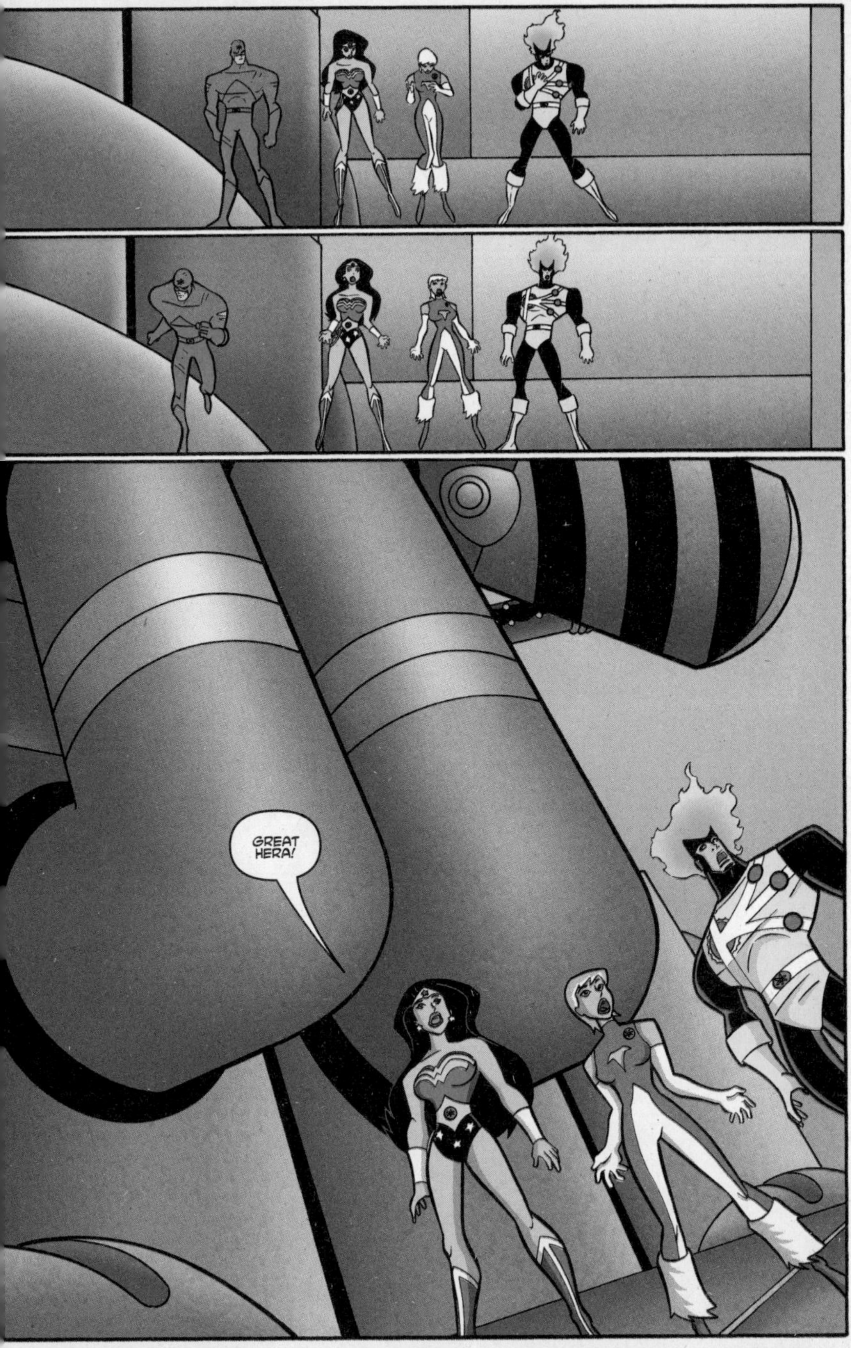
GREAT HERA!

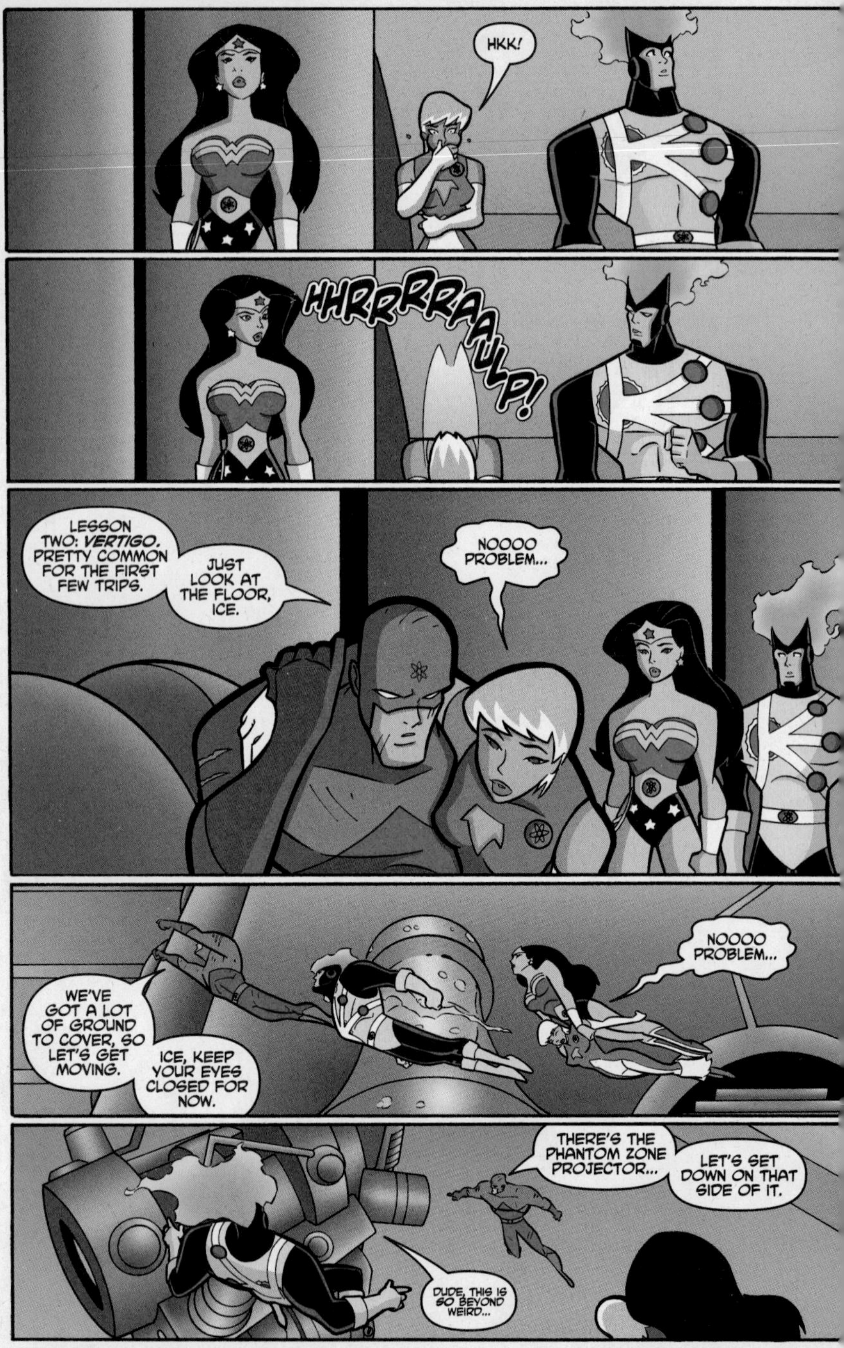
HKK!
HHRRRRAAULP!
LESSON TWO: VERTIGO. PRETTY COMMON FOR THE FIRST FEW TRIPS.
JUST LOOK AT THE FLOOR, ICE.
NOOOO PROBLEM...
WE'VE GOT A LOT OF GROUND TO COVER, SO LET'S GET MOVING.
ICE, KEEP YOUR EYES CLOSED FOR NOW.
NOOOO PROBLEM...
THERE'S THE PHANTOM ZONE PROJECTOR...
LET'S SET DOWN ON THAT SIDE OF IT.
DUDE, THIS IS SO BEYOND WEIRD...

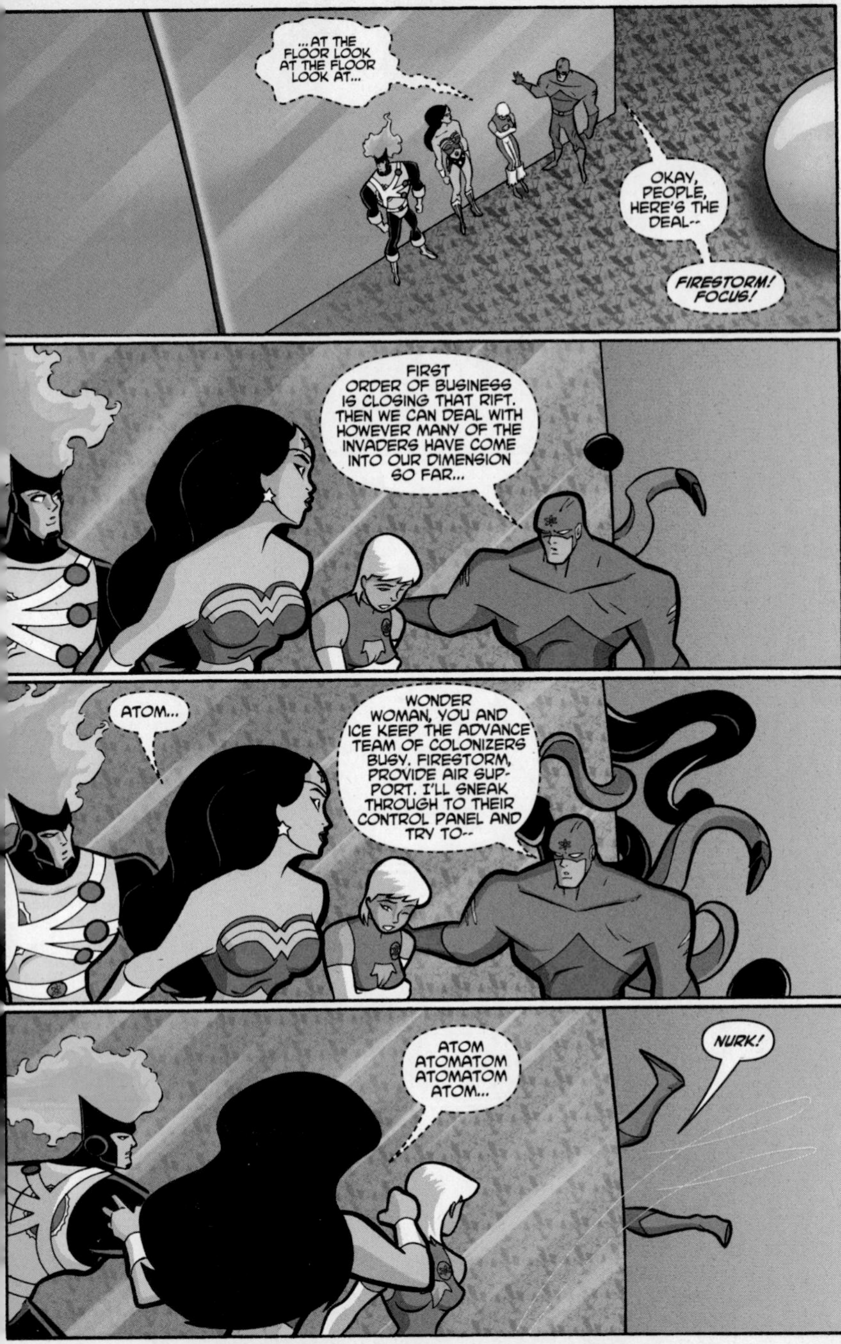
...AT THE FLOOR LOOK AT THE FLOOR LOOK AT...
OKAY, PEOPLE, HERE'S THE DEAL--
FIRESTORM! FOCUS!
FIRST ORDER OF BUSINESS IS CLOSING THAT RIFT. THEN WE CAN DEAL WITH HOWEVER MANY OF THE INVADERS HAVE COME INTO OUR DIMENSION SO FAR...
ATOM...
WONDER WOMAN, YOU AND ICE KEEP THE ADVANCE TEAM OF COLONIZERS BUSY. FIRESTORM, PROVIDE AIR SUP-PORT. I'LL SNEAK THROUGH TO THEIR CONTROL PANEL AND TRY TO--
ATOM ATOMATOM ATOMATOM ATOM...
NURK!

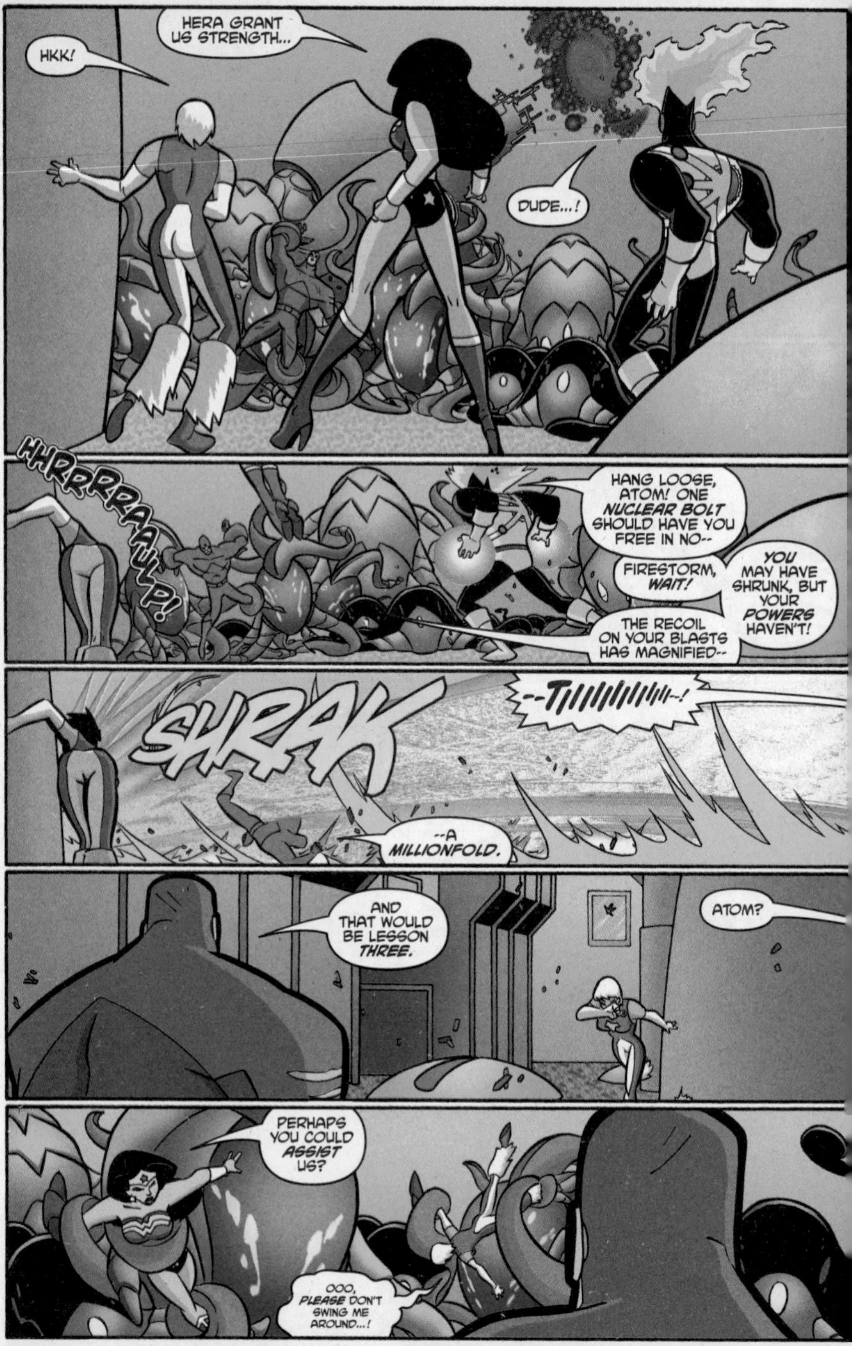

HERA GRANT US STRENGTH...
HKK!
DUDE...!
HHRRRRAAAULP!
HANG LOOSE, ATOM! ONE NUCLEAR BOLT SHOULD HAVE YOU FREE IN NO--
FIRESTORM, WAIT!
THE RECOIL ON YOUR BLASTS HAS MAGNIFIED--
YOU MAY HAVE SHRUNK, BUT YOUR POWERS HAVEN'T!
SHRAK
--T!!!!!!!--!
--A MILLIONFOLD.
AND THAT WOULD BE LESSON THREE.
ATOM?
PERHAPS YOU COULD ASSIST US?
OOO, PLEASE DON'T SWING ME AROUND...!

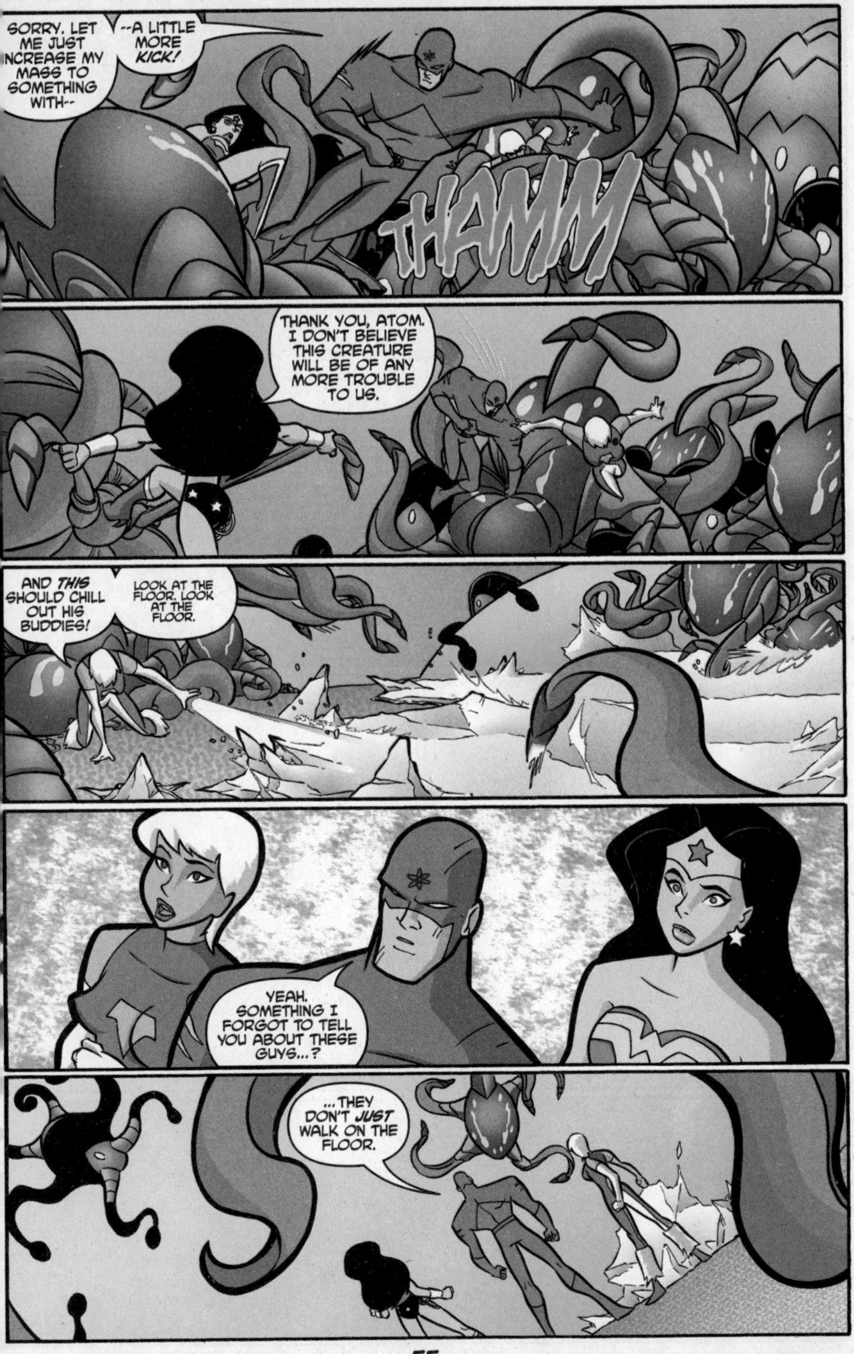
SORRY. LET ME JUST INCREASE MY MASS TO SOMETHING WITH--
--A LITTLE MORE KICK!
THAMM
THANK YOU, ATOM. I DON'T BELIEVE THIS CREATURE WILL BE OF ANY MORE TROUBLE TO US.
AND THIS SHOULD CHILL OUT HIS BUDDIES!
LOOK AT THE FLOOR. LOOK AT THE FLOOR.
YEAH. SOMETHING I FORGOT TO TELL YOU ABOUT THESE GUYS...?
...THEY DON'T JUST WALK ON THE FLOOR.

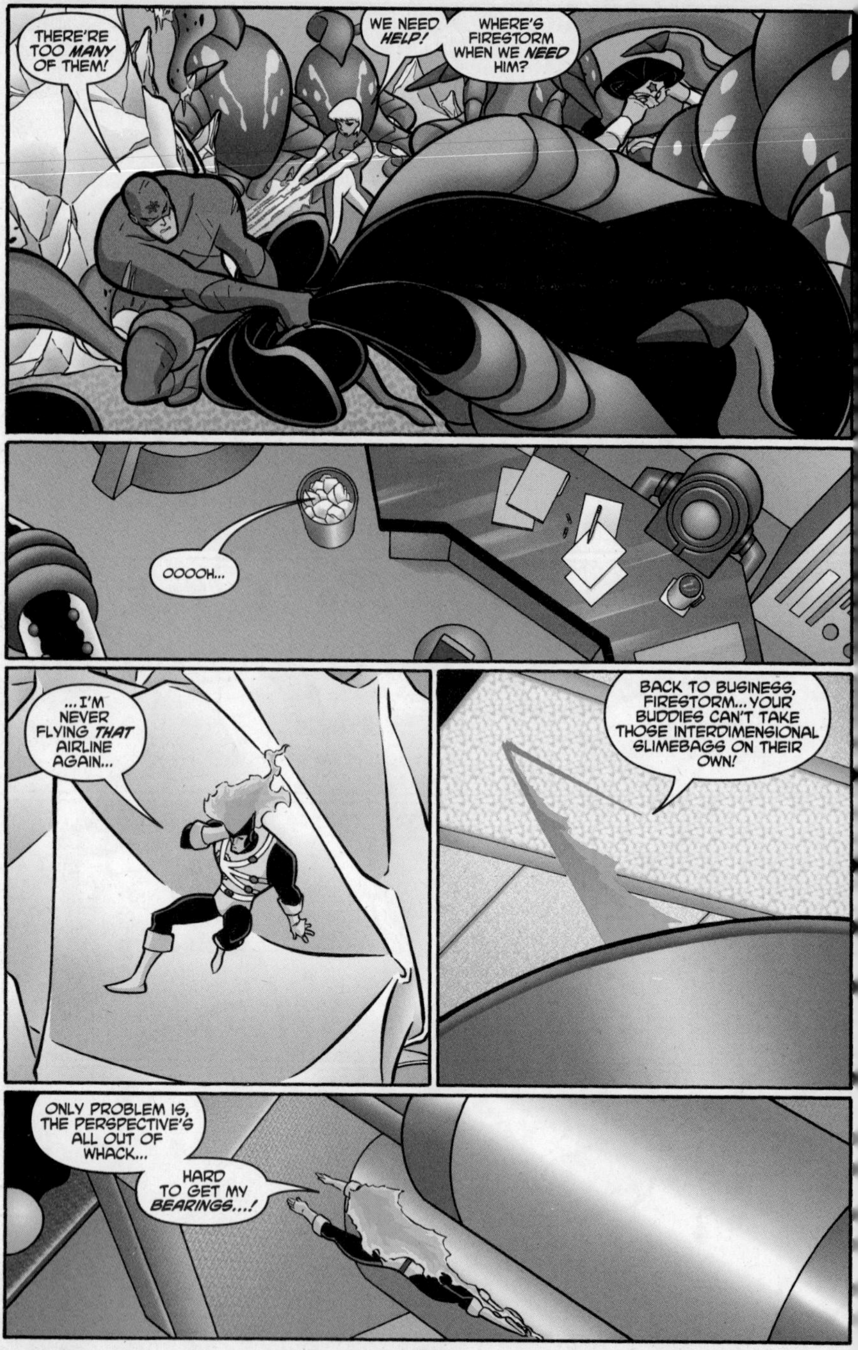
THERE'RE TOO MANY OF THEM!
WE NEED HELP!
WHERE'S FIRESTORM WHEN WE NEED HIM?
OOOOH...
...I'M NEVER FLYING THAT AIRLINE AGAIN...
BACK TO BUSINESS, FIRESTORM... YOUR BUDDIES CAN'T TAKE THOSE INTERDIMENSIONAL SLIMEBAGS ON THEIR OWN!
ONLY PROBLEM IS, THE PERSPECTIVE'S ALL OUT OF WHACK...
HARD TO GET MY BEARINGS...!

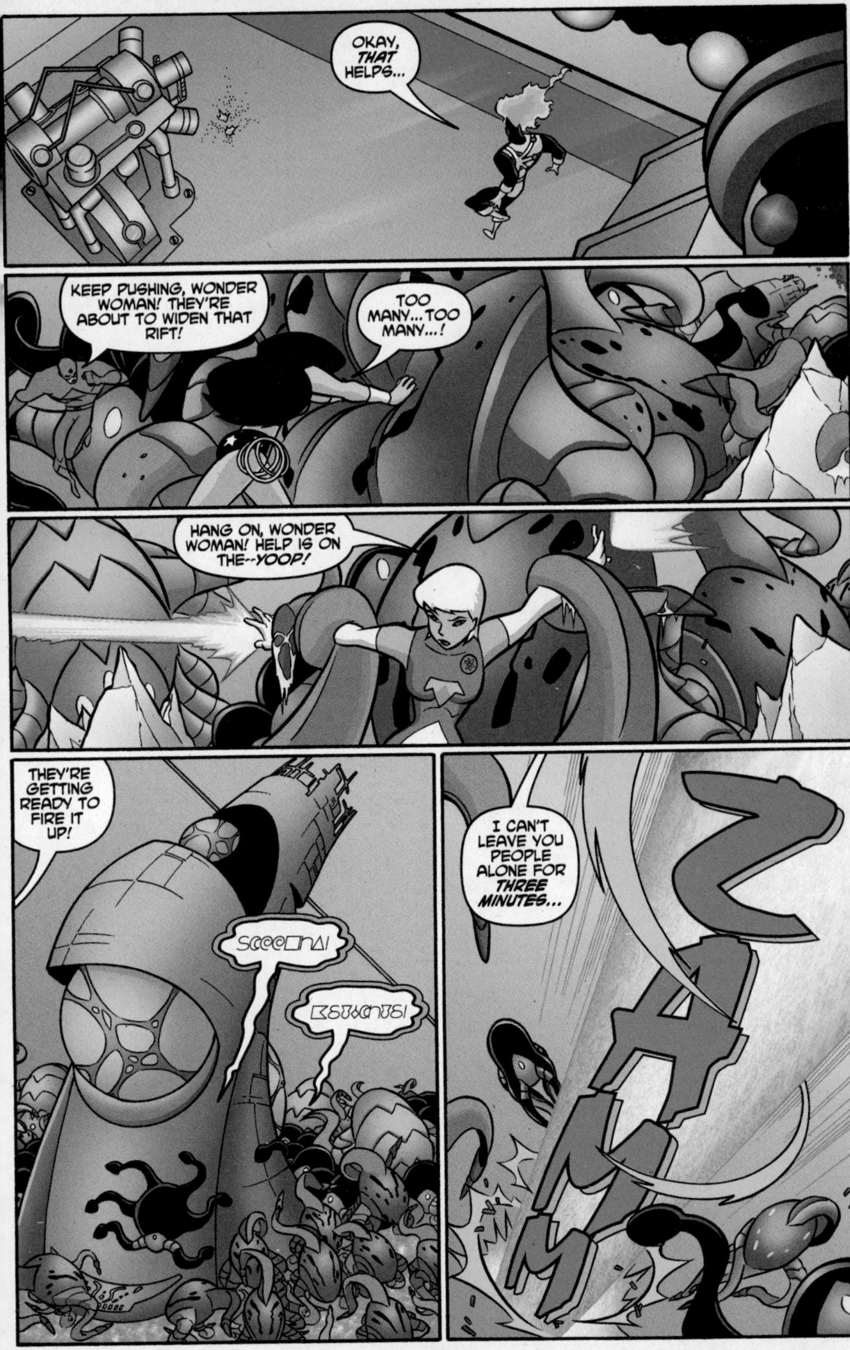

OKAY, THAT HELPS...
KEEP PUSHING, WONDER WOMAN! THEY'RE ABOUT TO WIDEN THAT RIFT!
TOO MANY...TOO MANY...!
HANG ON, WONDER WOMAN! HELP IS ON THE--YOOP!
THEY'RE GETTING READY TO FIRE IT UP!
I CAN'T LEAVE YOU PEOPLE ALONE FOR THREE MINUTES...
ZAM

GOOD WORK, FIRESTORM!

NOW, IF I CAN JUST MAKE SENSE OF THESE CONTROLS...

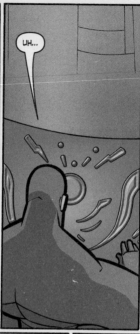

UH...

YOUR BEST GUESS WOULD BE APPRECIATED, ATOM...

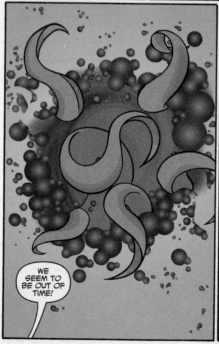

WE SEEM TO BE OUT OF TIME!

"GUESSING" ISN'T IN THE PHYSICIST'S VOCABULARY, WONDER WOMAN...

...BUT IN *THIS* CASE, I DON'T THINK THERE'S MUCH *CHOICE!*

WHUNNCH

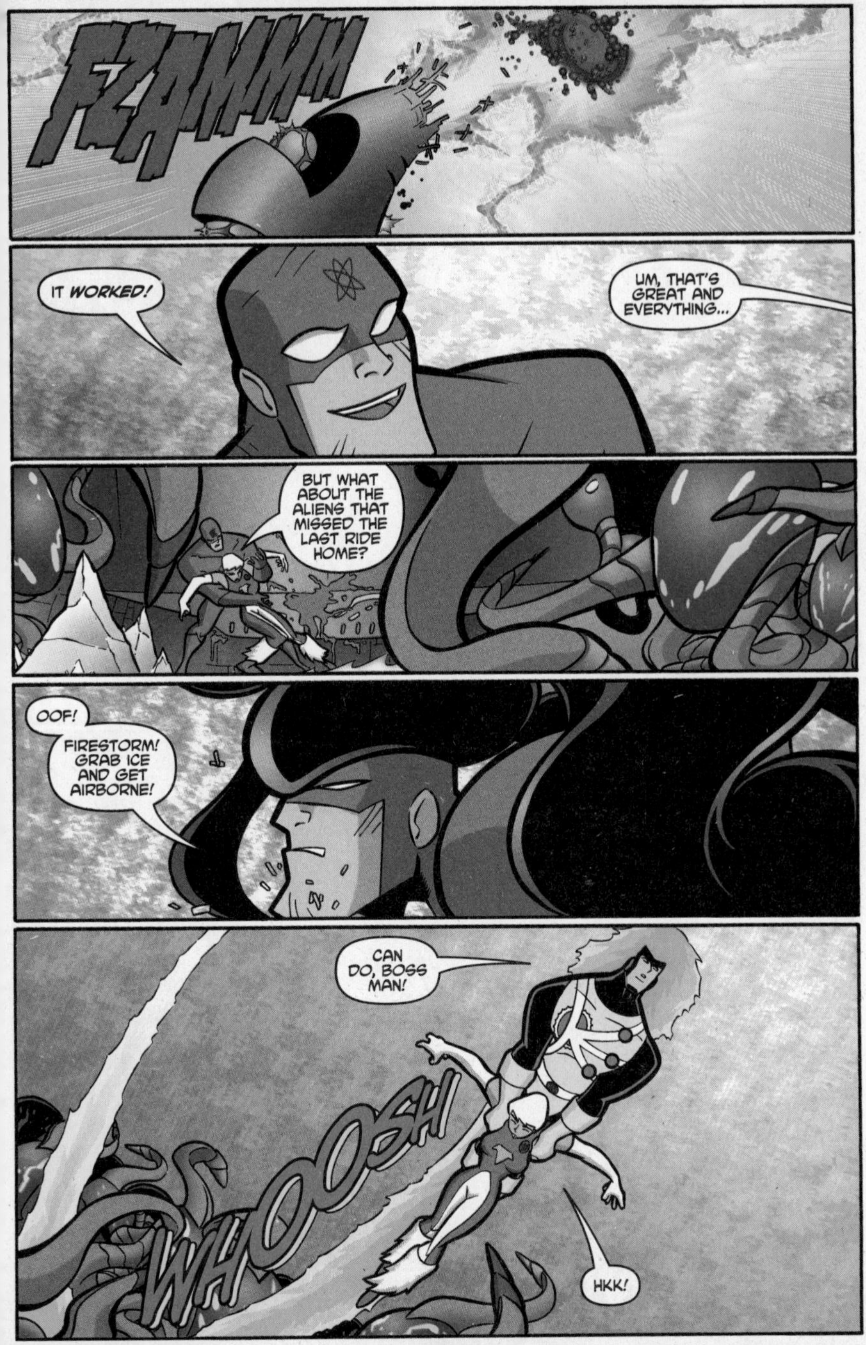
FZAMMMM
IT WORKED!
UM, THAT'S GREAT AND EVERYTHING...
BUT WHAT ABOUT THE ALIENS THAT MISSED THE LAST RIDE HOME?
OOF!
FIRESTORM! GRAB ICE AND GET AIRBORNE!
CAN DO, BOSS MAN!
WHOOOSH!
HKK!

WONDER WOMAN! CAN YOU HERD THE REMAINING ALIENS TOGETHER?

KAWHAM

WITHOUT QUESTION.

FIRESTORM! SWING THE PHANTOM ZONE PROJECTOR AROUND AND DOWN!

ICE, ACTIVATE THE MACHINE!

ANYTHING YOU SAY!

FZAMMM

CLICK

WHANG

SSHHKKK

DON'T HURL DON'T HURL DON'T HURL...

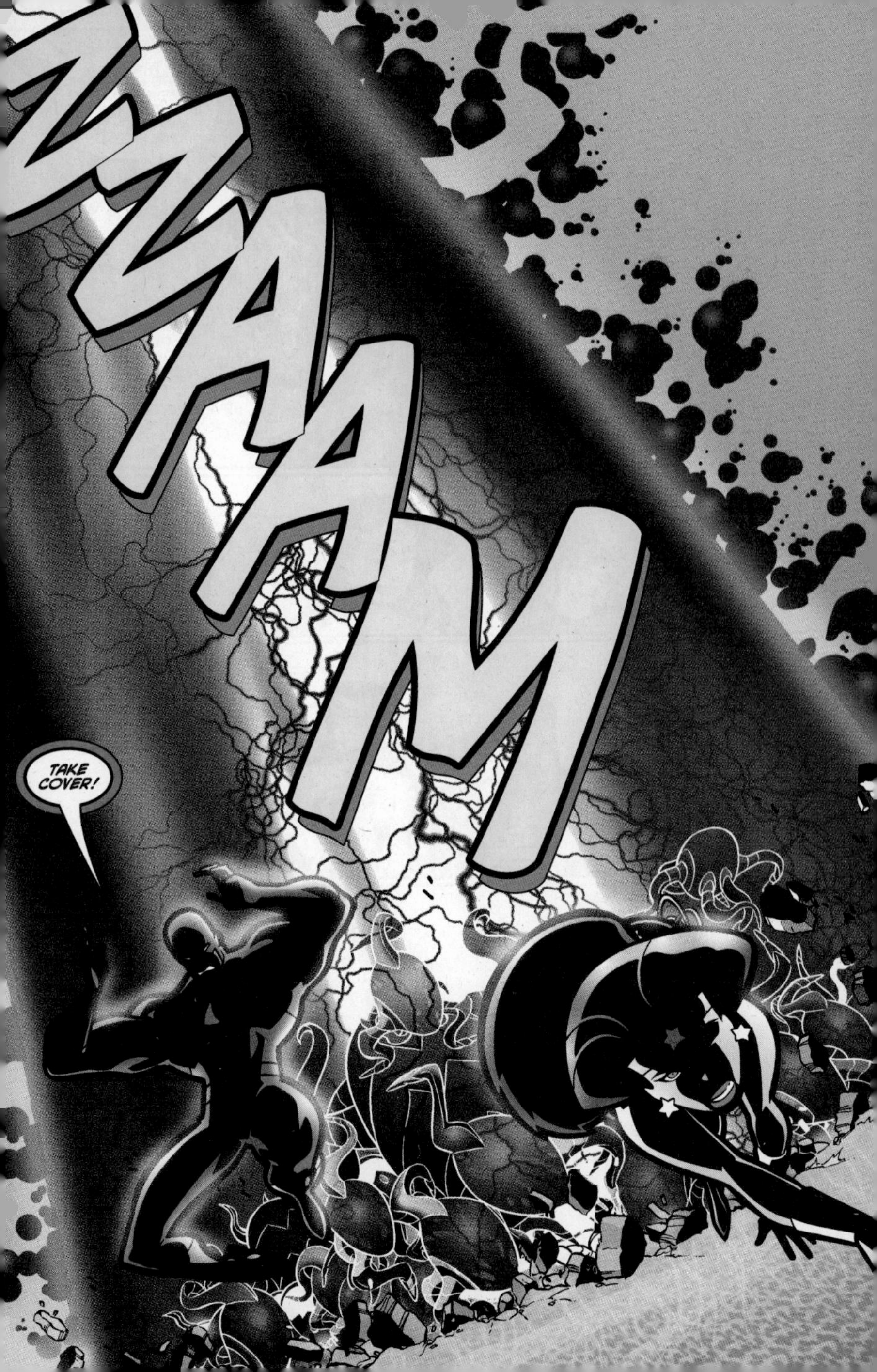

ZZAAM
TAKE COVER!

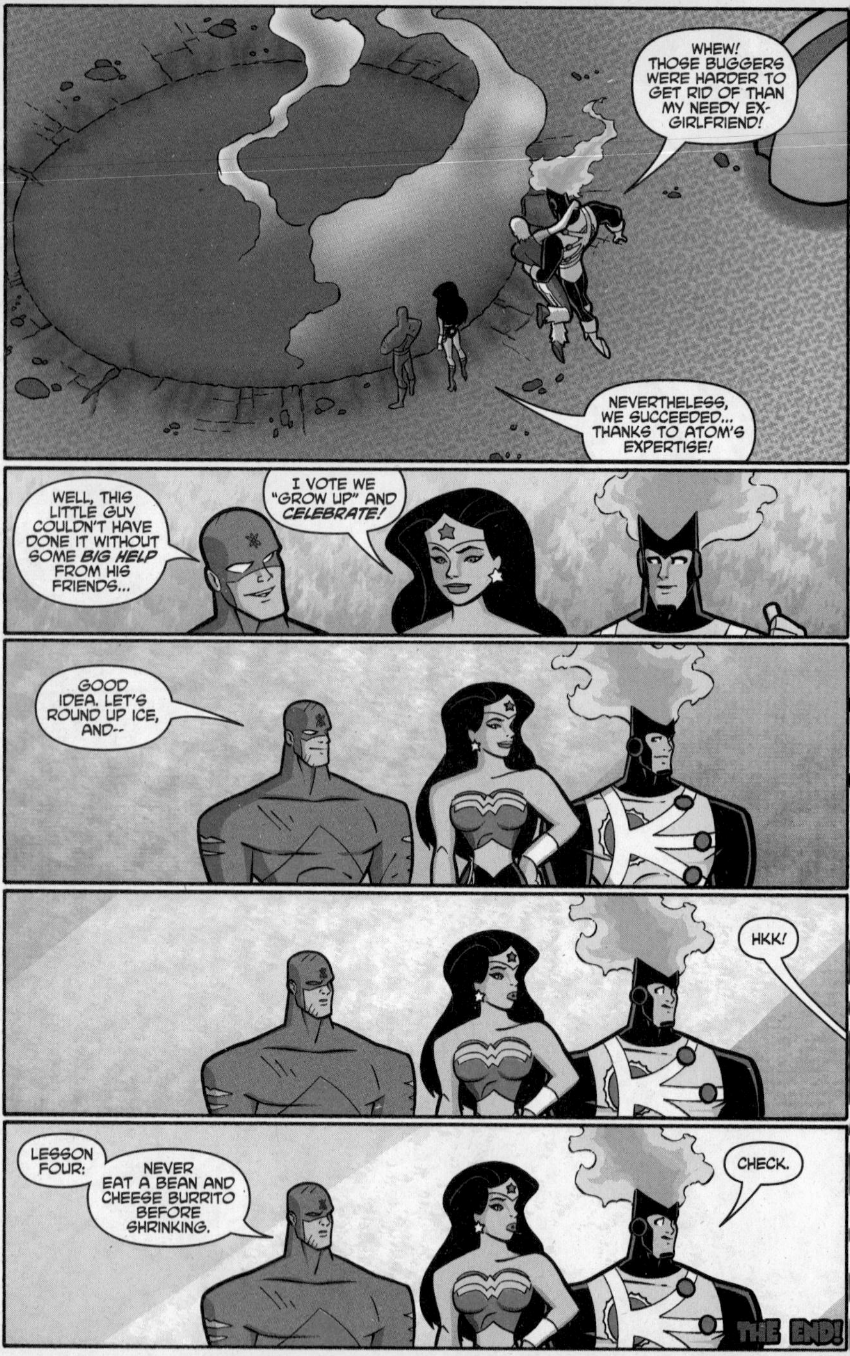
WHEW! THOSE BUGGERS WERE HARDER TO GET RID OF THAN MY NEEDY EX-GIRLFRIEND!
NEVERTHELESS, WE SUCCEEDED... THANKS TO ATOM'S EXPERTISE!
WELL, THIS LITTLE GUY COULDN'T HAVE DONE IT WITHOUT SOME BIG HELP FROM HIS FRIENDS...
I VOTE WE "GROW UP" AND CELEBRATE!
GOOD IDEA. LET'S ROUND UP ICE, AND--
HKK!
LESSON FOUR:
NEVER EAT A BEAN AND CHEESE BURRITO BEFORE SHRINKING.
CHECK.
THE END!

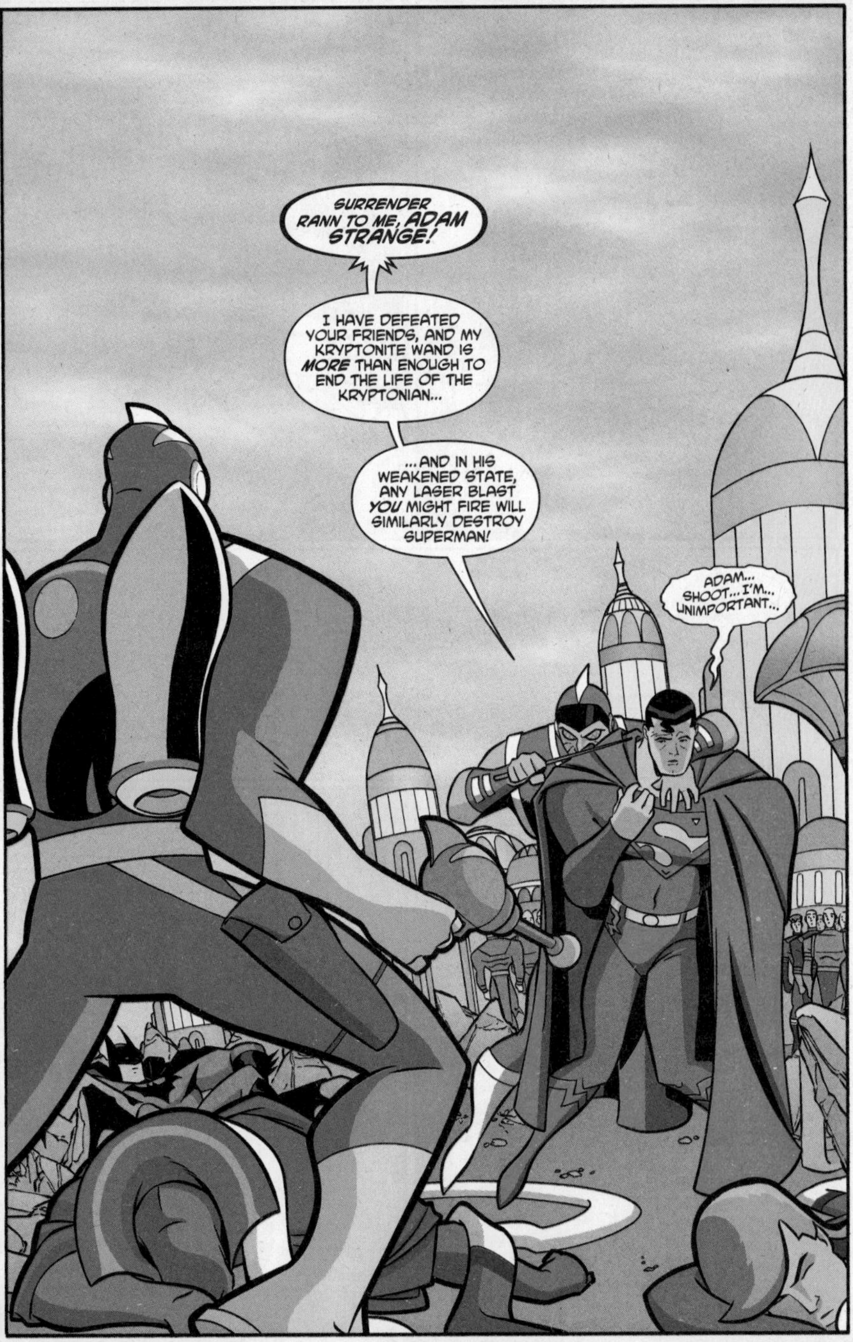
SURRENDER RANN TO ME, ADAM STRANGE!
I HAVE DEFEATED YOUR FRIENDS, AND MY KRYPTONITE WAND IS MORE THAN ENOUGH TO END THE LIFE OF THE KRYPTONIAN...
...AND IN HIS WEAKENED STATE, ANY LASER BLAST YOU MIGHT FIRE WILL SIMILARLY DESTROY SUPERMAN!
ADAM... SHOOT... I'M... UNIMPORTANT...

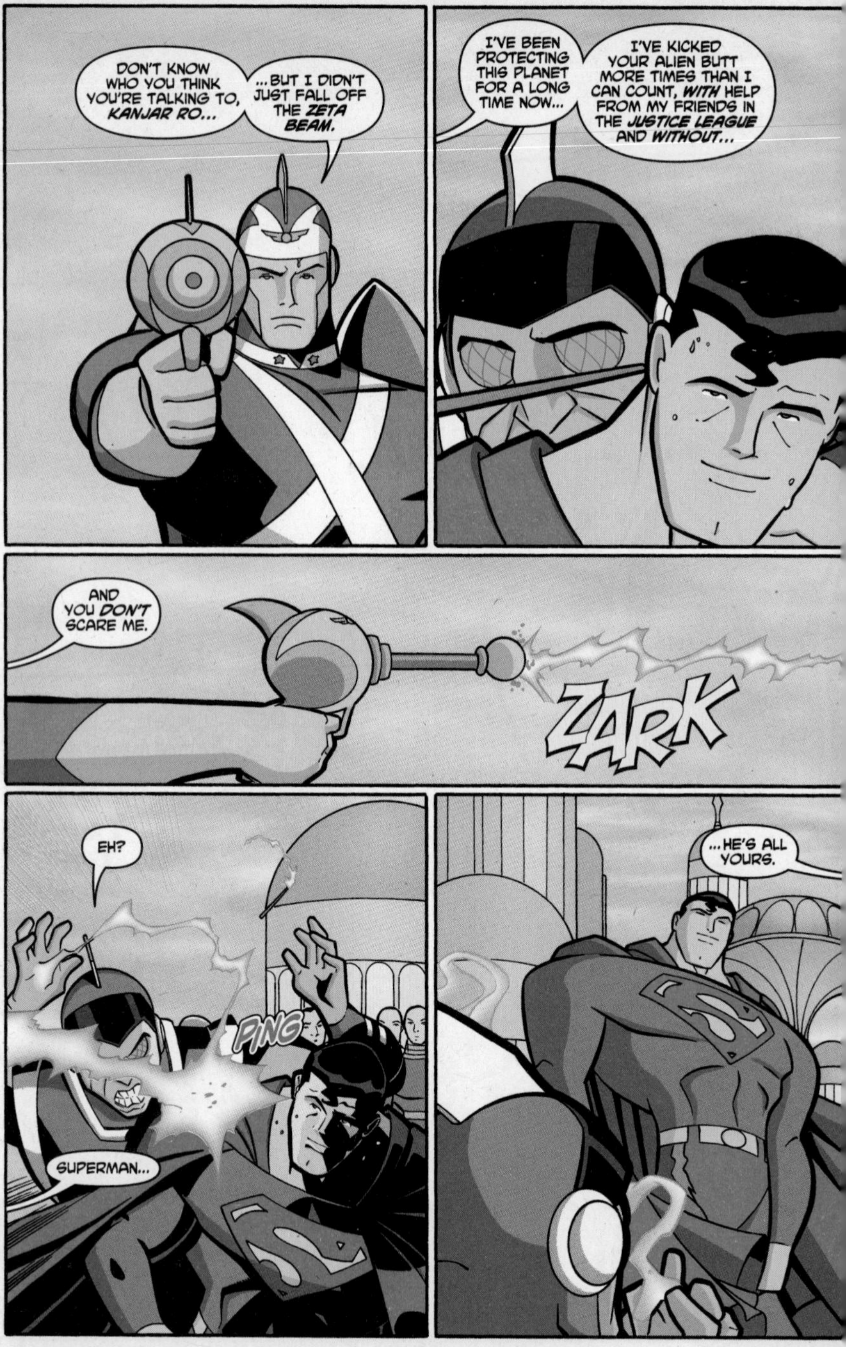
DON'T KNOW WHO YOU THINK YOU'RE TALKING TO, *KANJAR RO...*
...BUT I DIDN'T JUST FALL OFF THE *ZETA BEAM.*
I'VE BEEN PROTECTING THIS PLANET FOR A LONG TIME NOW...
I'VE KICKED YOUR ALIEN BUTT MORE TIMES THAN I CAN COUNT, *WITH* HELP FROM MY FRIENDS IN THE *JUSTICE LEAGUE* AND *WITHOUT...*
AND YOU *DON'T* SCARE ME.
ZARK
EH?
PING
SUPERMAN...
...HE'S ALL YOURS.

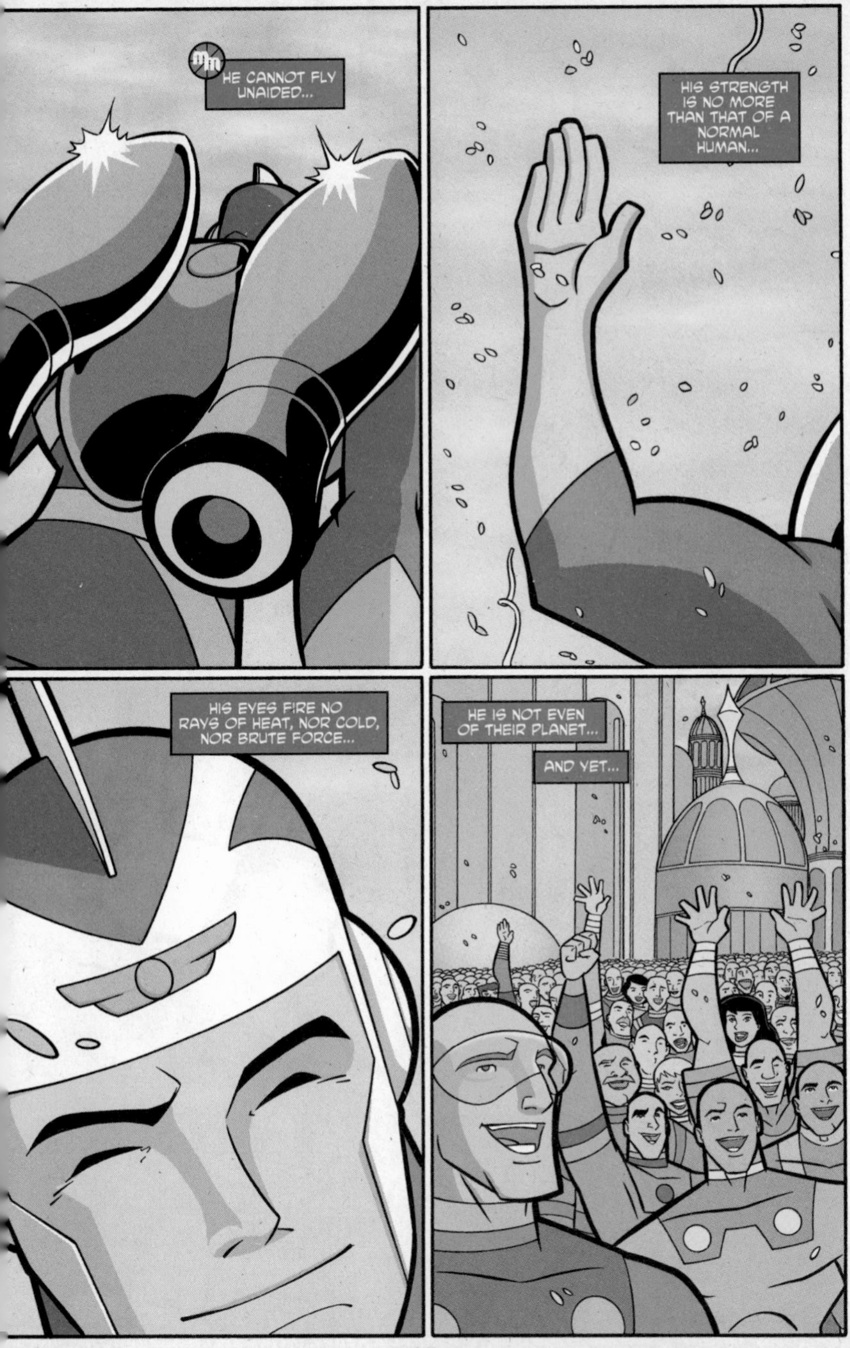
HE CANNOT FLY UNAIDED...
HIS STRENGTH IS NO MORE THAN THAT OF A NORMAL HUMAN...
HIS EYES FIRE NO RAYS OF HEAT, NOR COLD, NOR BRUTE FORCE...
HE IS NOT EVEN OF THEIR PLANET...
AND YET...

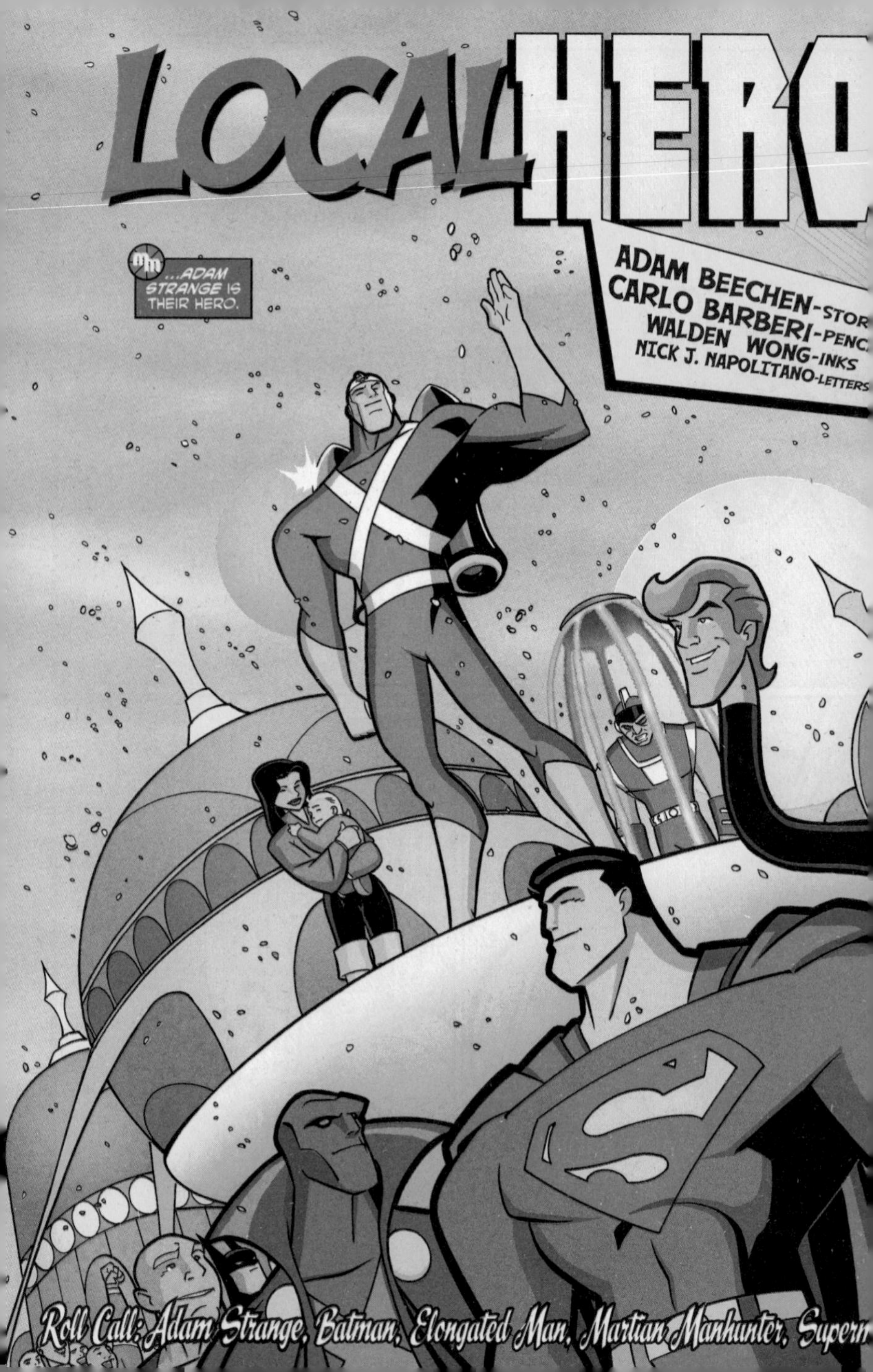
LOCAL HERO
...ADAM STRANGE IS THEIR HERO.
ADAM BEECHEN-STOR
CARLO BARBERI-PENC
WALDEN WONG-INKS
NICK J. NAPOLITANO-LETTERS
Roll Call: Adam Strange, Batman, Elongated Man, Martian Manhunter, Superm

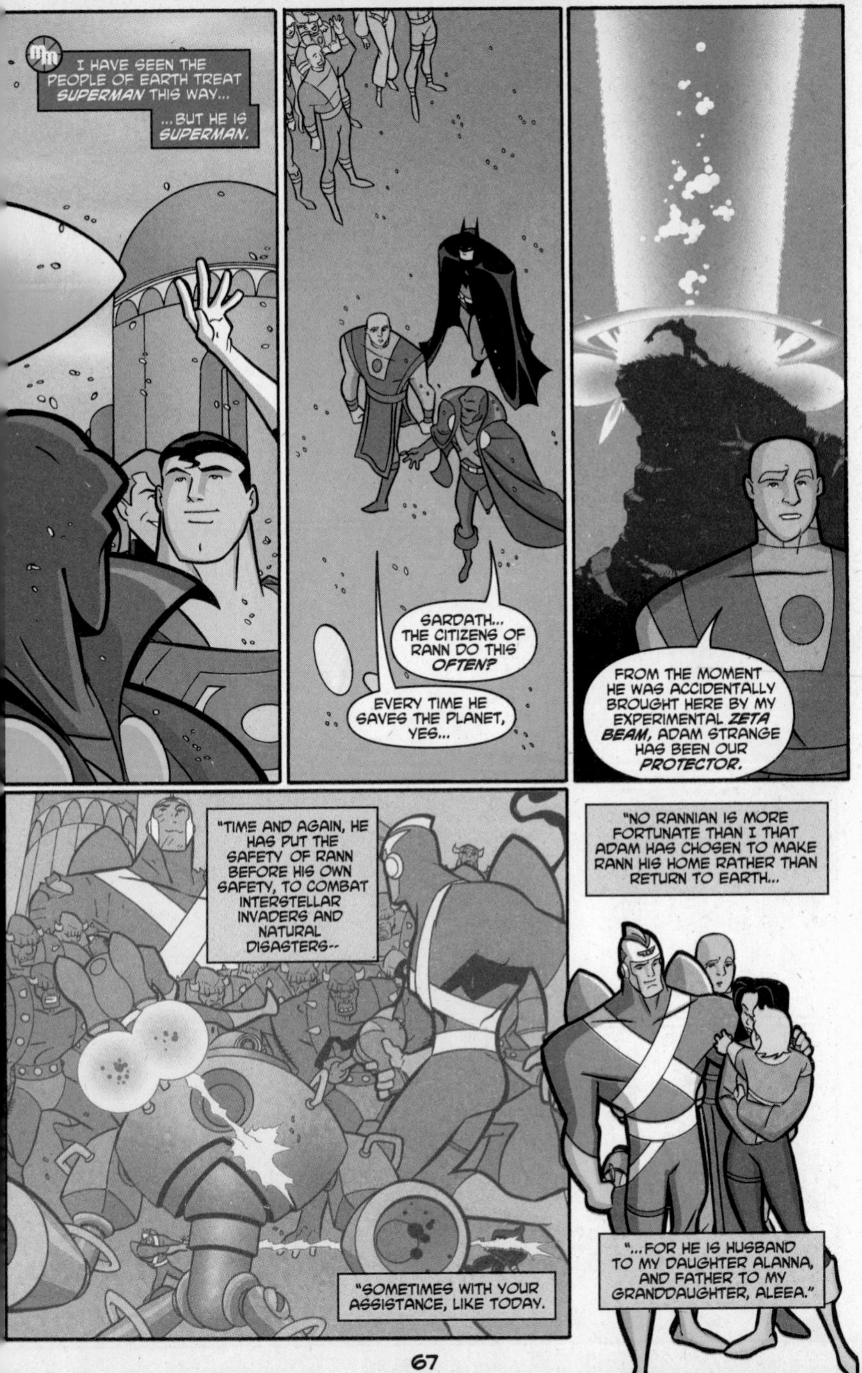
I HAVE SEEN THE PEOPLE OF EARTH TREAT SUPERMAN THIS WAY...
...BUT HE IS SUPERMAN.
SARDATH... THE CITIZENS OF RANN DO THIS OFTEN?
EVERY TIME HE SAVES THE PLANET, YES...
FROM THE MOMENT HE WAS ACCIDENTALLY BROUGHT HERE BY MY EXPERIMENTAL ZETA BEAM, ADAM STRANGE HAS BEEN OUR PROTECTOR.
"TIME AND AGAIN, HE HAS PUT THE SAFETY OF RANN BEFORE HIS OWN SAFETY, TO COMBAT INTERSTELLAR INVADERS AND NATURAL DISASTERS--
"SOMETIMES WITH YOUR ASSISTANCE, LIKE TODAY.
"NO RANNIAN IS MORE FORTUNATE THAN I THAT ADAM HAS CHOSEN TO MAKE RANN HIS HOME RATHER THAN RETURN TO EARTH...
"...FOR HE IS HUSBAND TO MY DAUGHTER ALANNA, AND FATHER TO MY GRANDDAUGHTER, ALEEA."

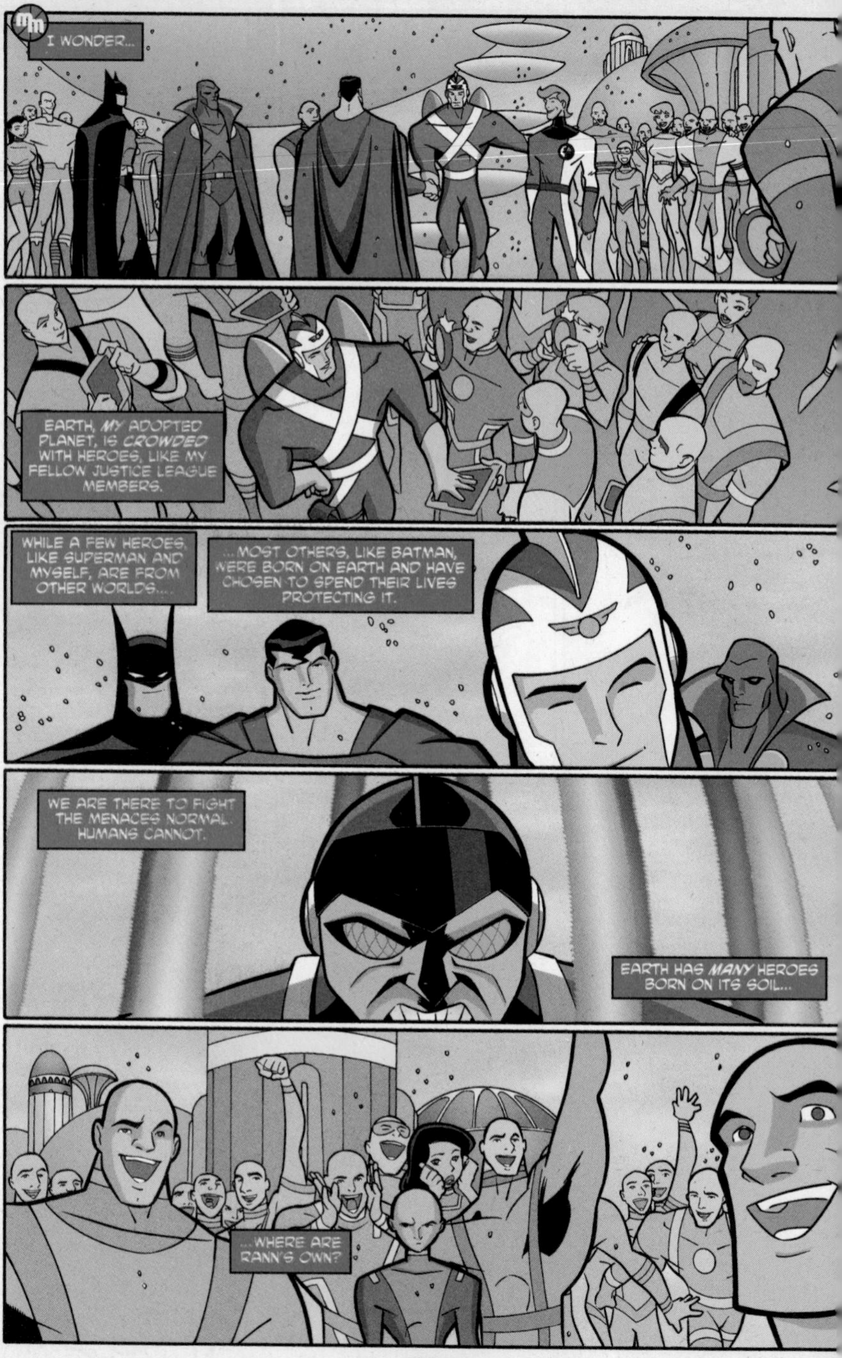
I WONDER...
EARTH, MY ADOPTED PLANET, IS CROWDED WITH HEROES, LIKE MY FELLOW JUSTICE LEAGUE MEMBERS.
WHILE A FEW HEROES, LIKE SUPERMAN AND MYSELF, ARE FROM OTHER WORLDS...
...MOST OTHERS, LIKE BATMAN, WERE BORN ON EARTH AND HAVE CHOSEN TO SPEND THEIR LIVES PROTECTING IT.
WE ARE THERE TO FIGHT THE MENACES NORMAL HUMANS CANNOT.
EARTH HAS MANY HEROES BORN ON ITS SOIL...
...WHERE ARE RANN'S OWN?

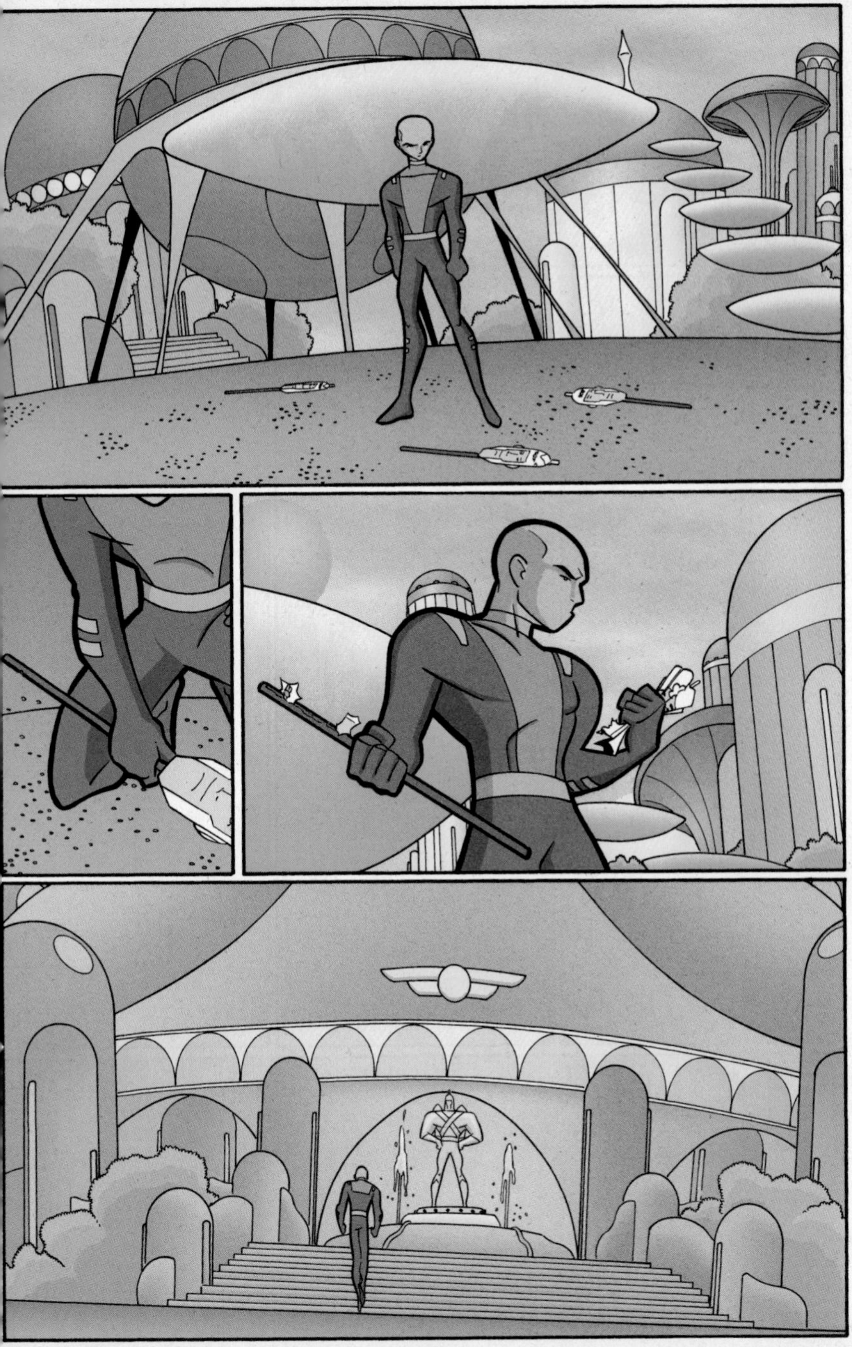

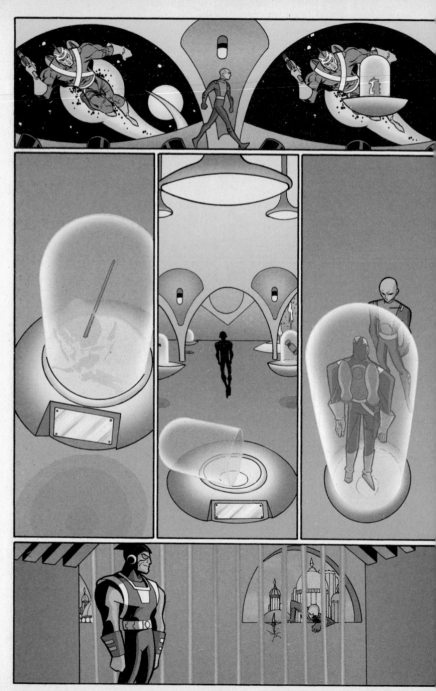

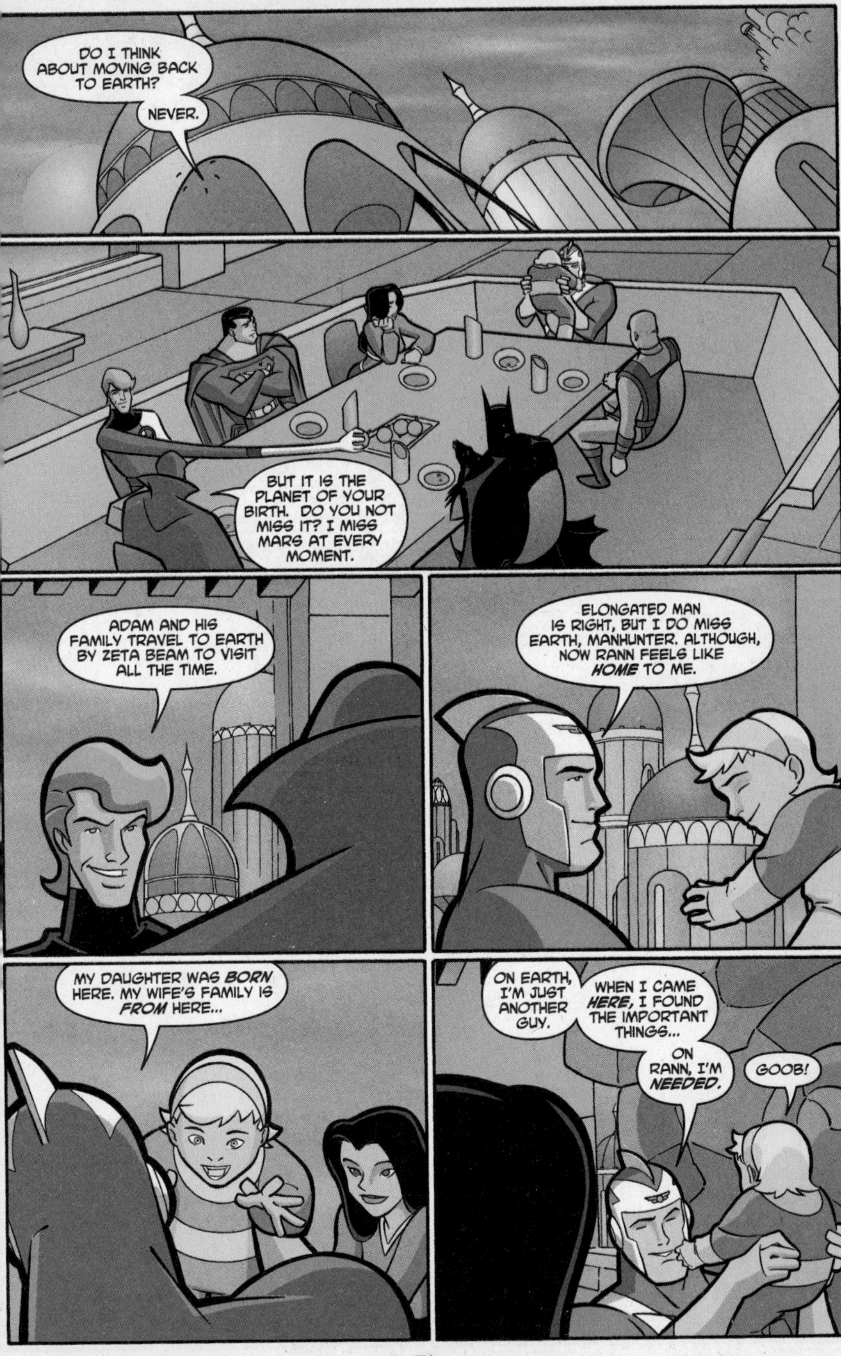
DO I THINK ABOUT MOVING BACK TO EARTH?
NEVER.
BUT IT IS THE PLANET OF YOUR BIRTH. DO YOU NOT MISS IT? I MISS MARS AT EVERY MOMENT.
ADAM AND HIS FAMILY TRAVEL TO EARTH BY ZETA BEAM TO VISIT ALL THE TIME.
ELONGATED MAN IS RIGHT, BUT I DO MISS EARTH, MANHUNTER. ALTHOUGH, NOW RANN FEELS LIKE *HOME* TO ME.
MY DAUGHTER WAS *BORN* HERE. MY WIFE'S FAMILY IS *FROM* HERE...
ON EARTH, I'M JUST ANOTHER GUY.
WHEN I CAME *HERE,* I FOUND THE IMPORTANT THINGS...
ON RANN, I'M *NEEDED.*
GOOB!

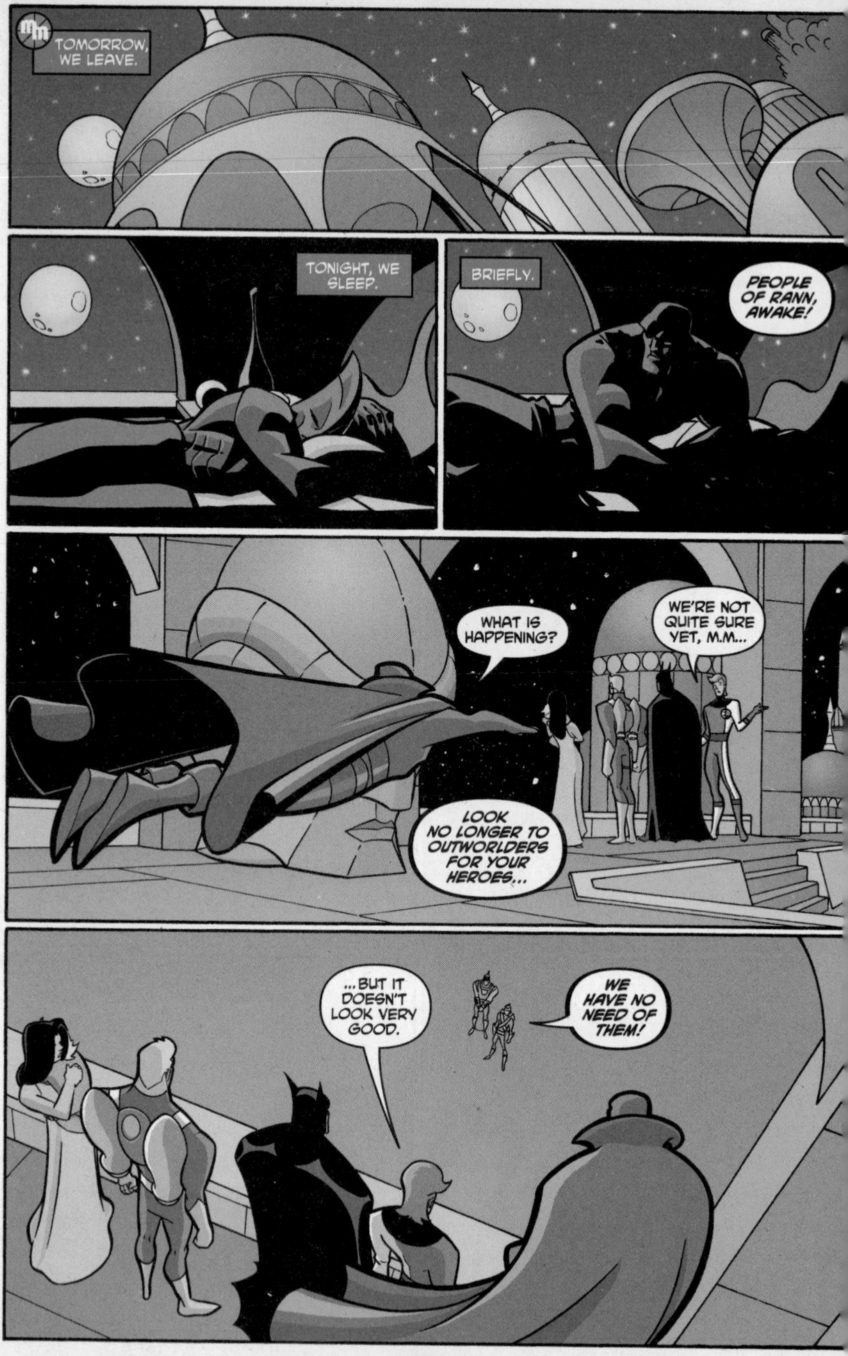
TOMORROW, WE LEAVE.
TONIGHT, WE SLEEP.
BRIEFLY.
PEOPLE OF RANN, AWAKE!
WHAT IS HAPPENING?
WE'RE NOT QUITE SURE YET, M.M...
LOOK NO LONGER TO OUTWORLDERS FOR YOUR HEROES...
...BUT IT DOESN'T LOOK VERY GOOD.
WE HAVE NO NEED OF THEM!

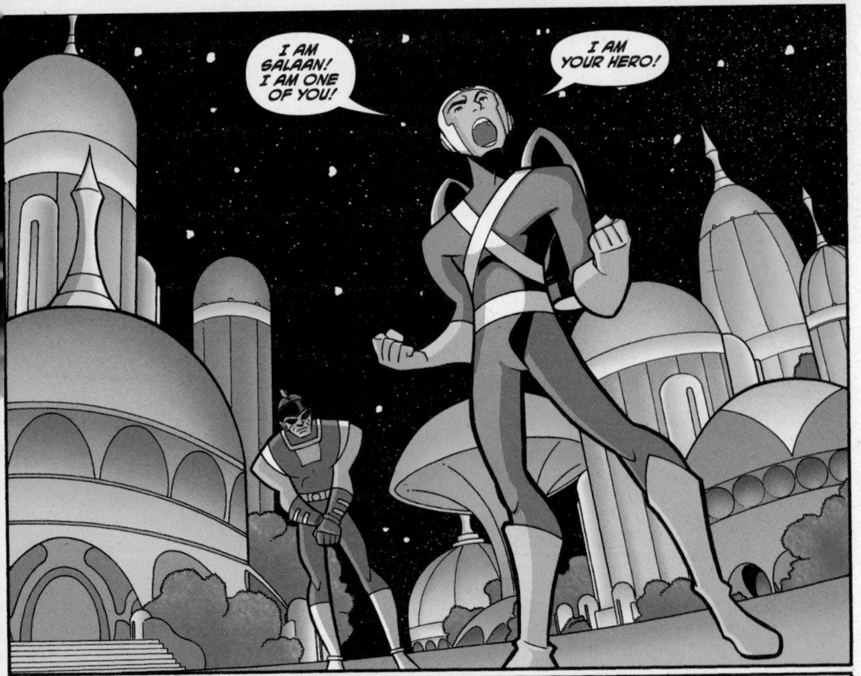
I AM SALAAN! I AM ONE OF YOU!
I AM YOUR HERO!

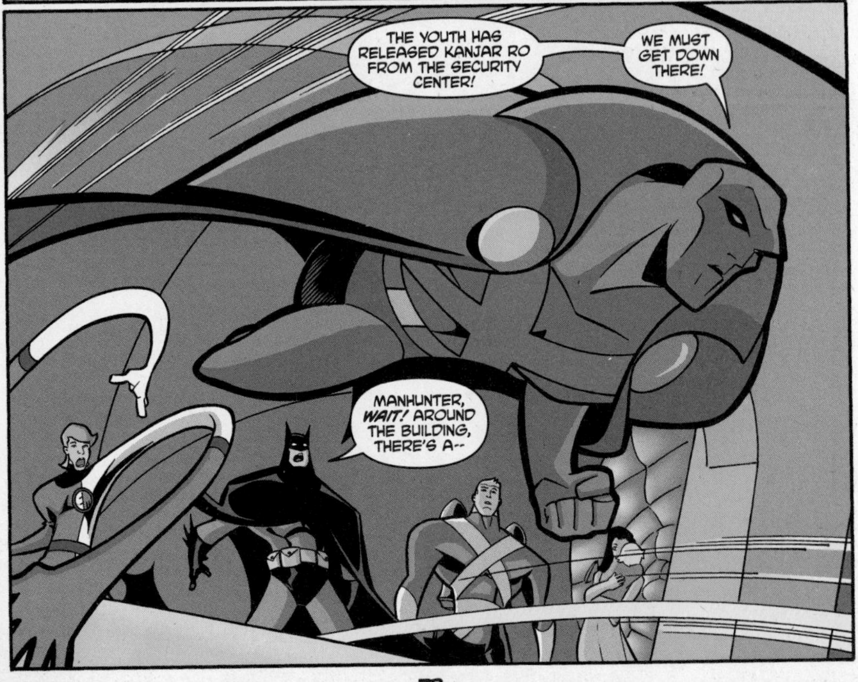
THE YOUTH HAS RELEASED KANJAR RO FROM THE SECURITY CENTER!
WE MUST GET DOWN THERE!
MANHUNTER, WAIT! AROUND THE BUILDING, THERE'S A--

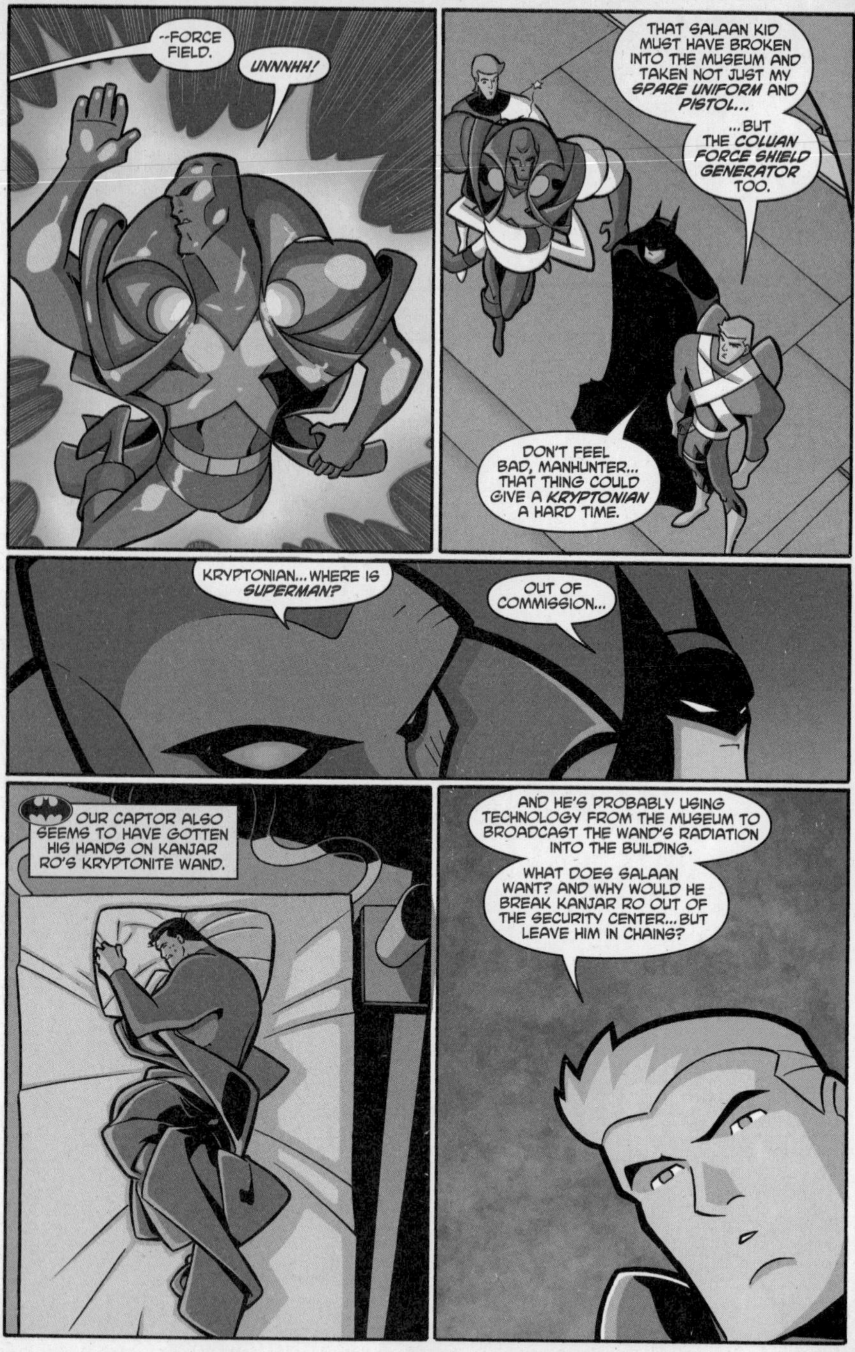
--FORCE FIELD.
UNNNHH!
THAT SALAAN KID MUST HAVE BROKEN INTO THE MUSEUM AND TAKEN NOT JUST MY SPARE UNIFORM AND PISTOL...
...BUT THE COLUAN FORCE SHIELD GENERATOR TOO.
DON'T FEEL BAD, MANHUNTER... THAT THING COULD GIVE A KRYPTONIAN A HARD TIME.
KRYPTONIAN... WHERE IS SUPERMAN?
OUT OF COMMISSION...
OUR CAPTOR ALSO SEEMS TO HAVE GOTTEN HIS HANDS ON KANJAR RO'S KRYPTONITE WAND.
AND HE'S PROBABLY USING TECHNOLOGY FROM THE MUSEUM TO BROADCAST THE WAND'S RADIATION INTO THE BUILDING.
WHAT DOES SALAAN WANT? AND WHY WOULD HE BREAK KANJAR RO OUT OF THE SECURITY CENTER... BUT LEAVE HIM IN CHAINS?

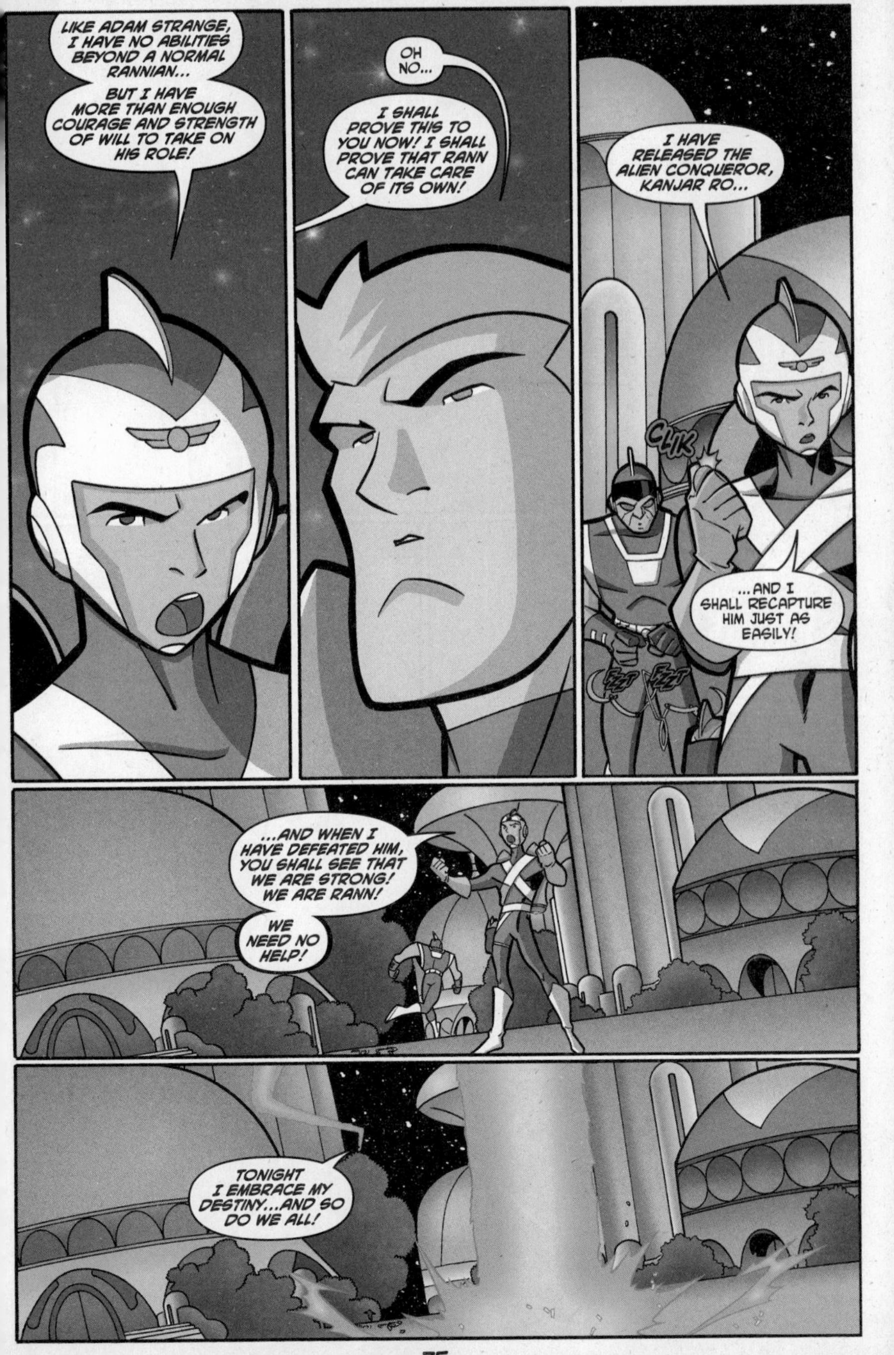
LIKE ADAM STRANGE, I HAVE NO ABILITIES BEYOND A NORMAL RANNIAN...
BUT I HAVE MORE THAN ENOUGH COURAGE AND STRENGTH OF WILL TO TAKE ON HIS ROLE!
OH NO...
I SHALL PROVE THIS TO YOU NOW! I SHALL PROVE THAT RANN CAN TAKE CARE OF ITS OWN!
I HAVE RELEASED THE ALIEN CONQUEROR, KANJAR RO...
CLIK
...AND I SHALL RECAPTURE HIM JUST AS EASILY!
FZZT
FZZT
...AND WHEN I HAVE DEFEATED HIM, YOU SHALL SEE THAT WE ARE STRONG! WE ARE RANN!
WE NEED NO HELP!
TONIGHT I EMBRACE MY DESTINY...AND SO DO WE ALL!

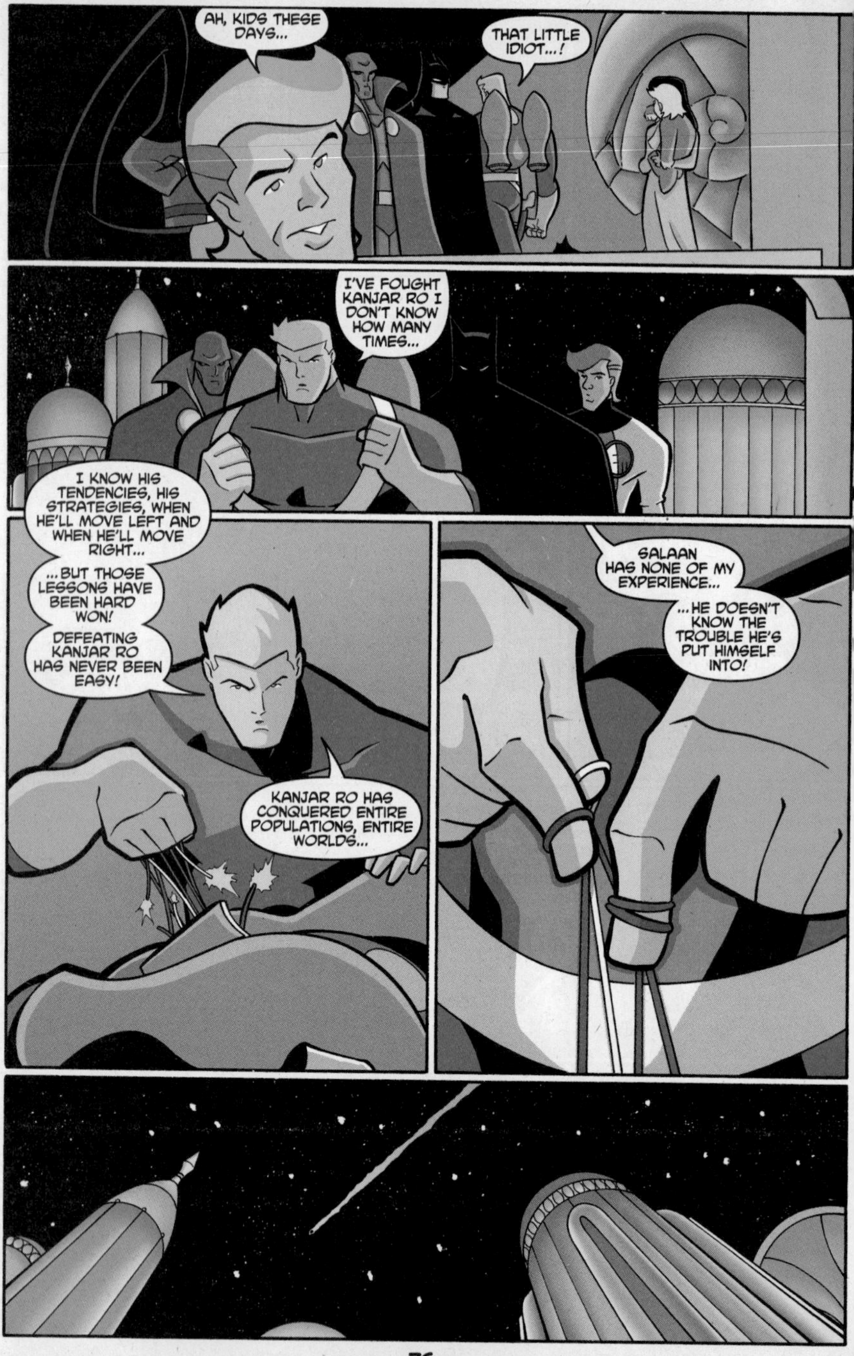
AH, KIDS THESE DAYS...
THAT LITTLE IDIOT...!
I'VE FOUGHT KANJAR RO I DON'T KNOW HOW MANY TIMES...
I KNOW HIS TENDENCIES, HIS STRATEGIES, WHEN HE'LL MOVE LEFT AND WHEN HE'LL MOVE RIGHT...
...BUT THOSE LESSONS HAVE BEEN HARD WON!
DEFEATING KANJAR RO HAS NEVER BEEN EASY!
KANJAR RO HAS CONQUERED ENTIRE POPULATIONS, ENTIRE WORLDS...
SALAAN HAS NONE OF MY EXPERIENCE...
...HE DOESN'T KNOW THE TROUBLE HE'S PUT HIMSELF INTO!

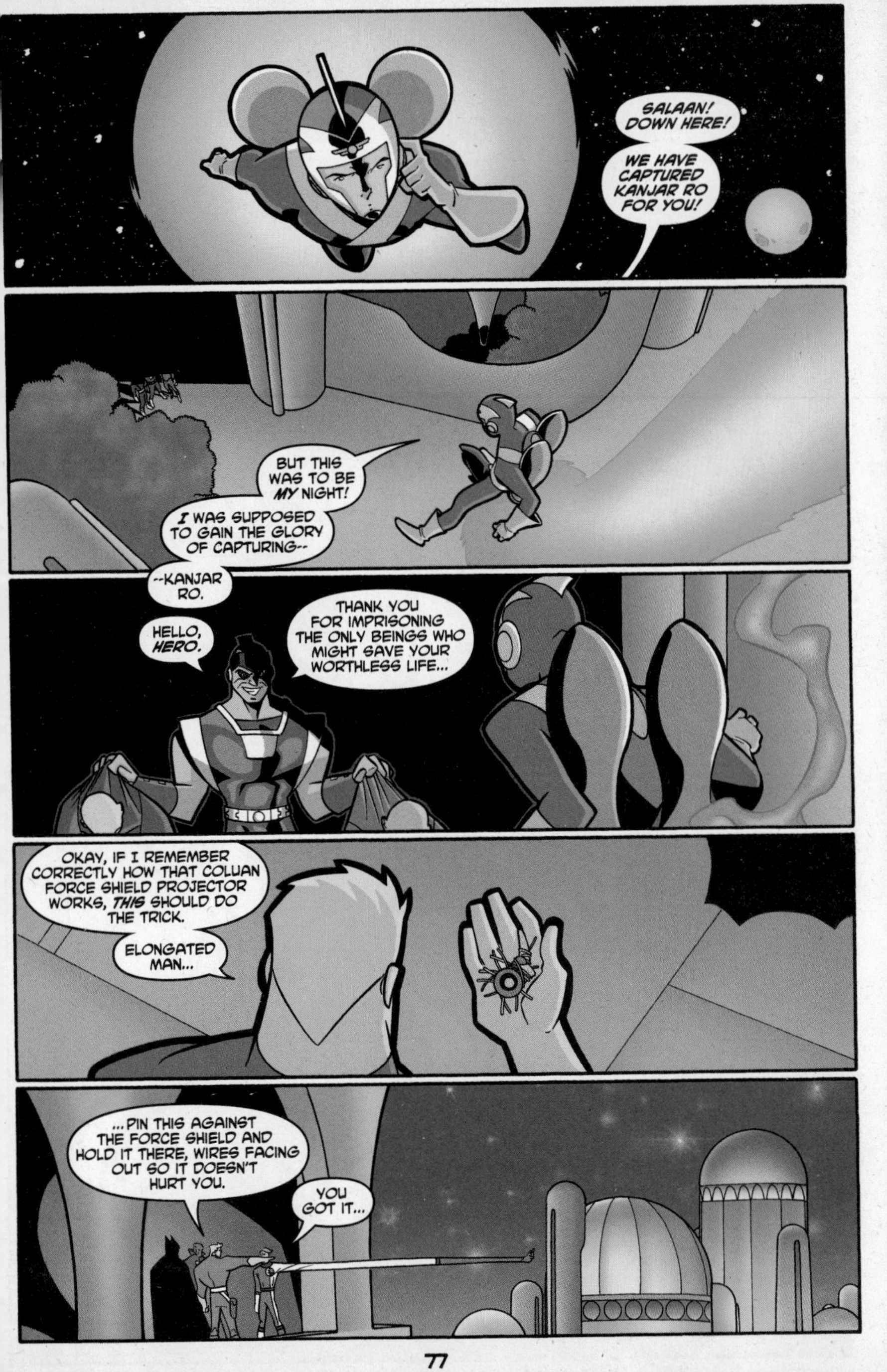
SALAAN! DOWN HERE!
WE HAVE CAPTURED KANJAR RO FOR YOU!
BUT THIS WAS TO BE *MY* NIGHT!
I WAS SUPPOSED TO GAIN THE GLORY OF CAPTURING--
--KANJAR RO.
HELLO, *HERO.*
THANK YOU FOR IMPRISONING THE ONLY BEINGS WHO MIGHT SAVE YOUR WORTHLESS LIFE...
OKAY, IF I REMEMBER CORRECTLY HOW THAT COLUAN FORCE SHIELD PROJECTOR WORKS, *THIS* SHOULD DO THE TRICK.
ELONGATED MAN...
...PIN THIS AGAINST THE FORCE SHIELD AND HOLD IT THERE, WIRES FACING OUT SO IT DOESN'T HURT YOU.
YOU GOT IT...

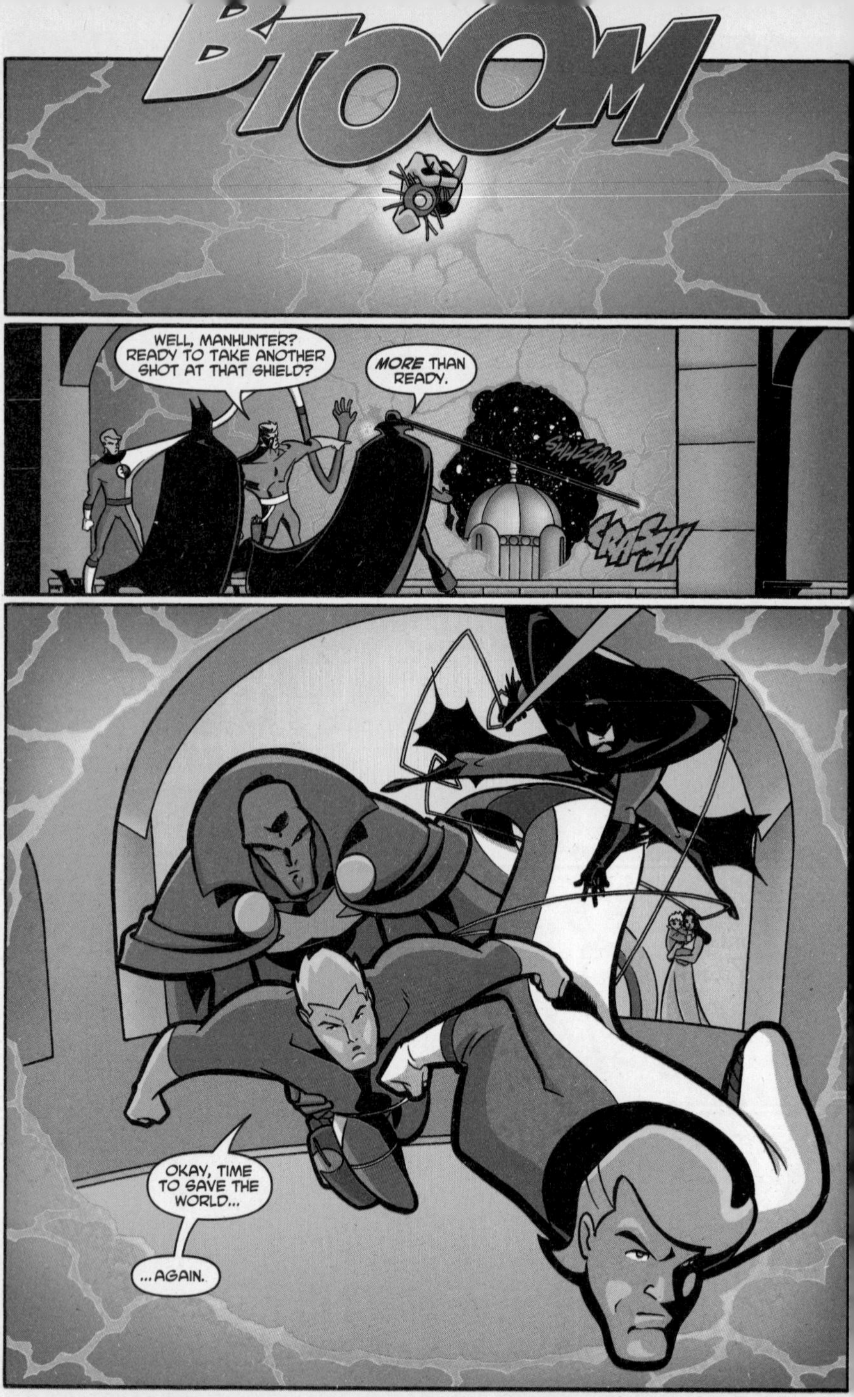
BTOOM
WELL, MANHUNTER? READY TO TAKE ANOTHER SHOT AT THAT SHIELD?
MORE THAN READY.
SHAZZAK!
CRASH
OKAY, TIME TO SAVE THE WORLD...
...AGAIN.

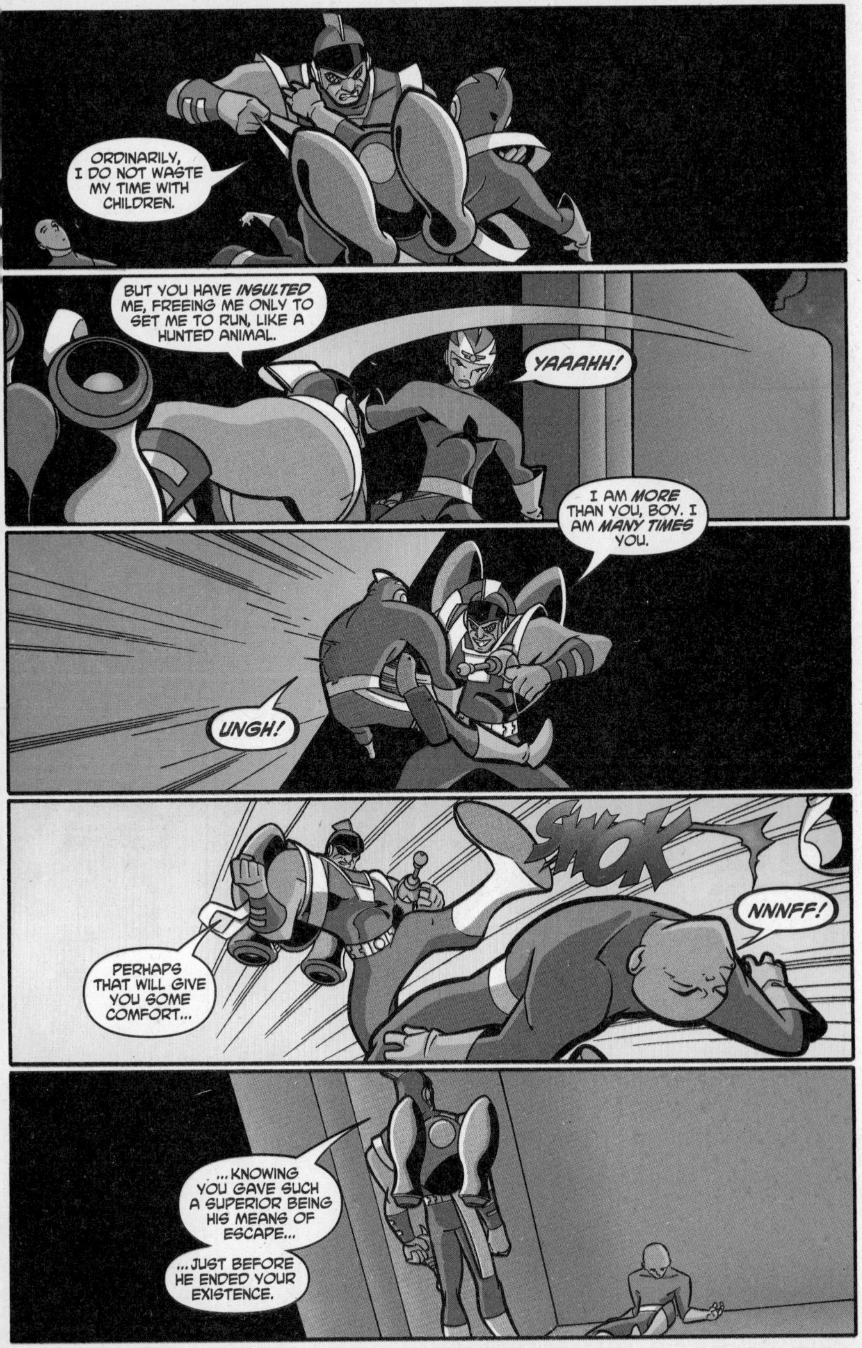
ORDINARILY, I DO NOT WASTE MY TIME WITH CHILDREN.
BUT YOU HAVE *INSULTED* ME, FREEING ME ONLY TO SET ME TO RUN, LIKE A HUNTED ANIMAL.
YAAAHH!
I AM *MORE* THAN YOU, BOY. I AM *MANY TIMES* YOU.
UNGH!
SHOK
NNNFF!
PERHAPS THAT WILL GIVE YOU SOME COMFORT...
...KNOWING YOU GAVE SUCH A SUPERIOR BEING HIS MEANS OF ESCAPE...
...JUST BEFORE HE ENDED YOUR EXISTENCE.

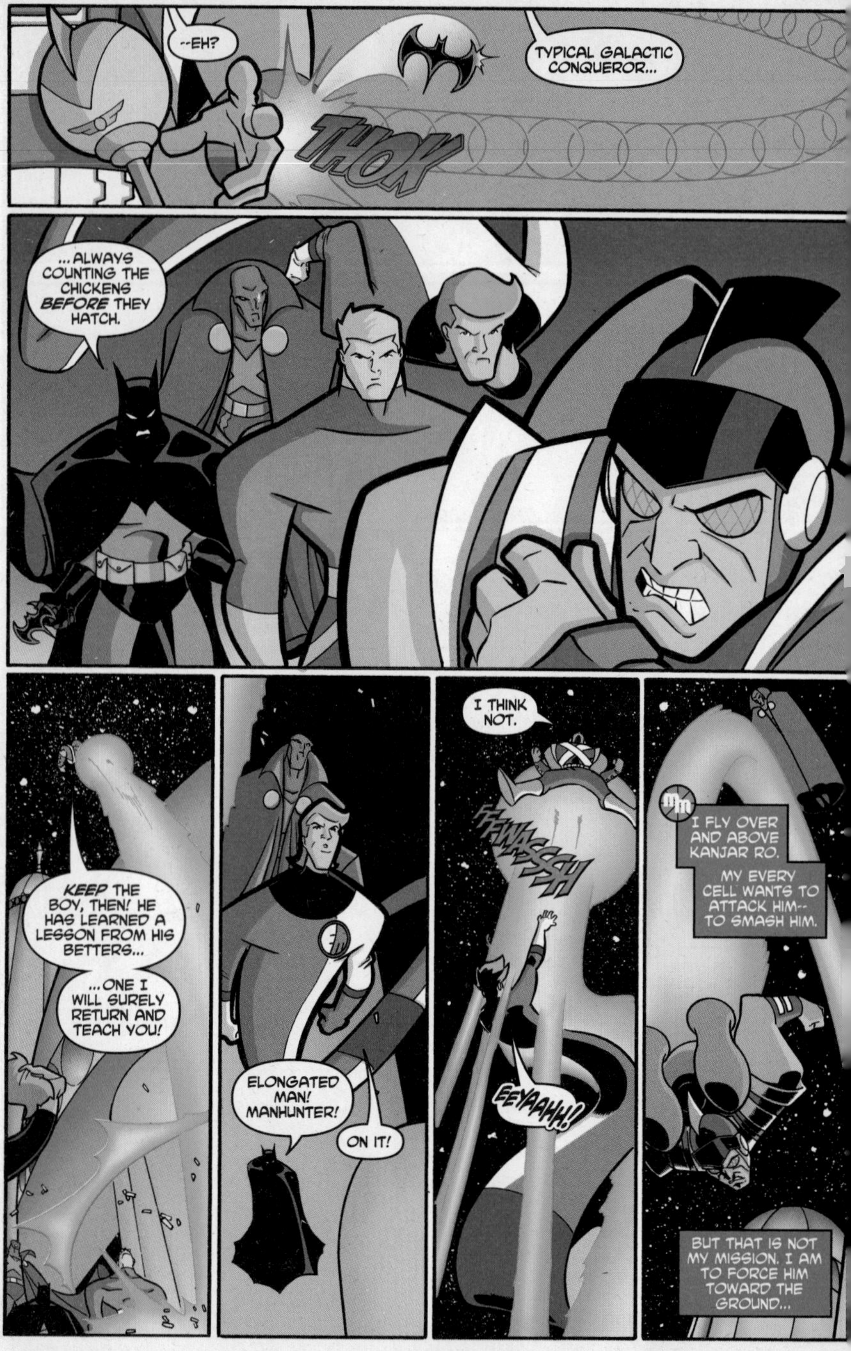

--EH?
TYPICAL GALACTIC CONQUEROR...
THOK
...ALWAYS COUNTING THE CHICKENS *BEFORE* THEY HATCH.
KEEP THE BOY, THEN! HE HAS LEARNED A LESSON FROM HIS BETTERS...
...ONE I WILL SURELY RETURN AND TEACH YOU!
ELONGATED MAN! MANHUNTER!
ON IT!
I THINK NOT.
FFFWASSSH
EEYAAAHH!
I FLY OVER AND ABOVE KANJAR RO.
MY EVERY CELL WANTS TO ATTACK HIM-- TO SMASH HIM.
BUT THAT IS NOT MY MISSION. I AM TO FORCE HIM TOWARD THE GROUND...

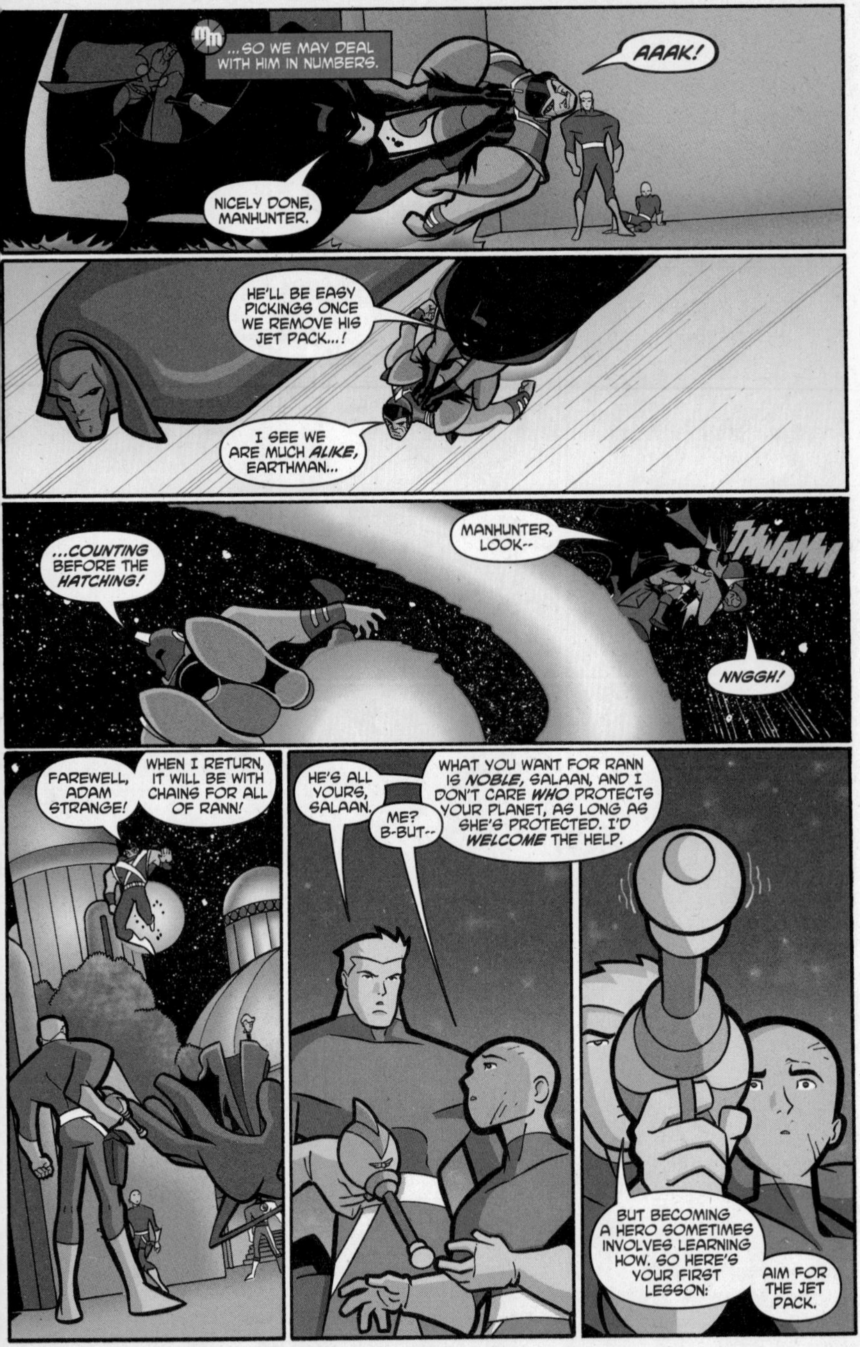
...SO WE MAY DEAL WITH HIM IN NUMBERS.
AAAK!
NICELY DONE, MANHUNTER.
HE'LL BE EASY PICKINGS ONCE WE REMOVE HIS JET PACK...!
I SEE WE ARE MUCH ALIKE, EARTHMAN...
...COUNTING BEFORE THE HATCHING!
MANHUNTER, LOOK--
THWAMM
NNGGH!
FAREWELL, ADAM STRANGE!
WHEN I RETURN, IT WILL BE WITH CHAINS FOR ALL OF RANN!
HE'S ALL YOURS, SALAAN.
ME? B-BUT--
WHAT YOU WANT FOR RANN IS NOBLE, SALAAN, AND I DON'T CARE WHO PROTECTS YOUR PLANET, AS LONG AS SHE'S PROTECTED. I'D WELCOME THE HELP.
BUT BECOMING A HERO SOMETIMES INVOLVES LEARNING HOW. SO HERE'S YOUR FIRST LESSON:
AIM FOR THE JET PACK.

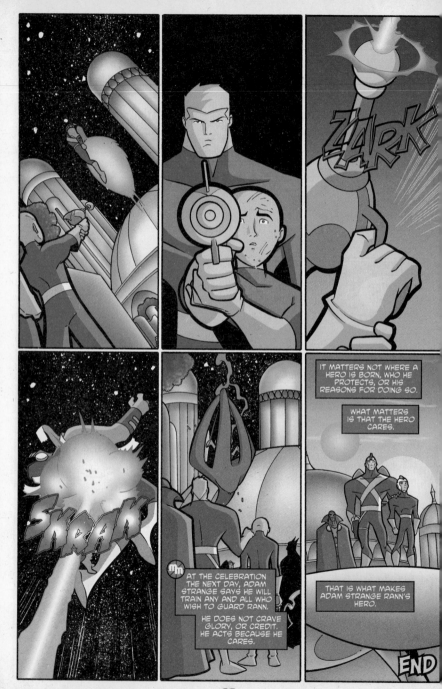

ZARK

KRAA

IT MATTERS NOT WHERE A HERO IS BORN, WHO HE PROTECTS, OR HIS REASONS FOR DOING SO.

WHAT MATTERS IS THAT THE HERO CARES.

AT THE CELEBRATION THE NEXT DAY, ADAM STRANGE SAYS HE WILL TRAIN ANY AND ALL WHO WISH TO GUARD RANN.

HE DOES NOT CRAVE GLORY, OR CREDIT. HE ACTS BECAUSE HE CARES.

THAT IS WHAT MAKES ADAM STRANGE RANN'S HERO.

END

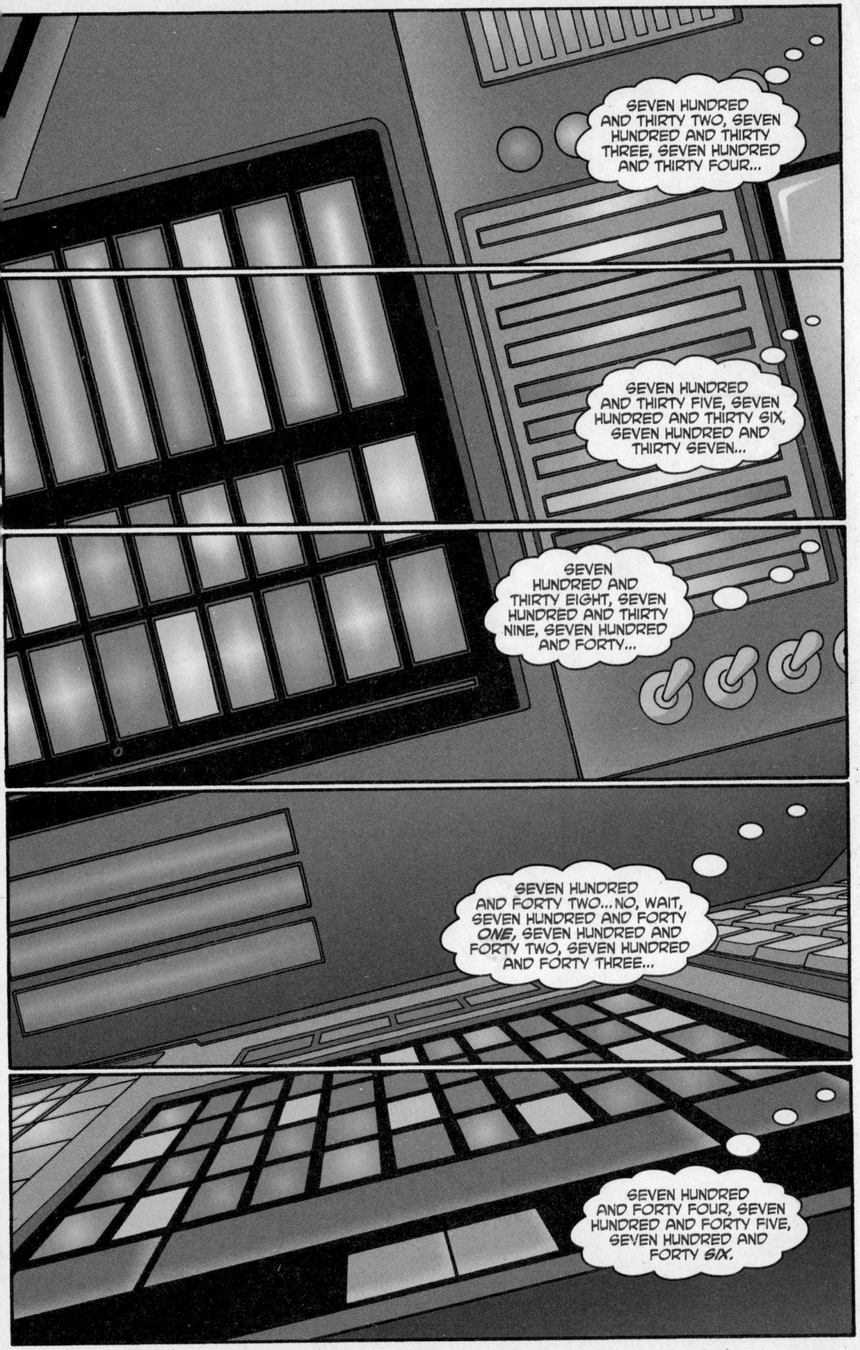
SEVEN HUNDRED AND THIRTY TWO, SEVEN HUNDRED AND THIRTY THREE, SEVEN HUNDRED AND THIRTY FOUR...
SEVEN HUNDRED AND THIRTY FIVE, SEVEN HUNDRED AND THIRTY SIX, SEVEN HUNDRED AND THIRTY SEVEN...
SEVEN HUNDRED AND THIRTY EIGHT, SEVEN HUNDRED AND THIRTY NINE, SEVEN HUNDRED AND FORTY...
SEVEN HUNDRED AND FORTY TWO...NO, WAIT, SEVEN HUNDRED AND FORTY *ONE,* SEVEN HUNDRED AND FORTY TWO, SEVEN HUNDRED AND FORTY THREE...
SEVEN HUNDRED AND FORTY FOUR, SEVEN HUNDRED AND FORTY FIVE, SEVEN HUNDRED AND FORTY *SIX.*

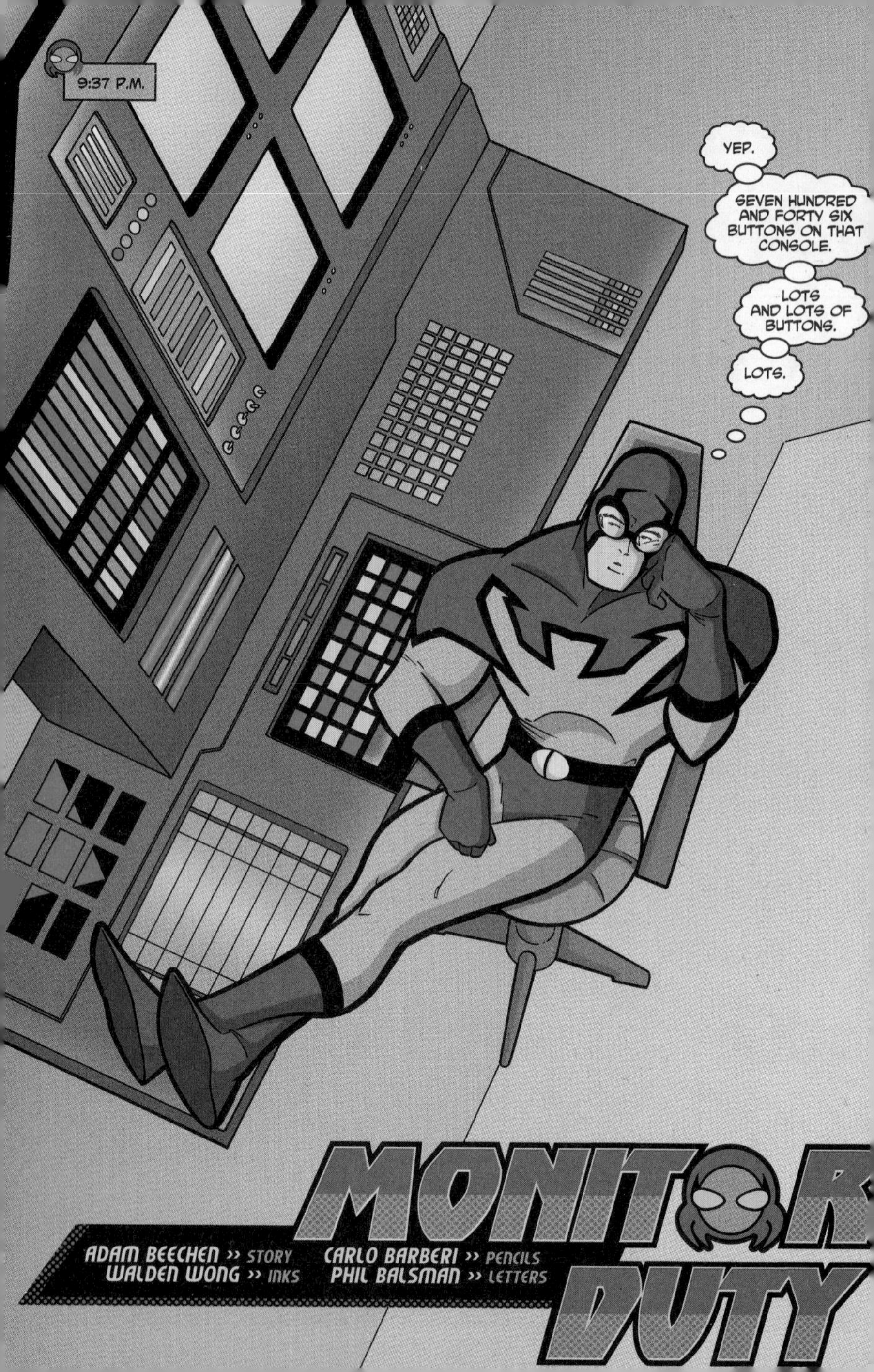
9:37 P.M.
YEP.
SEVEN HUNDRED AND FORTY SIX BUTTONS ON THAT CONSOLE.
LOTS AND LOTS OF BUTTONS.
LOTS.
MONITOR DUTY
ADAM BEECHEN » STORY CARLO BARBERI » PENCILS
WALDEN WONG » INKS PHIL BALSMAN » LETTERS

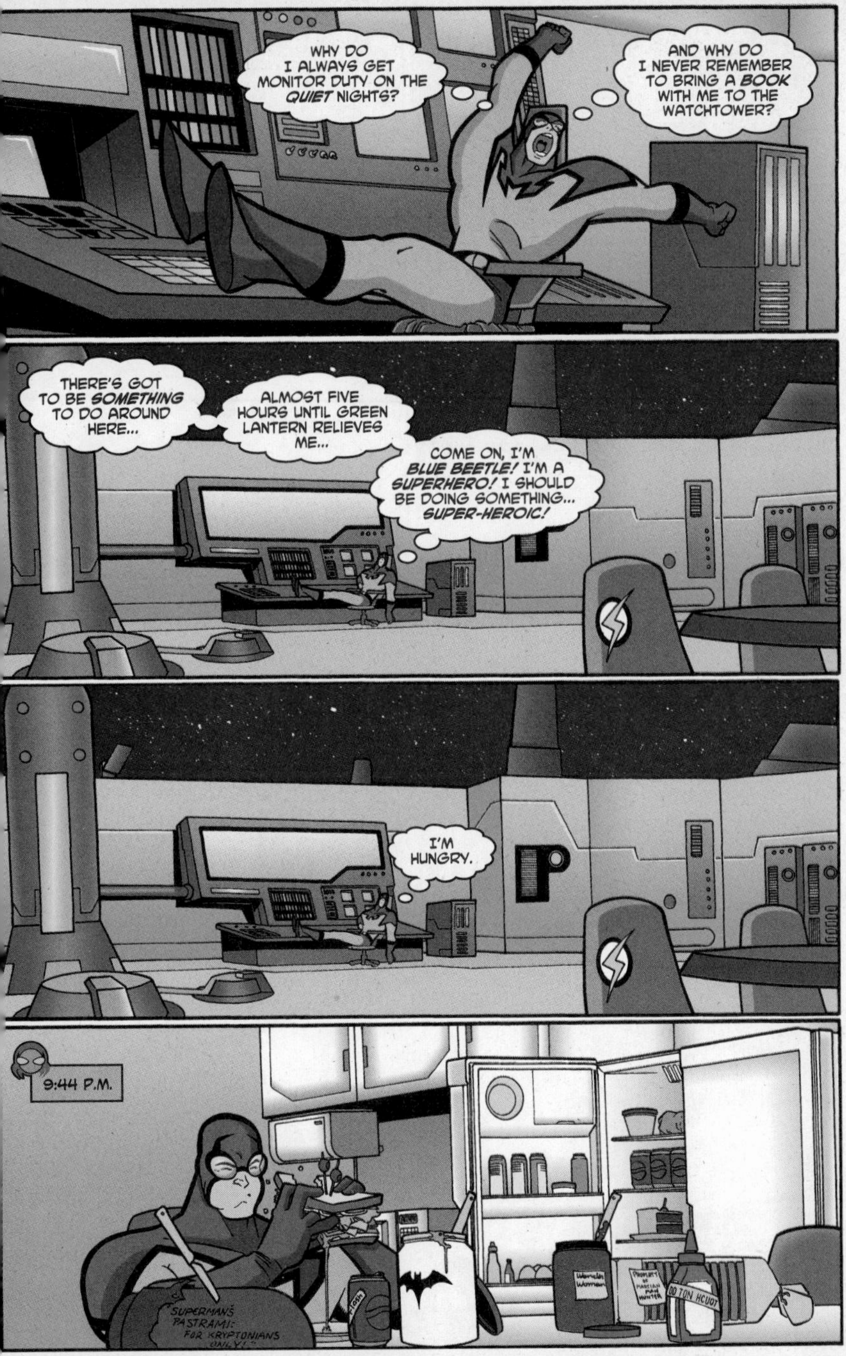
WHY DO I ALWAYS GET MONITOR DUTY ON THE *QUIET* NIGHTS?
AND WHY DO I NEVER REMEMBER TO BRING A *BOOK* WITH ME TO THE WATCHTOWER?
THERE'S GOT TO BE *SOMETHING* TO DO AROUND HERE...
ALMOST FIVE HOURS UNTIL GREEN LANTERN RELIEVES ME...
COME ON, I'M *BLUE BEETLE!* I'M A *SUPERHERO!* I SHOULD BE DOING SOMETHING... *SUPER-HEROIC!*
I'M HUNGRY.
9:44 P.M.
"SUPERMAN'S PASTRAMI: FOR KRYPTONIANS ONLY!"
Flash
Wonder Woman
PROPERTY OF MARTIAN MAN HUNTER
DO TON HCUOT

9:46 P.M.

URRRP.

NOW WHAT?

9:52 P.M.

WHUMPITY WHUMPITY WHUMPITY

10:12 P.M.

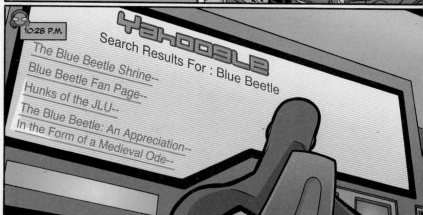

10:28 P.M.

YAHOOGLE

Search Results For : Blue Beetle

The Blue Beetle Shrine--

Blue Beetle Fan Page--

Hunks of the JLU--

The Blue Beetle: An Appreciation--

In the Form of a Medieval Ode--

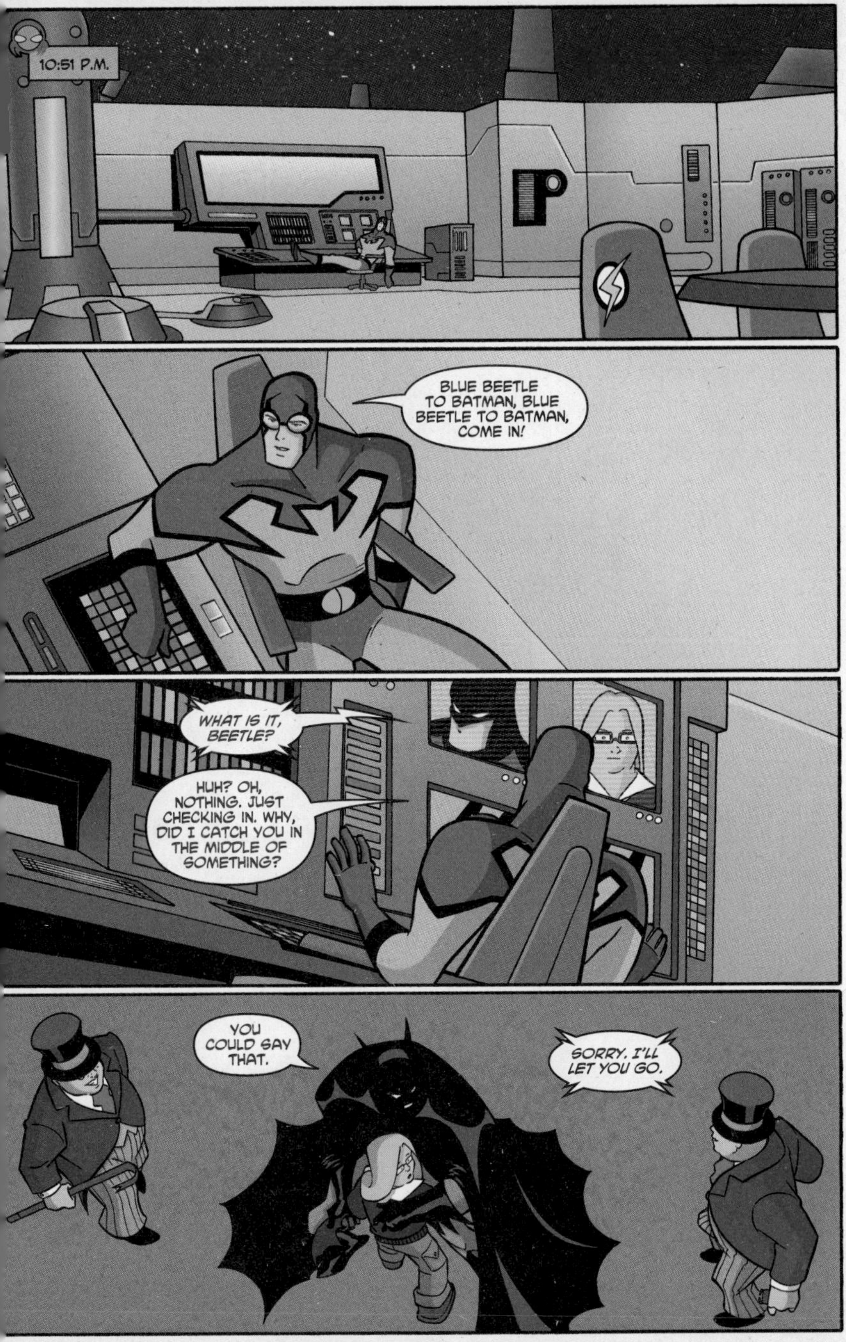

10:51 P.M.
BLUE BEETLE TO BATMAN, BLUE BEETLE TO BATMAN, COME IN!
WHAT IS IT, BEETLE?
HUH? OH, NOTHING. JUST CHECKING IN. WHY, DID I CATCH YOU IN THE MIDDLE OF SOMETHING?
YOU COULD SAY THAT.
SORRY. I'LL LET YOU GO.

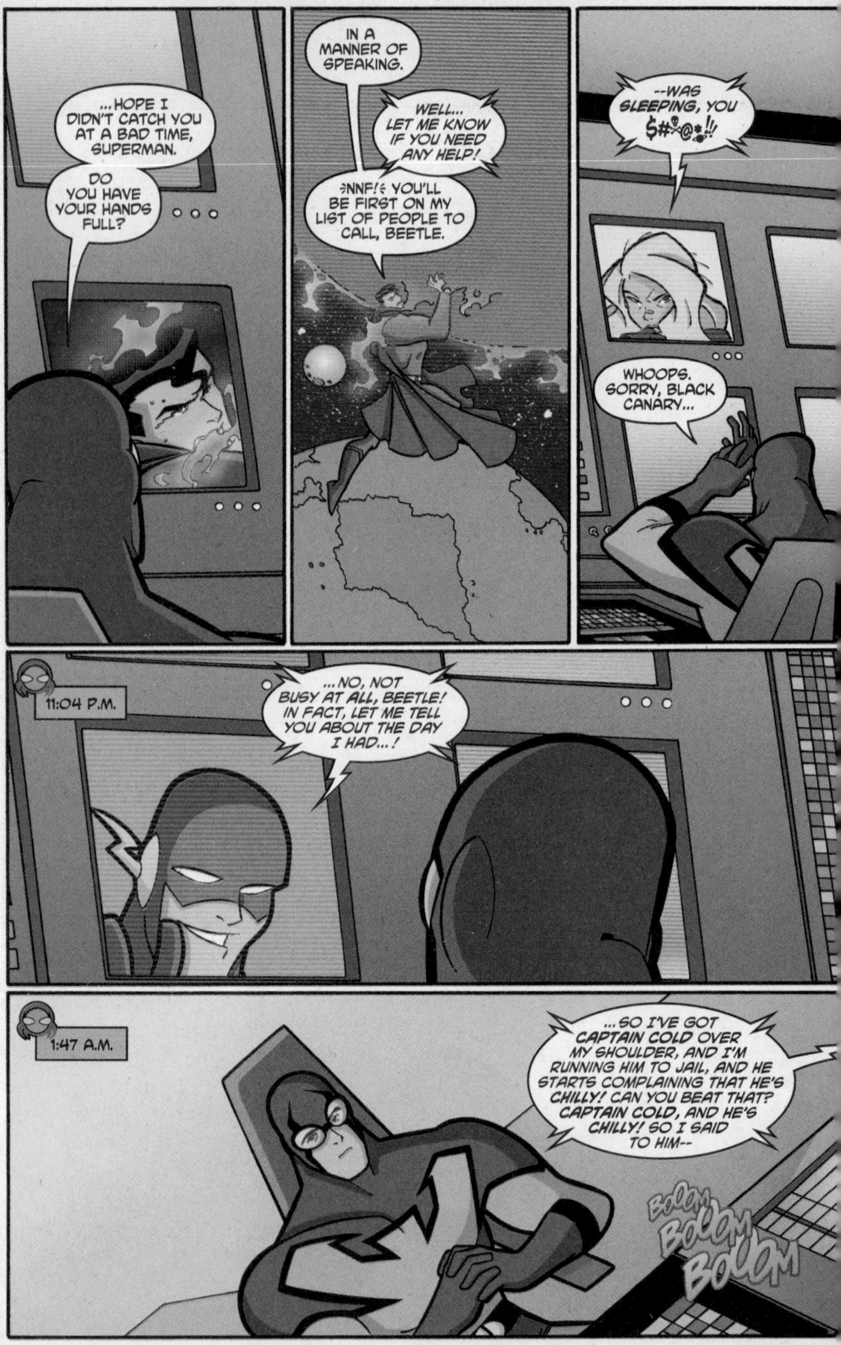
...HOPE I DIDN'T CATCH YOU AT A BAD TIME, SUPERMAN.
DO YOU HAVE YOUR HANDS FULL?
IN A MANNER OF SPEAKING.
WELL... LET ME KNOW IF YOU NEED ANY HELP!
NNF! YOU'LL BE FIRST ON MY LIST OF PEOPLE TO CALL, BEETLE.
--WAS SLEEPING, YOU $#*@*!!
WHOOPS. SORRY, BLACK CANARY...
11:04 P.M.
...NO, NOT BUSY AT ALL, BEETLE! IN FACT, LET ME TELL YOU ABOUT THE DAY I HAD...!
1:47 A.M.
...SO I'VE GOT CAPTAIN COLD OVER MY SHOULDER, AND I'M RUNNING HIM TO JAIL, AND HE STARTS COMPLAINING THAT HE'S CHILLY! CAN YOU BEAT THAT? CAPTAIN COLD, AND HE'S CHILLY! SO I SAID TO HIM--
BOOM BOOM BOOM

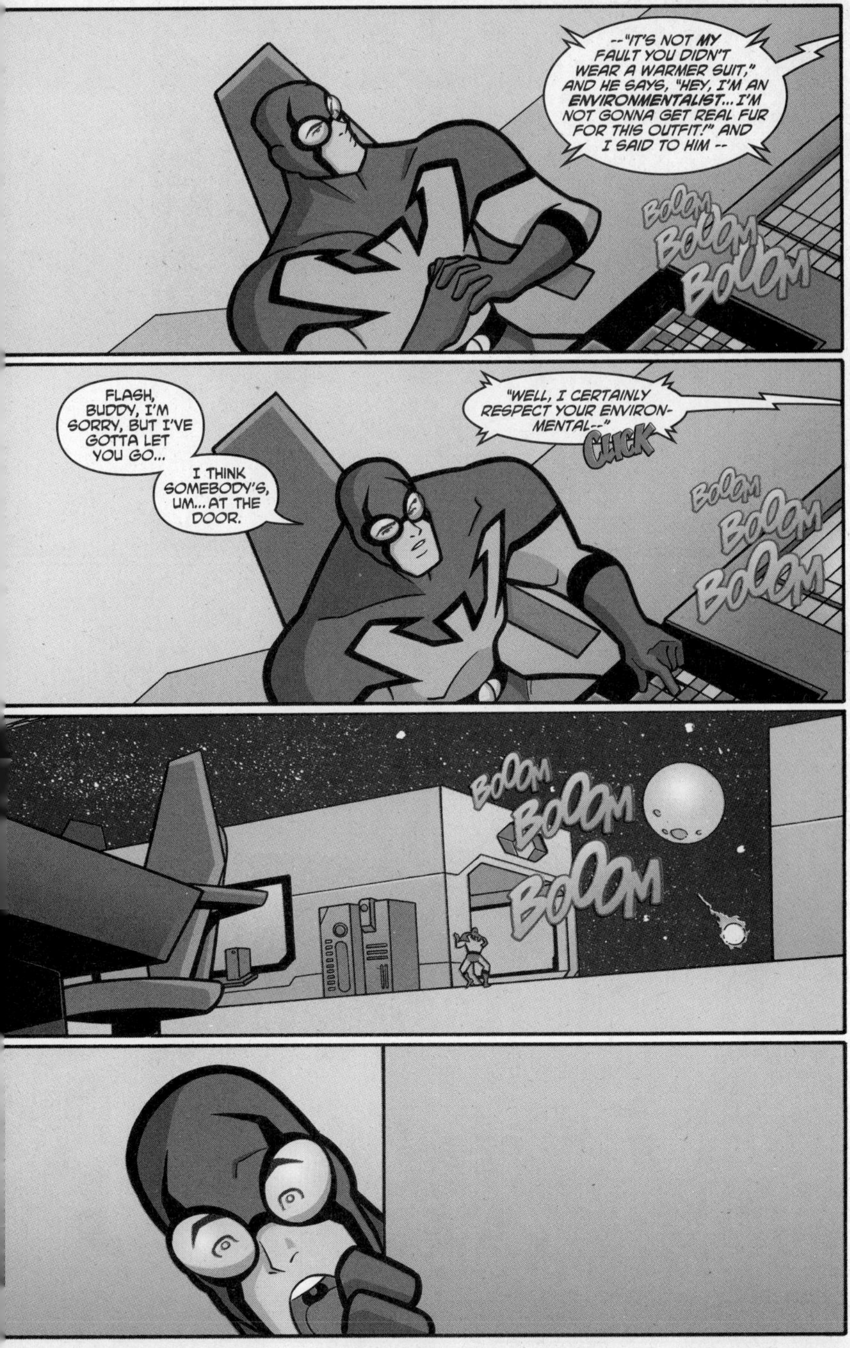
--"IT'S NOT MY FAULT YOU DIDN'T WEAR A WARMER SUIT," AND HE SAYS, "HEY, I'M AN ENVIRONMENTALIST... I'M NOT GONNA GET REAL FUR FOR THIS OUTFIT!" AND I SAID TO HIM --
BOOM BOOM BOOM
FLASH, BUDDY, I'M SORRY, BUT I'VE GOTTA LET YOU GO...
"WELL, I CERTAINLY RESPECT YOUR ENVIRON-MENTAL--"
CLICK
I THINK SOMEBODY'S, UM... AT THE DOOR.
BOOM BOOM BOOM
BOOM BOOM BOOM

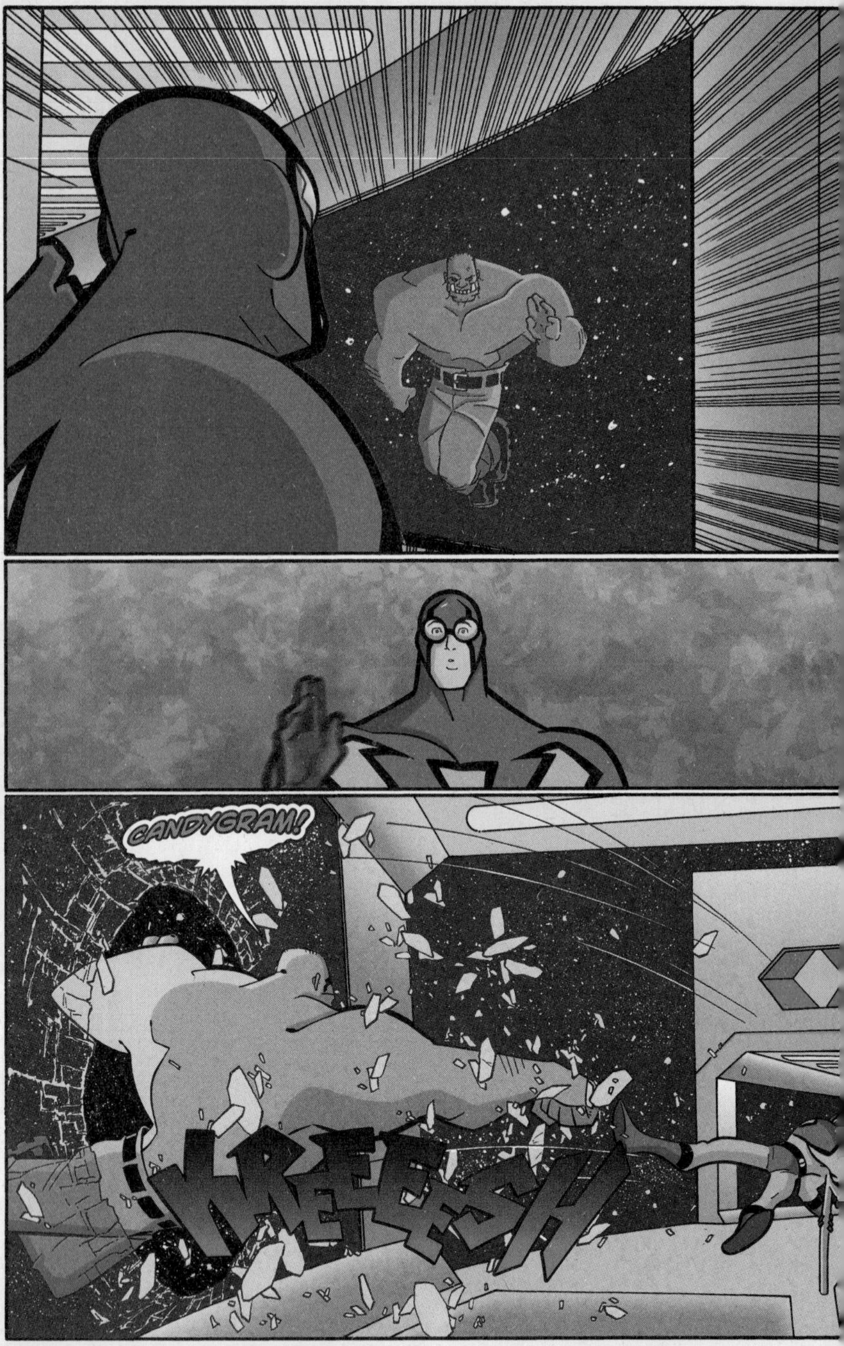
CANDYGRAM!
WREEESH

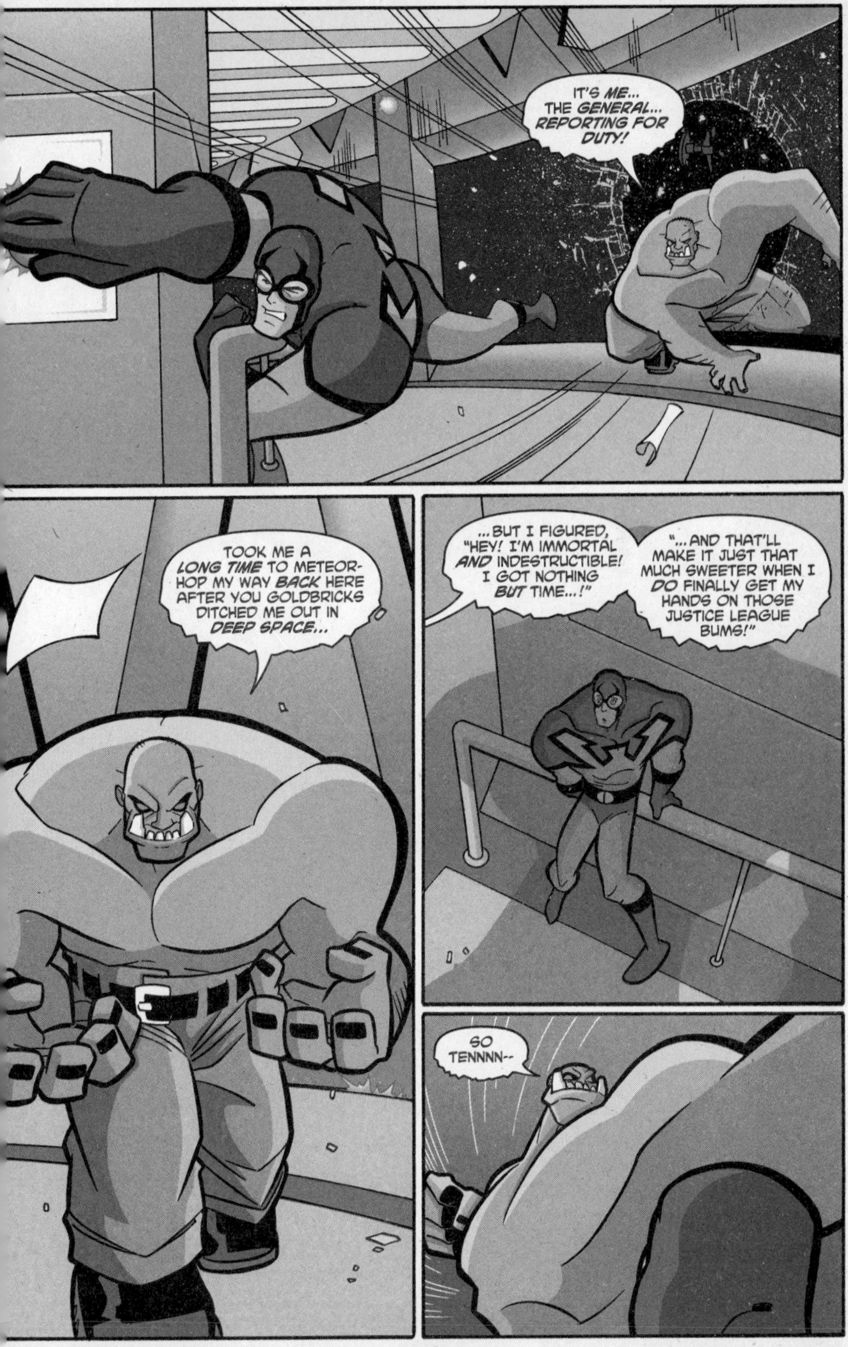
IT'S ME... THE GENERAL... REPORTING FOR DUTY!
TOOK ME A LONG TIME TO METEOR-HOP MY WAY BACK HERE AFTER YOU GOLDBRICKS DITCHED ME OUT IN DEEP SPACE...
...BUT I FIGURED, "HEY! I'M IMMORTAL AND INDESTRUCTIBLE! I GOT NOTHING BUT TIME...!"
"...AND THAT'LL MAKE IT JUST THAT MUCH SWEETER WHEN I DO FINALLY GET MY HANDS ON THOSE JUSTICE LEAGUE BUMS!"
SO TENNNN--

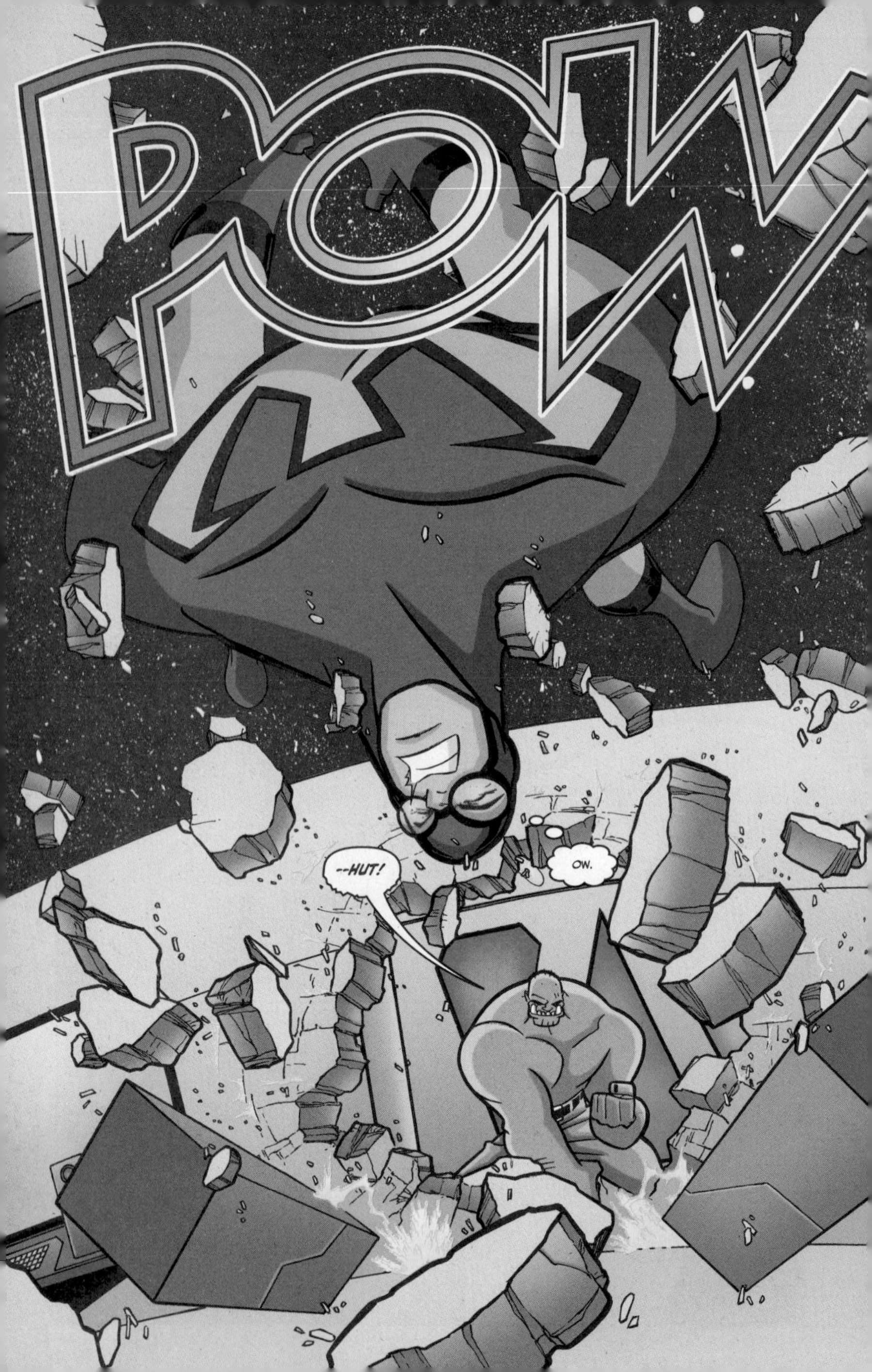
POW
--HUT!
OW.

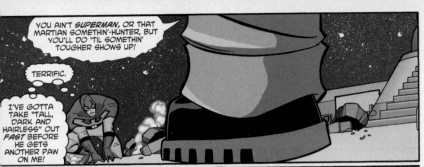

YOU AIN'T *SUPERMAN*, OR THAT MARTIAN SOMETHIN'-HUNTER, BUT YOU'LL DO 'TIL SOMETHIN' TOUGHER SHOWS UP!

TERRIFIC.

I'VE GOTTA TAKE "TALL, DARK AND HAIRLESS" OUT *FAST* BEFORE HE GETS ANOTHER PAW ON ME!

I'LL JUST CONSIDER YOU A *TRAINING EXERCISE!*

THA-BUMP

OW.

THAT'S IT, SOLDIER! TEST THOSE ABS!

TURN YOUR *HIPS* WHEN YOU PUNCH! GET SOME *POWER* BEHIND IT!

BAP BAP BAP BAP BAP

OW. OW. OW. OW. OW. OW.

OWWWW!

SORRY, SON, YOU'RE OUTMATCHED BY GOOD OL' AMERICAN MUSCLE AND KNOW-HOW!

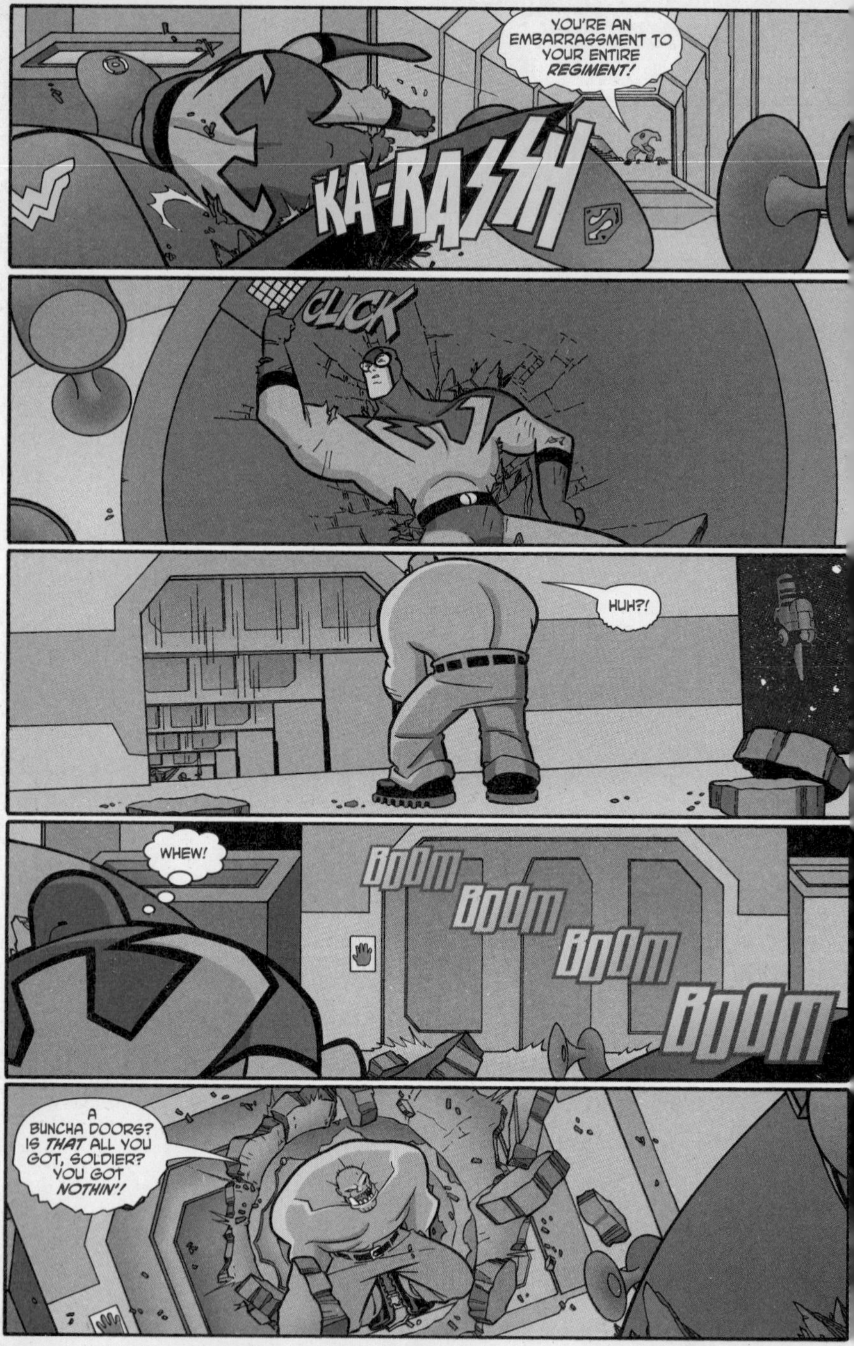
YOU'RE AN EMBARRASSMENT TO YOUR ENTIRE REGIMENT!
KA-RASSH
CLICK
HUH?!
WHEW!
BOOM
BOOM
BOOM
BOOM
A BUNCHA DOORS? IS THAT ALL YOU GOT, SOLDIER? YOU GOT NOTHIN'!

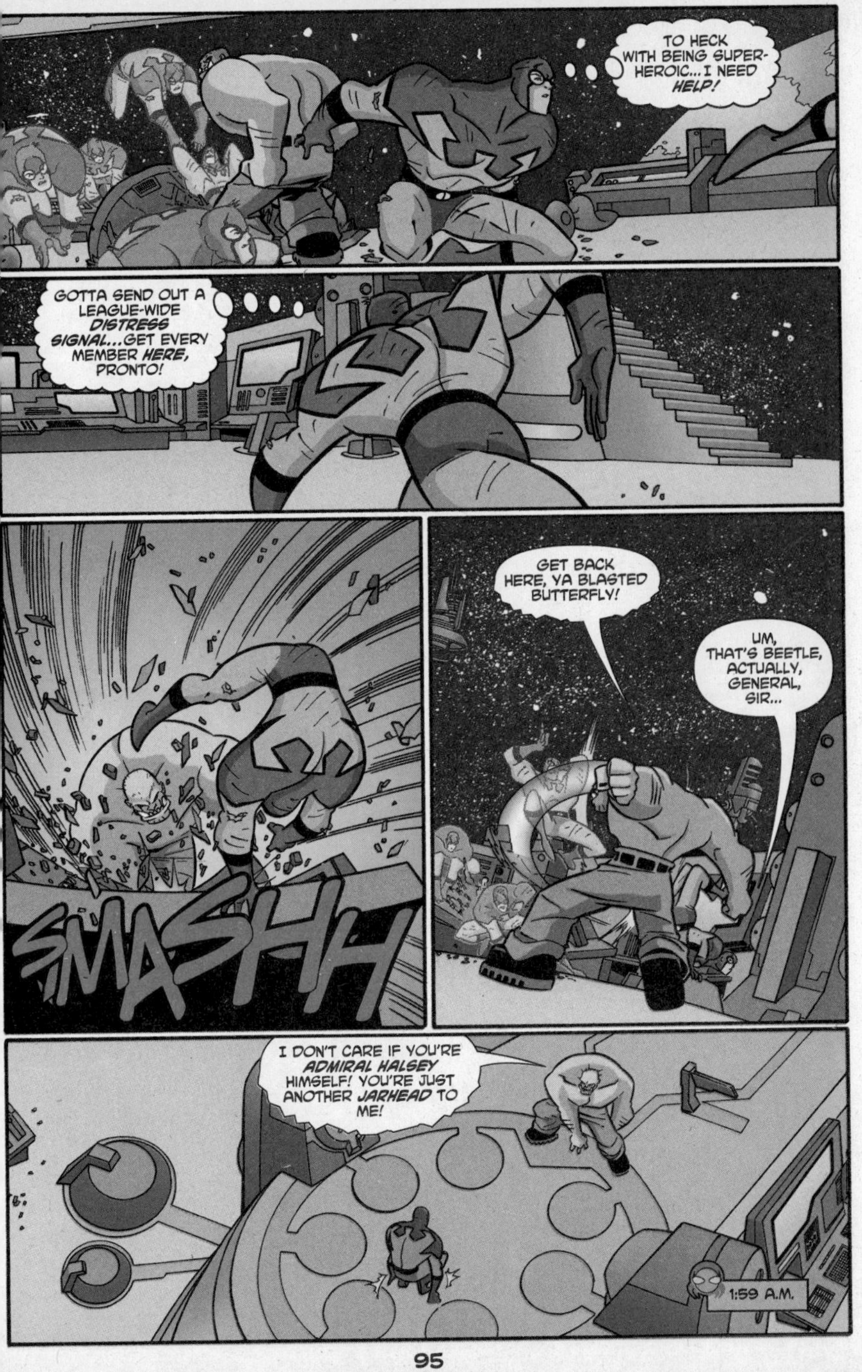
TO HECK WITH BEING SUPER-HEROIC... I NEED HELP!
GOTTA SEND OUT A LEAGUE-WIDE DISTRESS SIGNAL... GET EVERY MEMBER HERE, PRONTO!
SMASHH
GET BACK HERE, YA BLASTED BUTTERFLY!
UM, THAT'S BEETLE, ACTUALLY, GENERAL, SIR...
I DON'T CARE IF YOU'RE ADMIRAL HALSEY HIMSELF! YOU'RE JUST ANOTHER JARHEAD TO ME!
1:59 A.M.

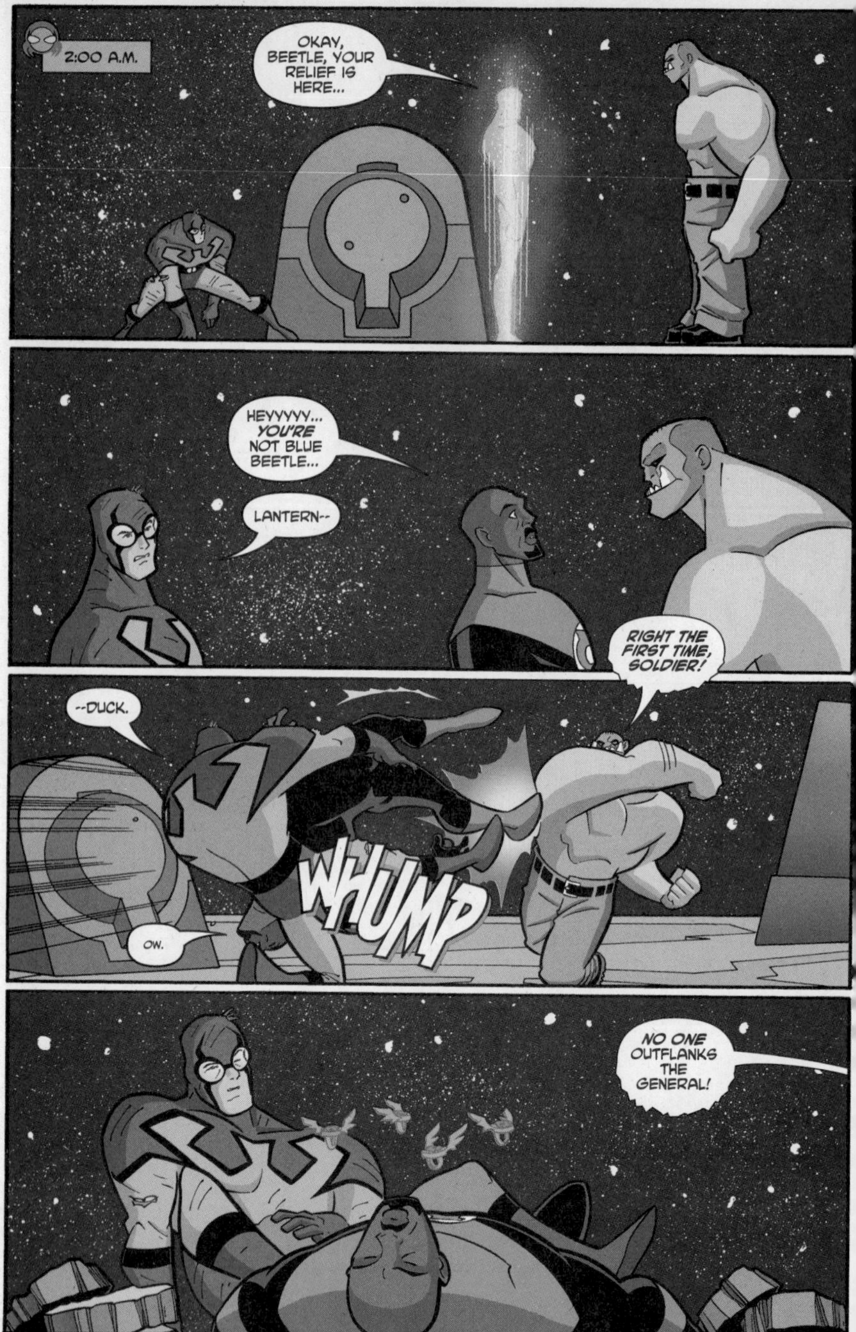

2:00 A.M.
OKAY, BEETLE, YOUR RELIEF IS HERE...
HEYYYYY... YOU'RE NOT BLUE BEETLE...
LANTERN--
RIGHT THE FIRST TIME, SOLDIER!
--DUCK.
WHUMP
OW.
NO ONE OUTFLANKS THE GENERAL!

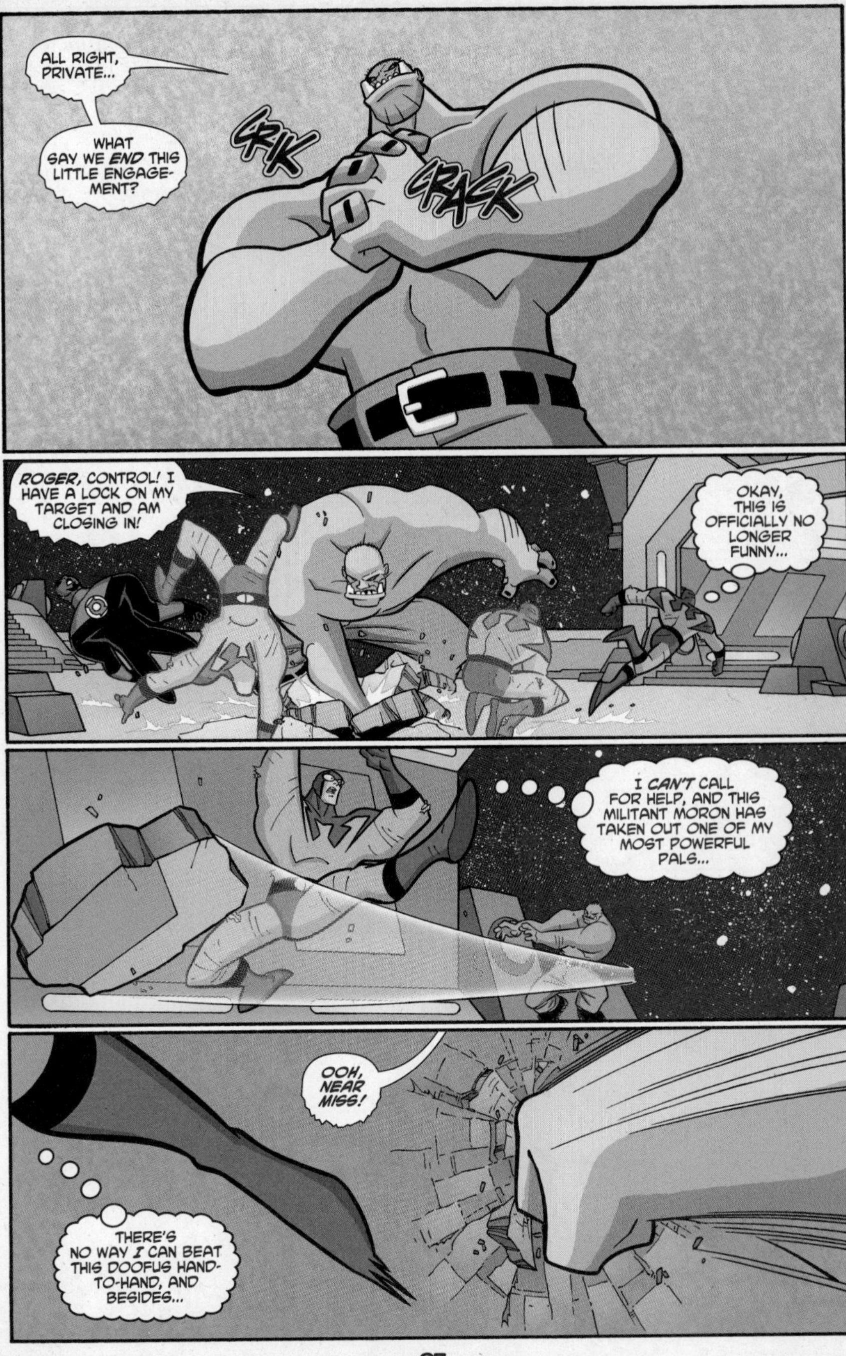

ALL RIGHT, PRIVATE...
WHAT SAY WE *END* THIS LITTLE ENGAGE-MENT?
CRIK
CRACK
ROGER, CONTROL! I HAVE A LOCK ON MY TARGET AND AM CLOSING IN!
OKAY, THIS IS OFFICIALLY NO LONGER FUNNY...
I *CAN'T* CALL FOR HELP, AND THIS MILITANT MORON HAS TAKEN OUT ONE OF MY MOST POWERFUL PALS...
OOH, NEAR MISS!
THERE'S NO WAY *I* CAN BEAT THIS DOOFUS HAND-TO-HAND, AND BESIDES...

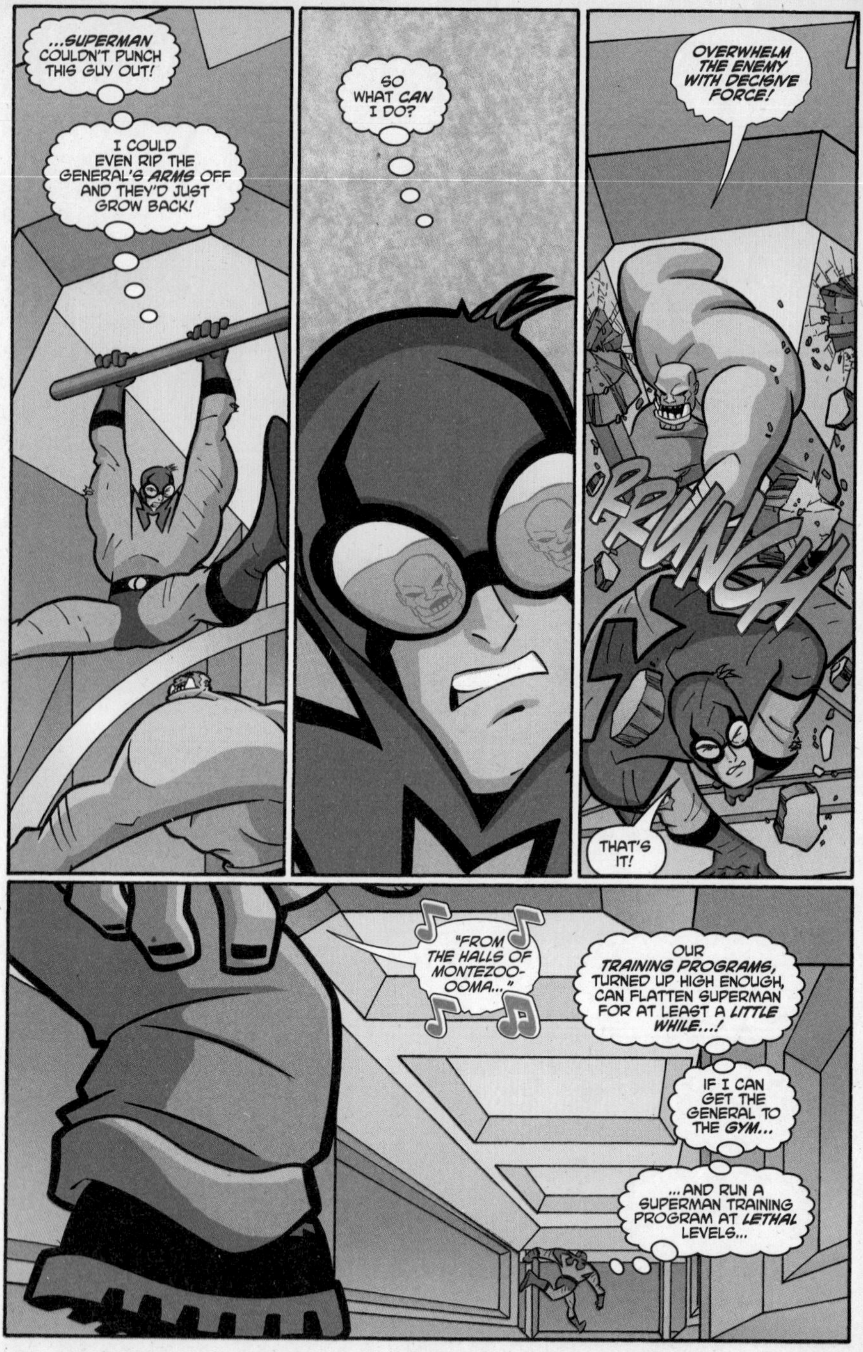
...SUPERMAN COULDN'T PUNCH THIS GUY OUT!
I COULD EVEN RIP THE GENERAL'S ARMS OFF AND THEY'D JUST GROW BACK!
SO WHAT CAN I DO?
OVERWHELM THE ENEMY WITH DECISIVE FORCE!
KRRUNCH
THAT'S IT!
"FROM THE HALLS OF MONTEZOOO-OOMA..."
OUR TRAINING PROGRAMS, TURNED UP HIGH ENOUGH, CAN FLATTEN SUPERMAN FOR AT LEAST A LITTLE WHILE...!
IF I CAN GET THE GENERAL TO THE GYM...
...AND RUN A SUPERMAN TRAINING PROGRAM AT LETHAL LEVELS...

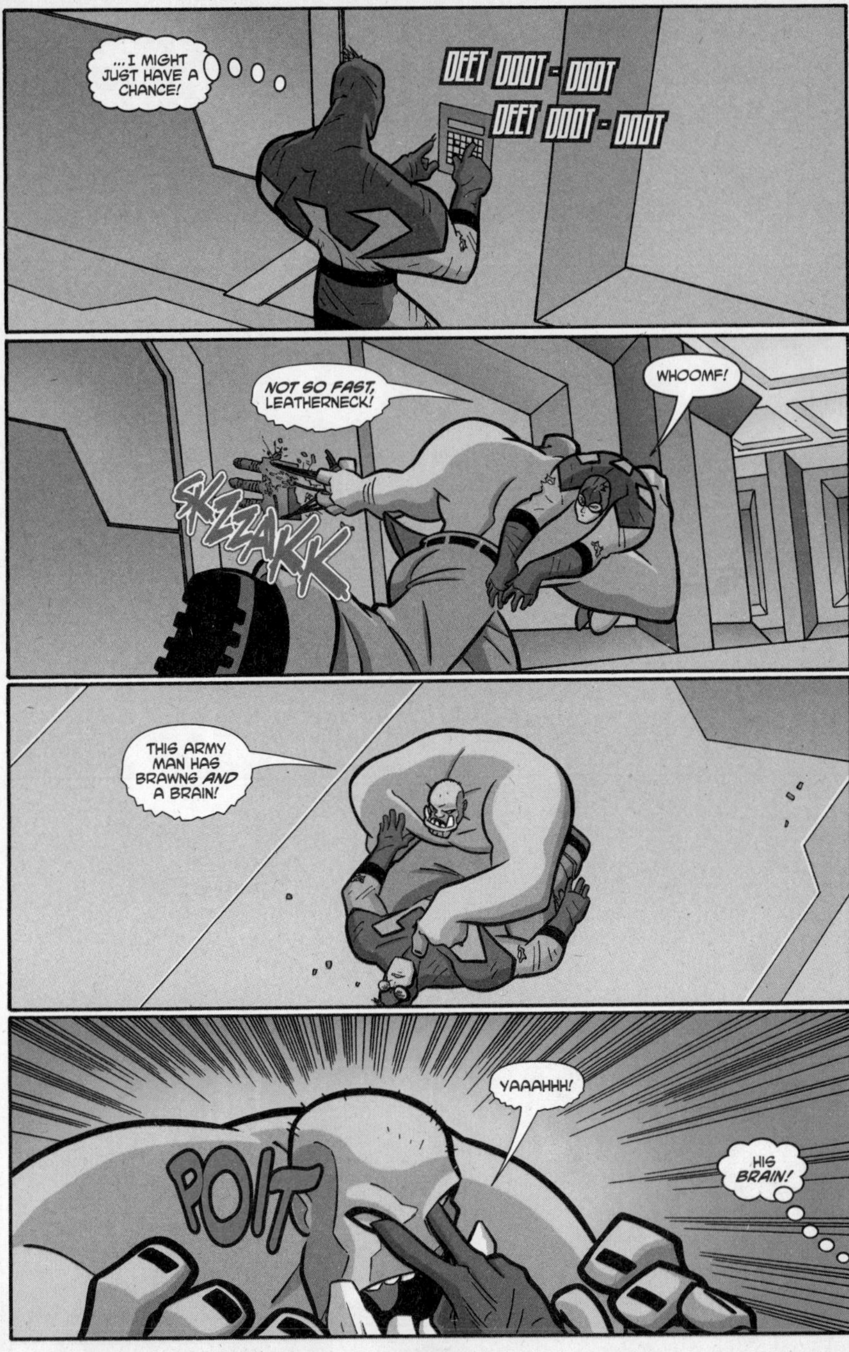
...I MIGHT JUST HAVE A CHANCE!
DEET DOOT-DOOT
DEET DOOT-DOOT
NOT SO FAST, LEATHERNECK!
WHOOMF!
SKZZZAKK
THIS ARMY MAN HAS BRAWNS AND A BRAIN!
YAAAHHH!
POIT
HIS BRAIN!

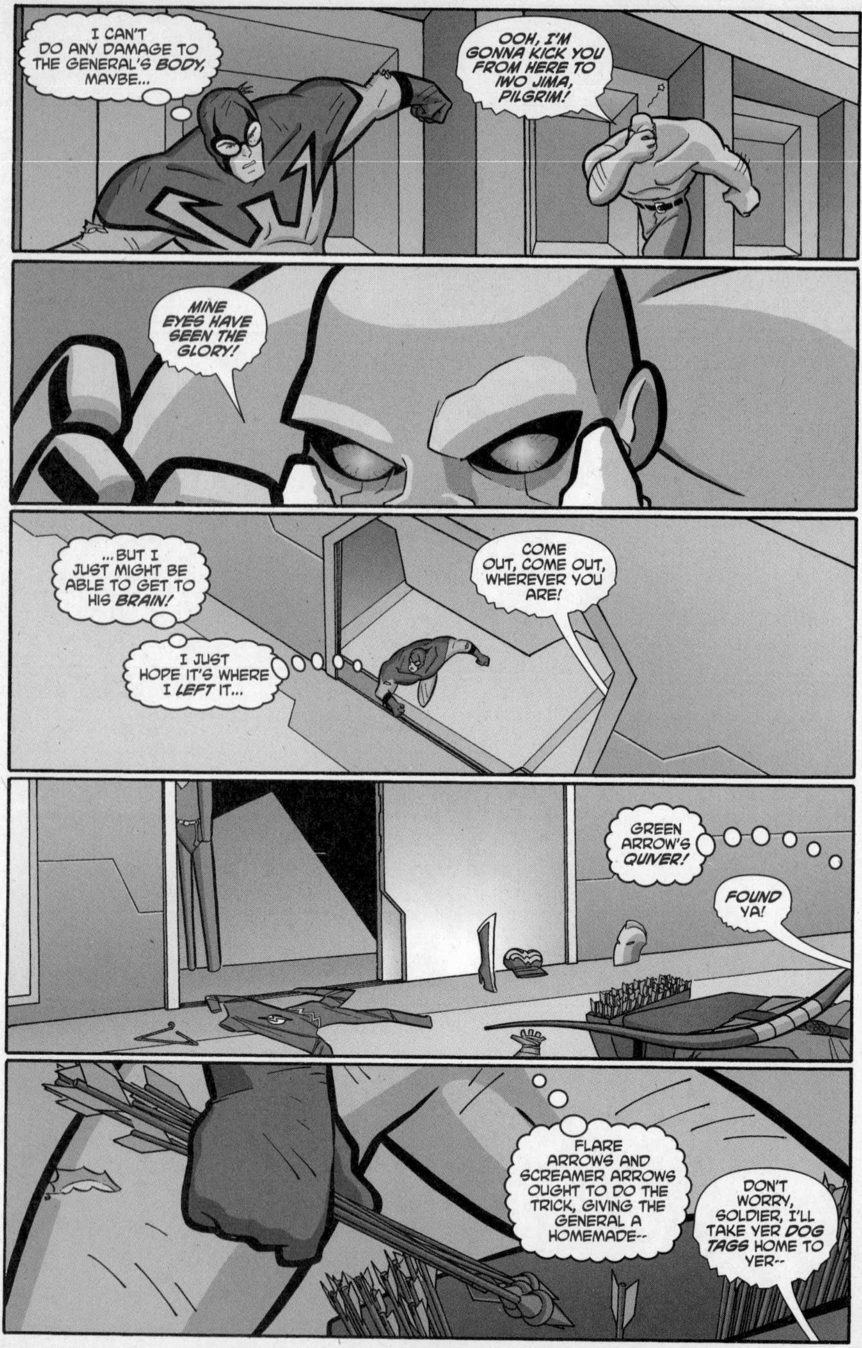

I CAN'T DO ANY DAMAGE TO THE GENERAL'S BODY, MAYBE...
OOH, I'M GONNA KICK YOU FROM HERE TO IWO JIMA, PILGRIM!
MINE EYES HAVE SEEN THE GLORY!
...BUT I JUST MIGHT BE ABLE TO GET TO HIS BRAIN!
COME OUT, COME OUT, WHEREVER YOU ARE!
I JUST HOPE IT'S WHERE I LEFT IT...
GREEN ARROW'S QUIVER!
FOUND YA!
FLARE ARROWS AND SCREAMER ARROWS OUGHT TO DO THE TRICK, GIVING THE GENERAL A HOMEMADE--
DON'T WORRY, SOLDIER, I'LL TAKE YER DOG TAGS HOME TO YER--

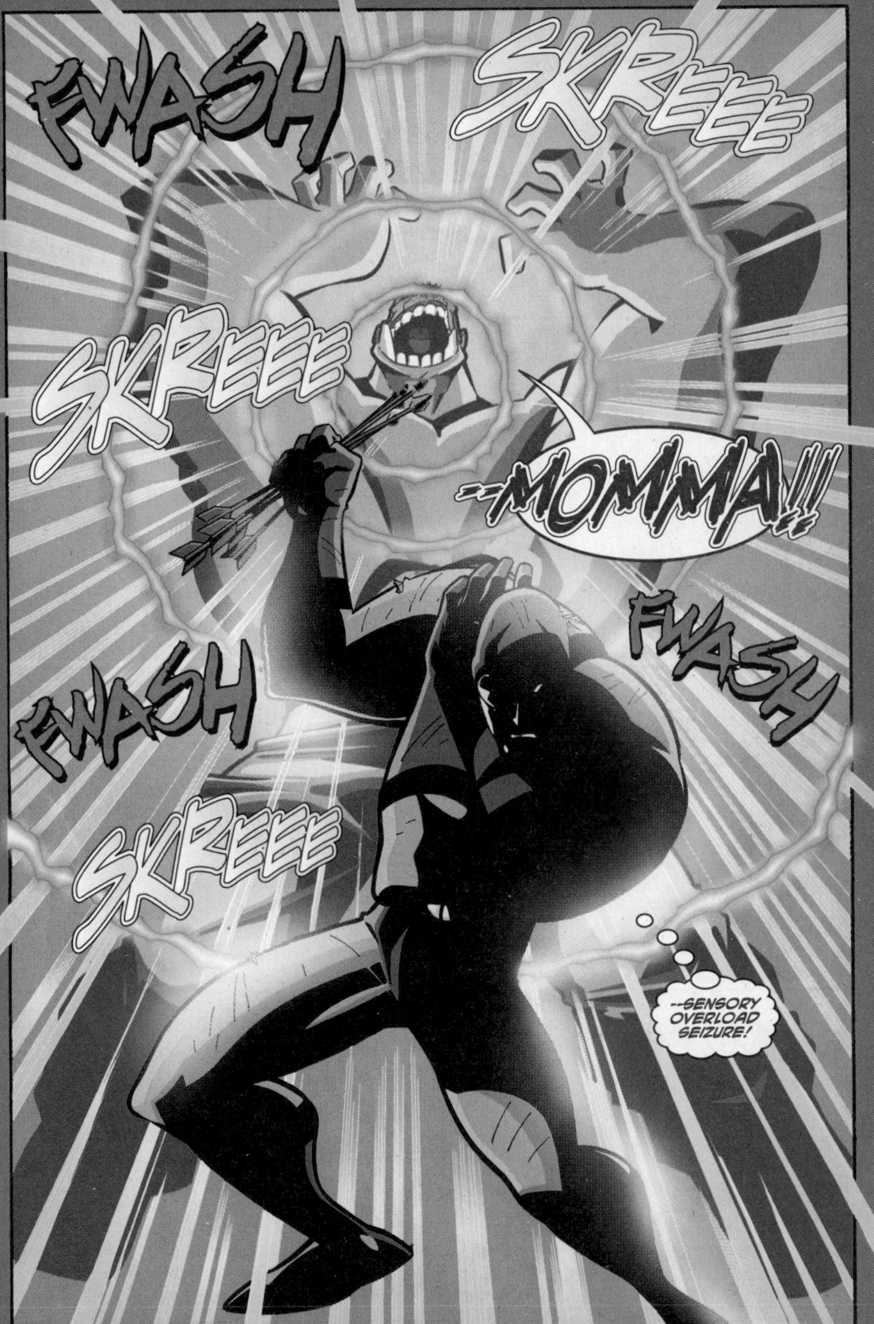
FWASH
SKREEE
SKREEE
--MOMMA!!
FWASH
FWASH
SKREEE
--SENSORY OVERLOAD SEIZURE!

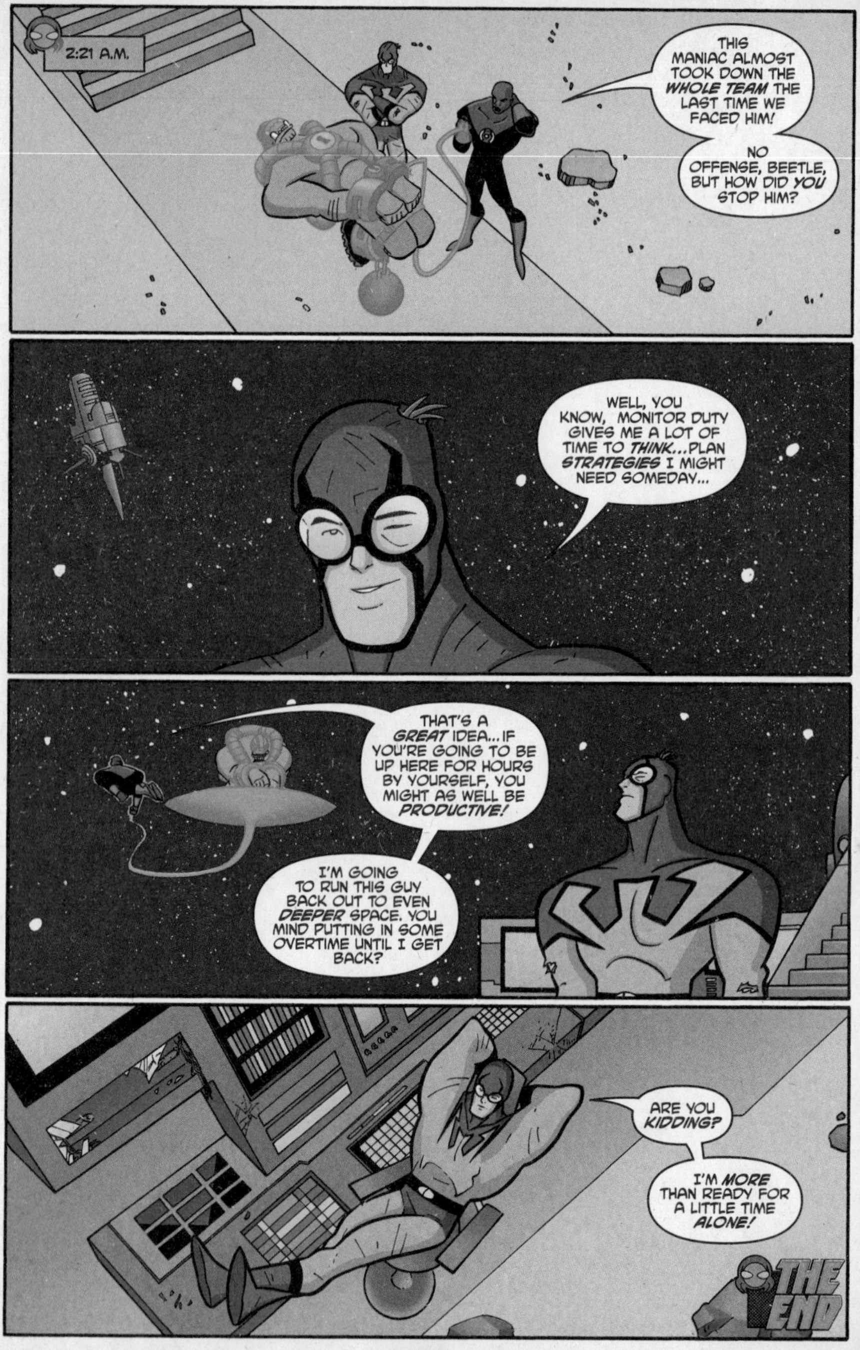
2:21 A.M.
THIS MANIAC ALMOST TOOK DOWN THE *WHOLE TEAM* THE LAST TIME WE FACED HIM!
NO OFFENSE, BEETLE, BUT HOW DID *YOU* STOP HIM?
WELL, YOU KNOW, MONITOR DUTY GIVES ME A LOT OF TIME TO *THINK*...PLAN *STRATEGIES* I MIGHT NEED SOMEDAY...
THAT'S A *GREAT* IDEA...IF YOU'RE GOING TO BE UP HERE FOR HOURS BY YOURSELF, YOU MIGHT AS WELL BE *PRODUCTIVE!*
I'M GOING TO RUN THIS GUY BACK OUT TO EVEN *DEEPER* SPACE. YOU MIND PUTTING IN SOME OVERTIME UNTIL I GET BACK?
ARE YOU *KIDDING?*
I'M *MORE* THAN READY FOR A LITTLE TIME *ALONE!*
THE END